I0526008

CONTENTS

RAVAGE MC #19

BOUND

by

temptation

bound #10

RYAN MICHELE

1st edition published: December 13, 2022

eBook IBSN: 978-0-9981280-9-2

AISN: B0BCXS4VQ4

Paperback IBSN: 978-1-951708-28-3

RAVAAGE MC FAMILY TREE

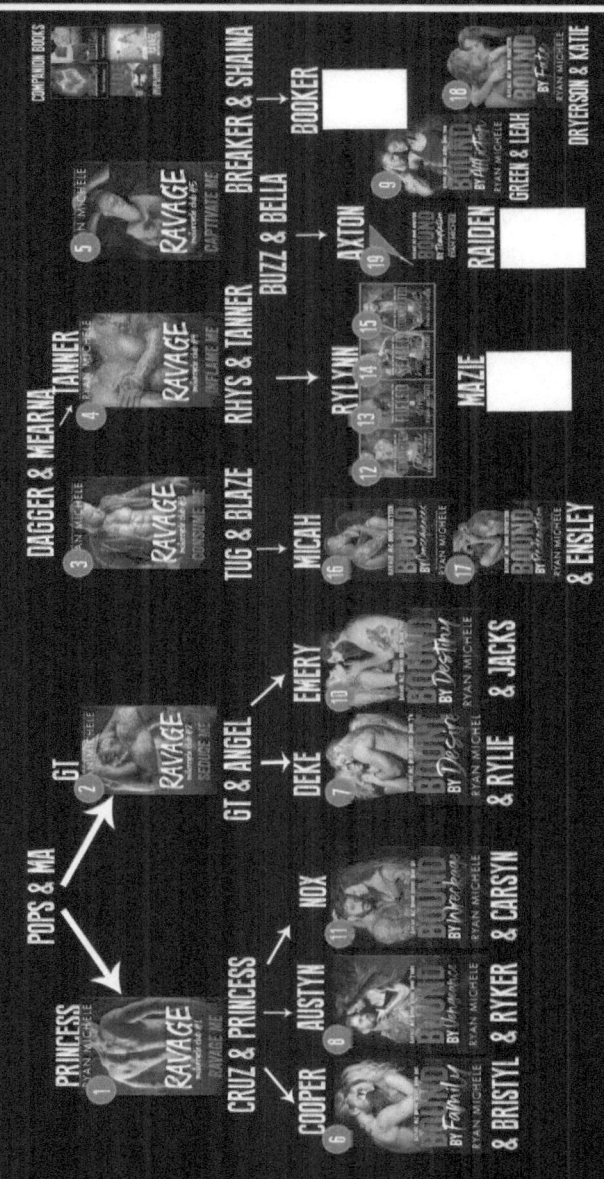

1. Ravage Me
2. Seduce Me
3. Consume Me
4. Inflame Me
5. Captivate Me
6. Bound by Family
7. Bound by Desire
8. Bound by Vengeance
9. Bound by Affliction
10. Bound by Destiny
11. Bound by Wreckage
12. Connected in Pain
13. Fueled in Fire
14. Sealed in Strength
15. Connected in Code
16. Bound by Consequences
17. Bound by Redemption
18. Bound by Fate
19. Bound by Temptation

COMPANION BOOKS

POPS & MA

PRINCESS

GT

DAGGER & MEARNA

TANNER

BREAKER & SHAINA

BOOKER

CRUZ & PRINCESS

GT & ANGEL

TUG & BLAZE

RHYS & TANNER

BUZZ & BELLA

COOPER   AUSTYN   NOX   DEKE   EMERY   MICAH   RYLYNN   AXTON   GREEN & LEAH

& BRISTYL & RYKER & CARSYN   & RYLIE & JACKS   MAZIE   RAIDEN   DRYERSON & KATIE

& ENSLEY

BLURB

Tik Tok ...

Every morning I entered Fallon's Bakery.

Coffee. That was what I told myself. I was only here for the coffee and sweets.

It had absolutely nothing to do with the woman who always had flour on her face, her hair in a messy bun on the top of her head, and a wide smile to greet every single person who entered the store.

Except for me. It always fell at the sight of me.

The man who ripped out her heart and walked away, never to look back. I was an a$$hole.

Now, all I could do was order my coffee, smile at her and leave.

Too bad considering all I could think about was her.

Too bad I was read to right the wrongs.

She would forgive me. No matter what I had to do.

I was Ax Monroe a brother of the Ravage Motorcycle Club and we never gave up.

She didn't know what was going to hit her because time was up and I was coming...for her.

It has taken me 52 books to come to the realization that I have talent when it comes to writing stories. I always thought my stories were blah ... until this one. Now I can see the gift I was given to write. Here's to more stories to come.

PROLOGUE

A PRICKLE HIT ME AND SLITHERED DOWN MY BACK. Someone was watching me. I hated that feeling. It always took me back to a time I never wanted to revisit. A time that taught me to always watch my surroundings.

CHAPTER ONE
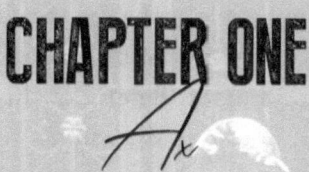

Walking through the door, the smell of smoke, booze, and sex assailed me. Three of the greatest smells if you asked me. Nothing made me feel more at home. It was a deeply heady concoction that stuck around the clubhouse daily.

Music hit my ears and thumped on in the background as barely dressed women, which I didn't mind one bit, danced on the makeshift floor in the center of the worn bar. Arms in the air, they shook their bodies and ground on anyone near them, getting lost in the rhythm. Several eyes came my way as I lifted my chin in acknowledgment yet didn't stop to say a word to anyone. Sure, I knew most people here; it was Sumner after all.

Ravage knew the lay of the land here.

They, meaning everyone, knew Ravage.

Enough said.

Checking out the booths on the far right of the building, Raid, my twin, sat nursing a longneck with two women standing at the end of the table smiling and oozing sex. Raid was sly, and no doubt he'd have one or both warming his bed later tonight. From the looks of their tits almost falling out of their flimsy tops, they were all in for that ride.

It was Ravage.

The cut, tattoos, bikes, arms made of steel, not giving two shits to fuck you up if you crossed us—all of it wrapped up in a leather package that no woman could resist.

Cocky? Sure, but I'd yet to have a woman complain. We'd grown up living this life, and it was all we knew.

The attention came wherever we went; hell, even the grocery store which I had to say was one of my least favorite things ever. I actually had a woman who did that shit for me now, so I didn't have to step foot in the store. If I did step into there, though, gazes would all be on me. It was the patch. The life. It drew people in. It piqued their curiosity.

Eyes continually scanning the crowd, there appeared to be no one ready to give us shit or cause us any problems. That was another part of this life; one never knew friend or foe. It kept you on your toes and alert. I'd been taught since birth the ways of the Ravage Motorcycle Club. Now, it was second nature. It was me.

Bimbos was one of the few bars in Sumner that Ravage visited that wasn't owned by the club. The place ran a tight ship and Bingo, Bimbo's old man, ran the joint. The club was on good terms with them, and we'd yet to have any issues here. Still, eyes were always open when it came to the others here.

There was always Studio X, the strip bar the Ravage MC owned and where we lived, where we could've met, but every once in a while, we needed a break. We lived and worked there, and this was our break.

Raid saw me coming closer and got up from the table. The two women thought he was rising for them, and their postures leaned into Raid's touch. But when he ignored them and turned to me, the girls shoulders deflated, and they followed his every move. Their eyes lit up once again—spotting me, no doubt—with some fucking twin fantasies or some shit. Seemed every woman had that dream at some point in their lives. Eighteen or eighty women seemed to love the idea. Damn well knew Raid, and I'd filled quite a few of those.

Never had a woman turn us down yet.

Hand out, Raid grabbed it and pulled me into a hug where he slapped me on the back twice and pulled away. "'Bout fuckin' time. You're late," he said with a grin.

We released each other and scooted into either side of the booth with the two women still standing there staring at us, waiting. "Looks like you weren't hurtin' for my delay."

Raid shook his head, smug as fuck. He was always giving me shit for anything and everything he could come up with. We both dished out what we gave. Fucking loved this man in front of me and nothing would tear that apart. Nothing. He was my brother more than in blood which made the bond untouchable.

Anything for this man. No questions asked.

If he told me to meet him somewhere with a pickax and zip ties, I'd be there in a heartbeat and smile doing whatever needed to be done. He was part of me.

"Well, hello..." the woman on the right purred as her tongue reached out over her bottom lip. Normally I'd be all for this attention since my cock couldn't fuck enough, but right now, Raid and I needed to talk family business. That meant bitches had to go.

"Hey. Go. We'll catch up later." Their demeanor changed at the tone in my words. If they wanted hearts and fucking flowers, I was not the man for that. A hard fuck they'd remember until they were ninety, that I could make happen. Loving words? Fuck that shit.

The dismissal made the girls pout for a moment, then a wide come-hither smile came to their lips, not ready to give up quite yet. "Don't forget us. We can be a lot of fun," she said then bit her lip seductively again. It must have been her come-on, telling us we could do anything we wanted with the both of them, and neither would say a fucking word. Gotta love that shit.

"I'm sure you are," I replied as the women hung

around a beat longer just to see if we honestly meant for them to move their asses. When we said nothing to the contrary and I lifted my brow making the ball cap on my head rise just a touch, silently telling them to get the fuck away, they finally got the hint and took off.

Pussy was pussy, and it was all around for the picking.

"Any reason you wanted to come here for this shit?" I asked my brother just as the waitress came over to the table.

"What can I get ya?" she asked, and I couldn't help appreciating the red leather corset that pushed up her breasts and tight black leather pants that hugged each of her curves and rode low on her hips. With blonde hair and brown eyes, she was definitely my type.

"Bud bottle with the cap on and you ridin' me later tonight," I answered as Raid just held up his bottle for another and shook his head at my antics.

"Bud it is," she said, turning away completely and dismissing the come-on. No doubt she was propositioned at every table she stopped at, including the women.

"Damn, bro. You got shot the fuck down," Raid teased.

"Nah. Momentary lapse in judgment." She posed a challenge, not fawning over us. That shit was hot. Easy pussy was just that—easy. When you had to work for it, it tasted so much sweeter. She was going to make me work. I was down for that.

Business first.

"Right. As for your question, just needed to get away for a bit."

This wasn't unusual for Raid. He had a bit of nomad in him at times, wanting to just be by himself on the open road. He said he thought better that way, but I knew he liked solitude too. Been that way since we were kids.

While I loved being in the thick of everything going on around me, he was more in the background. We might be identical twins, but personality wise, we were two completely different people. I was the loud to his quiet. His predictability to my impulsiveness. My need for eyes on me to his wanting to be on the sidelines.

We were the yin to each other's yang. Cut from the same cloth yet split down the middle so we balanced each other out.

Looking at Raid, everything about him was like looking into a mirror, except for the scar by his right eye. It was deep and gnarly, never healing right even though he had it stitched up and taken care of. Mom gooped that shit up at every turn, but it never went away. It actually caused part of his brow to not have hair.

To me it was badass. And he didn't seem to give two shits about it being on him. Actually never said a word about it or discussed with anyone how it happened. All I knew for sure was it was one of the very few ways to tell us apart.

"Right. What's up? You texted something about

family shit. Whose family, and who do I have ta kill?" I asked, and Raid chuckled even knowing I was serious as fuck.

The waitress came right then and set the two bottles down on the table, both with the caps firmly in place. I even grabbed it and made sure it was tight before nodding her off and giving her a wink to which she didn't acknowledge.

We both opened the beers and tossed the caps on the table with a tink to the wooden top. Whenever we were somewhere that wasn't exclusively Ravage, we opened our own shit. We'd learned our lesson on that one, and no chances were taken for history to repeat itself. People could be sneaky fuckers, and that was what got men like us killed. So, fuck that.

"Ours," Raid started. "Nick's back."

Fucking hell. "What the fuck does that dick want?" I asked, taking a huge pull on my beer, the coldness seeping into my bones. More than likely, though, this talk would need something stronger than beer. Anything that had to do with Nick needed Jack or Jim.

"Called me yesterday out of the fuckin' blue sayin' he wanted to come by the clubhouse and talk to the club. I told him fuck no, but you know Uncle dick. He's pushin'."

My head shook at the man's audacity. "Doesn't he ever fuckin' learn? He just wants to get his ass dead. Cruz will never forget the shit he pulled decades ago. Even suggesting coming to the club is asinine. He's lost his fuckin' mind."

Back when Cruz and Princess were getting together twenty or thirty years ago, Nick thought it would be a good idea to fuck Princess in a bathroom at the clubhouse. Granted she asked him too, but it didn't go over well. Cruz ended up tearing the door off the hinges, pulling my uncle away from his woman and Nick barely got out of the clubhouse without his ass kicked.

Nick wasn't allowed back in the clubhouse for any reason afterward. It had been said the actual fucking between the two never happened, but it was enough for Cruz to put a ban on Nick. No one fucked with his woman ever, even if she didn't know she was his at the time.

Even though Nick tried many times over the years to come back into the Ravage fold, since he was trying to be a Prospect before the bathroom incident, he eventually stopped pushing hard yet would bring up the Prospecting idea from time to time, putting a bug in our ear so maybe we'd change our mind. Yeah, fuck that.

Normally Nick would call his brothers—my father, Buzz, and Uncle Breaker, who were also twins and wouldn't give him an inch when it came to the club. They kept a tight leash around the man when it came to Ravage.

Looked like now he intended to drag Raid and myself into his craziassness. The question was, why?

We'd had "family" dinners over the years at my folks' home with Nick in attendance. Nothing too much, but enough to keep him in the family loop and our lives at least a little. The sad thing was when he brought up wanting to be part of the club, he just sounded pathetic. It had been fucking decades, dude—get the fuck over it. Wasn't gonna happen. Not only because of our President, Cruz, but because of the rest of the club.

Raid's mouth quirked up at the sides. "And when I asked him why the clubhouse and not just Dad's place, he said he needed to talk to the club, but he wouldn't give me the fuckin' reason, so he got another no."

I nodded. I knew my brother could handle it, not that he needed Nick's shit any more than the rest of us did. Raid was a good man. "Yeah. Good call. So, why am *I* here talkin' about this shit? You coulda texted and let me know the dick was callin'." Nick was par for the course and nothing justified this *we must meet in secret* bullshit.

"Because I got curious. He seemed to push harder than before. More insistent. Poking. Prodding. Trying my fuckin' patience. So, I did some digging." This was Raid calculating. He was the smart one, thinking shit through. Analyzing it. Coming up with information and putting a plan together to handle it. He was a lot like our father.

Me, I would have easily lost my shit on Uncle without taking pause to realize something was definitely off and needed more attention. I would've cussed his ass out and told him to leave us alone with all the club bullshit. Probably would've gone into the *haven't you learned over the years* shit.

A smile widened my face. Loved how smart my brother was. It was something I truly admired about him. "Of course, you did." Raid was thorough. Whenever something happened in the club, he'd learn the ins and outs backward and forward. The risks and benefits. He'd voice things when he had concerns, but if he felt it was a good call, he didn't say a word. It was just the type of man he was. He'd always taught me that knowledge was power, and I was lucky as fuck he had my back on that.

My memory was nowhere near as good as his. Raid, on the other hand, could remember shit from when we were five. I wouldn't be surprised if he didn't have it all written down somewhere under lock and key.

That'd be a hell of a read someday.

"Nick's in some serious shit out in Vegas." His face grew very serious, pulling my attention.

"What's happenin' now?" I asked, taking another long pull. It tasted like water. The way this was going, I'd need to get back home or to the clubhouse so I could have a full bottle of Jack ready and waiting.

"Brother…" Raid paused and shook his head, looking down at the table and then back to me. His eyes completely hard and serious. "Two hundred seventy-three thousand, four hundred seventeen dollars and seventy-two cents in the hole to be exact."

My eyes rolled back in my head as my lids shut. This fucker was going to get himself killed and not by Ravage. "Fucking hell. Bookie?" I asked, opening my eyes.

Because he sure as fuck didn't have anywhere near that kind of cake on hand to dish out. He was an electrician by trade, and while he made decent money, he sure as shit didn't make over two hundred thousand.

"Yep. Old Red."

It was my turn to stare at my brother. "Fucker's fucked." That wasn't even the half of it. Old Red had been in the bookie business for three, maybe four decades. Had cash coming out of everywhere from all of his dealings. Some shit legal. Some not. But whatever he had going on, no one fucked with him.

He had the best reputation as a bookie in Vegas because he didn't take any shit from anyone. He gave you money, you signed a contract and paid his fees—that were non-negotiable—and you paid him back at a specific time and date. But he didn't take that contract to the courts; nope, he'd destroy your life and wring every bit of cash he could, even if he had to sell you. He had no qualms with any of it.

There was an old saying "you couldn't squeeze blood from a turnip." Well, Red would squeeze and squeeze until blood magically appeared.

Even here in Georgia we knew who the man was. Didn't have any dealings with him, but Ravage knew who key players in our world were.

Yeah, Old Red was an evil fucker. One I sure as shit would never go to for fucking money. Ever.

Nick was a fucking idiot. Always knew he was a few bricks shy of a full load, but this was taking it to an entirely different level.

And if that fucker of an uncle used our names or the Ravage MC to get ahold of the funds, I'd kill him myself. Considering he was calling Raid, it was a crap shoot if Nick did or not.

"Nick wants us to give him the cake to cover that? I mean, since I just have that in my sock drawer or some shit."

Raid chuckled. We both knew we could get our hands on that much cash easily, hell we probably did have it at home, but it was always nice to have a mood break to laugh, especially with this topic. "Don't know the answer to that one because he didn't elaborate when I told him no. I'm thinkin' he either wants us to pay, or he wants to work for Ravage to get the funds. Either way is a no go."

Fuck yeah that was a no go.

"You tell Dad about this shit?" I asked, pulling on my beer once again.

His head shook in the negative. "Nope. We're goin' together to talk about this shit."

"Thanks so fuckin' much. What I've always fuckin' wanted," I grumbled. There was a reason that Nick didn't go directly to my dad or Uncle Breaker. That meant it was a possibility of being worse than Raid thought, and more along the lines of my thoughts of using the Ravage name which didn't sit well with me one bit.

Raid smiled. "I can't have all the fun when it comes to family shit."

"Yeah, but you're better than I am with it," I responded, pointing my bottle at him.

"Bullshit," he shot back immediately. "You just know I'll handle it, so you don't even fuckin' try."

I shrugged on a smile, then took another swig from the bottle. He wasn't wrong. He did just that all the time. "Damn straight. So, when we meetin' with our old man?"

"Tomorrow mornin' at his place. Just thought you needed a heads-up on what I was about to drop down on the old man."

"Fuckin' perfect. Let's find some pussy and get the fuck outta here."

On a smile, we both got up from the booth. At least there would be some good shit tonight to drown out all the bullshit.

CHAPTER TWO
Indie

A WIDE SMILE CROSSED MY FACE AS THE BELL OVER THE door rang, alerting me to the arrival of another customer. I'd almost thought of taking the offending metal down once upon a time because it rang constantly throughout the day, never taking a break all day long and giving me the occasional headache.

This technically wasn't a bad thing. It meant that customers were coming in, and that equaled money in the register. Who the hell wouldn't like that? So, I got over it and kept my bell.

Having your own business wasn't a walk in the park; that was for damn sure. But I loved my not so little bakery on the corner in downtown Sumner, Georgia. *Fallon's Bakery* to be exact.

I named it after my grandmother, and since my last name was Fallon too, it was considered both of ours. Gram Olive was the reason I started this place up two and a half years ago. I'd always loved to bake. But I really loved to design cakes. Ever see that TV show where the man makes those huge come to life cakes? That was me. One could call it a passion. GramO pushed me to have fun in life and always said, "Work is just that—work. Now passion, it can bring a paycheck and make you feel like you're floating on air."

So, I turned my passion into my job.

GramO was the reason I'd done and changed several things throughout my life. Loved that woman to bits, and the vat of knowledge in that woman's head was priceless. Every drop I soaked up like a sponge because she was always right. Always. Not joking. She could predict something years from now and kid you not, it would happen.

The bell over the door rang, and my head rose automatically with a "Welcome!" coming from my lips along with a smile. Every guest who entered this place was greeted because I wanted the bakery to feel like home. Like a place where people wanted to be. Where they could get some sweets and a coffee and go sit in one of the many tables, chairs, or couches to kick back with friends.

The bakery took a bit to get going. Sumner wasn't really the ideal place to have such a thing considering the town was smaller and there were a wide range of people. But once people came in and tasted what I had to offer, the place blew up. More than I'd ever thought possible. People came from neighboring towns to eat, drink, and hang out.

When I bought the building, it was a blank canvas completely at my whim, and I took every advantage with that. It was pretty funny the décor I chose, because it was the complete opposite as to what I had in my home.

Whereas my house was color and vibrance, hell I even had an orange fridge, this place was on the flip side of that. Modern with warm tones. When you entered there were two levels to the place, but the top loft was open and set back a bit with a clear railing so people up there could look down upon the people ordering.

The main level had gray tiled floors that appeared to look like wooden planks. I loved the look of it and bonus—it cleaned up with ease. The walls were a greenish blue tone that was calming and relaxing. Or, at least, that was what I'd hoped it did for customers.

I tried so many different swatches, and my brain kept going to emerald green, then I'd take a step back and remember, this was a business. Not my home. Emerald green would be for my house, not here. Even on the flip side of my home tastes, I still loved it. It was my yin and yang all rolled into one.

On the right side of the large space stood the glass cases full of my sweets, along with the register and the coffee bar. Off to the left were a variety of tables in a variety of sizes and shapes of circles, squares, and rectangles. All different, but all working well together. The chairs were a variety as well. Some had cushions, while others were wood, chrome, or steel.

They didn't match each other one bit, but yet it all

seemed to mesh well. I guessed that was putting my spin on the place to remind me of home. Huh ... never thought of that before. My twist of unique flowing through the bakery.

In the back of the place there were two large open areas. The first had one large table that would fit between eight to ten people, solid wood painted just a bit darker than the flooring. Off to the side of that were couches. Three to be exact, all in a U shape with a large ottoman in the middle.

Lamps warmed the place up, giving off a yellow hue when the blinds were closed.

The other room in the far back was for parties. Instead of one large table, it had three and room to expand. There were two recliners in the corner with a few bean bags for extra seating. This was an excellent idea from my mother, Dalilah, and had brought in extra funds. You'd be amazed how many people were looking for a place to have a party that they didn't have to set up or clean up. Even in Sumner. That part of the business alone was a huge success.

Back out in the front behind the glass cabinets was where all the magic happened. It was open so customers could see what was going on in the kitchen, such as if I were making one of my cakes. They could watch me design it from start to finish. I didn't mind the eyes on me while I worked, because when I was in the zone, only someone speaking to me directly made me pull out of it.

This setup gave the place a family feel. I was inviting you to come along and be a part of the experience that was Fallon Bakery. Be part of my process and part of my family.

The loft, which was the second floor, was the best part for me to create. The ceilings in this place were so tall that when I first saw it, I knew instantly I wanted another level added. Up there was comfort upon comfort. Yes, there were tables and chairs just like below, there was one large section that was just couches, bean bags, and other odds and ends I'd found that could be used for additional seating.

We also had a fireplace in the loft in the far corner. It was a great place to kick back, read, and stay a while. Which was what I wanted my customers to do. And they did. Some stayed all day. Some came and brought their laptops to work or even have meetings.

There were even game tables. I'd put a lot of love, time, and money into this place and I loved every inch of it.

"What can I get for ya?" I asked the next person in line. It was typical to have a long line here, especially in the mornings, and customers for the most part were cool about waiting. There were always a select few who were not. Those were the ones I wanted to sprinkle a little something else in their tasty treats, even though here in Georgia it was illegal to mellow them out a bit. Not that I would, but it could help them get the sticks out of their asses.

Just like the woman standing in front of me needed a bit of chill in her life. Not really chill. More like a tub of ice water to take a bath in and stay in until she was blue.

Mrs. Corbo, or as I knew her in high school—Lexi Jones. She married right out of high school and started popping out babies. She also decided to never grow up.

She didn't come in here often, but when she did it took every bit of restraint to be nice.

I continued speaking after recognizing her and added, "A grande caramel macchiato upside down with extra caramel at 180 (degrees)." The order she'd recited every time she came into the bakery. Even though I knew it by heart, she always *had* to repeat it to me as if she thought I'd forget part of it. So I waited, stiff smile intact for that very thing to begin. Over the years, I fully admit my patience had more than a crack in it, but customer service was the key to success and all that. It was soon to run out.

GramO said that with age came not giving a fuck. Yes, she used those exact words. She gave zero fucks which was only one reason I loved her. My time to give zero fucks was getting closer by the day. What that had to say about my business, I didn't know. Only one way to find out—one day at a time and hope I didn't snap before then.

Truthfully, I just wanted to make my cakes, but helping with the coffee line when it was outrageously long was my duty as the owner.

"No, I want a Grande Caramel Macchiato upside down with extra caramel at 180(degrees)," she demanded, and I'd just stopped myself from telling her that I'd said that exact thing moments before and from rolling my eyes with a huge sigh added in for shits and giggles.

She wouldn't care, though, and it wasn't worth my breath. If she wanted to have a shitty day—hell, shitty life from what I'd heard around town—that was on her. It wouldn't dim my day because I wouldn't let it. Sun was out, and there was a cake on the horizon that I needed to work on in a bit.

She was incredibly grouchy, but it was an "all the time thing" instead of a "give me my caffeine fix" thing. It was permanently scratched onto her psyche and on her pinched off face. Life was way too short to be pissed off all the time, but it was hers to live. If she wanted to be miserable, her call.

Everyone had a choice on how to live their lives, and this one didn't make a very good one, but again, that was her choice.

I got busy making Mrs. Corbo's drink and heard the bell go off once more. Turning my head, I greeted the next customer, then turned my focus back to the coffee.

I finished the drink and turned back to Mrs. Corbo, gave her the total, and handed her the coffee once she put the money in my hand. Needless to say, I didn't trust this woman any further than I could throw her.

Trying to keep whatever smile I could muster for her, I gave her the change from her twenty dollar bill.

She crumbled up the bills and put them in her

huge purse that could fit a small dog easily. Each time she came in, she had a different one.

"Whore," she coughed under her breath, and my eyes narrowed. It had been a long time since I'd been called that, and my ass was not going back there.

"Excuse me?" I asked her as she turned away from me and started toward the door.

It pissed me off when she didn't stop, and my happy bubble appeared to pop as I said rather loudly, "Heard the gas station has some great coffee. Perfect 180(degrees). You should go there next time."

It was then she turned to me. "Pardon me? Are you kicking me out of your bakery?" She huffed.

"Appears so. And keep your comments to yourself. Being an asshole doesn't make you pretty."

She turned on a huff and stormed out the door.

"Nothin' like pissin' off the regulars," my brother Marley commented as he came from the back of the bakery holding two boxes.

"Here ya go." Marley handed over the two white boxes with "Fallon's Bakery" in a teal script font over the top of them to a waiting customer. I'd worked endlessly on the logo for this place. It had to be official, legible, and fun. Fallon was written neatly in a cursive, loopy font, and the word bakery was in bold block letters underneath. I absolutely loved it.

"Thanks, and Indie." Julie another woman who attended my high school asked.

"Yes?"

"She's a bitch. To everyone. Never take shit from people like her."

A smile came to my lips. "Amen sister."

Julie turned and left the store, and only then did I breathe not realizing I hadn't in a few beats.

Marley started to go back to his hidey hole, but I grabbed his arm. "Can you clean up the tables out there really quick? Meadow won't be in for another hour, and I need your help." I gave him my most dazzling smile.

Seeing the look on his face, I knew that he was going to say something about cleaning. Instead of letting him go on his little word vomit, I put my finger on his lips. "Please," I said, giving him my best stern look which he thought was hilarious and showed as much when he started laughing.

"Fine."

My smile widened in triumph.

GramO said you catch more flies with honey than vinegar.

Family was family. Being the boss, though, wasn't always easy. Especially with those who were late.

CHAPTER THREE

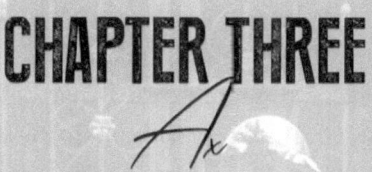

CUTTING THE ENGINE TO THE TAHOE, I LOOKED UP TO see Fallon's Bakery in curvy and bold letters scrolled on top of the building awning. The actual building had been in Sumner forever, or at least as far as I could remember. Dad said it used to be an old mill but sat empty for years until Indie took it over.

Indigo Jamison Fallon.

The one who would not get out of my head even after all these years.

She was like a drug to me. Every morning, I came here and ordered coffee and one of her blueberry muffins. Every morning, she smiled tightly at me. Every morning, I'd turn around and walk back out the door. Every. Single. Morning.

It was my own brand of torture. An addiction. One that I was unable to stop or control.

Entering the building, my eyes went immediately to the beauty who lifted her head to greet her customers every time she heard that bell ring, even when she was in the back. Not when she was working on the cakes, but any other time. She seemed to be in her own world with those.

"Welcome!" Indie called out, wide smile directed at me. The full force of it could knock the strongest man on his ass. Talk about beautiful and downright sexy. Her lips told her feelings. Smiling, flat, tipped, quirked, down, frown—all of them. If you put a mask over her face and just showed me her lips, I'd know who she was in a glance.

Not a stitch of makeup and her hair up in a messy thing on top of her head, no one could compare to her beauty. Ever. I'd known that even as an asshole teen she was special. She was unique.

There was nothing I wouldn't do to protect this woman. I'd kill without blinking an eye, but she couldn't stand to be anywhere around me. When our eyes connected, hers danced for just barely a moment, then the look was washed away as if it was never there in the first place and was replaced with an indifference I fucking couldn't stand.

She hated me. I knew it. Hell, everyone knew it. It was well deserved. I was a dick to her years ago, and it was something a woman like her would never forget or forgive.

Every action had a consequence. I knew that better than most in my line of work.

But she was a temptation that I had to get my fix

of every morning, come hell or high water. I needed her like I needed air, even if it were for her to barely give me the time of day.

She wasn't a "challenge" like the woman at the bar. No, Indie was on a pedestal so high, she was now unreachable for me. She deserved better, and it was the way things had to be. She was heaven while I remained in hell.

Today must've been my lucky day with Indie working the register. Normally she had others do that task, while she was in the back working on her beautiful cakes. She was a creative genius. I'd seen several of her cakes, and they looked like 3D magic.

Currently, though, it was nice to have her full attention if only for a minute. It'd been a long damn time since I'd felt the full effects of Indie with just a look.

"What can I get ya?" Indie asked, making eye contact, but she felt so far away, closed off. Cordial but not herself either. She erected an enormous wall between us to protect herself. I understood it, and I didn't see it ever coming down. "Your usual?"

A smirk came to my lips. How she remembered everyone who stepped into the bakery's orders when most of the time she wasn't even up front was beyond me. Especially some of the shit people ordered these days. Two pumps whatever, foam and milk ... blah, blah, blah.

Between the sweets and coffee, she deserved a fucking medal for remembering shit.

In my case, part of me would give anything for her to forget the bad shit that came from me.

"Two of those, two black coffees, and whatever in the hell my mom gets when she's here."

Her demeanor relaxed at the mention of my mother. My mother, Bella, and Indie loved each other once upon a time. They'd go shopping and do girl shit when I had shit to do. Truthfully, Mom still loved her to this day. I'd fucked that up too.

Their relationship had my mother so pissed at me for my actions. She didn't talk to me for a while, but I knew she still talked to Indie. I wasn't a stupid man; I just never brought it up.

"Sure thing. Anything else?" she asked writing with a black marker on the five cups in front of her.

"Yeah. Give me a dozen mixed donuts, a dozen of those cherry and apple things, and mixture of those sweet lemon bars you make." God the woman could bake. She was truly amazing at her gift.

Her hand holding the sharpie went to her hip, and her brow tilted in question. "You havin' a party?"

"Nah, family meetin'. Thought I'd try and sweeten' them up," I said, giving her my smile. Fuck, was I flirting with her?

I must've been because she turned around and started getting my order ready without another word. That was the shit I hated, her utter dismissal. But I had no one to blame but myself. She wasn't rude by any means. More professional.

Her, baker. Me, customer.

Nothing more.

Nothing like years before.

She buzzed along, my eyes going to her round ass. That ass was so perfectly peach shaped women around the world aspired to have one like it. I'd had the ass in my bed and kissed every damn inch of it. She always tasted sweet like honey straight from the hive. It felt as though it was just for me. As if she was made just for me.

My cock started to stir. It always did around Indie, but especially when her ass jumped out at me. Hell, it happened just breathing the same air as her.

If I grabbed her and fucked her against the wall, would anyone here stop me? Would she let me? Fuck.

She came to the glass case I'd moved to and started stacking boxes along with the coffees. There was no way in hell I'd be able to carry all of it at once. Which was fine. It was why I drove the Tahoe and not my bike.

The register beeped as she added up my total, still polite, but distant.

"That's ninety-two twenty-six," she said looking up expectantly.

"No family discount, huh?" I teased, trying to get a rise out of her. Just something. Anything but that voided mask.

That apparently was the wrong thing to say because her face fell.

No more smiling Indie. No, this was the enraged lit Indie who had a strong bite. She was two sides of a coin, just depended on what end came up once it was flipped. She could be nice as a kitten one moment, and in the next a fierce panther ready to claw your eyes out. I loved them both. Missed them both.

And since I was one of the lucky ones to piss her off, the panther was ready to attack, and I was ready for her bite. It was a craving that hit hard. If she'd just give me a snippet, I'd take it.

"Cash?" she asked instead of responding to me or commenting, but I could hear the bite in her tone.

I grabbed my wallet and pulled out two hundred-dollar bills, handing them to her. She did what she always did. Cashed it out without a word and put the rest in the tip jar. So what if I way overpaid to make sure her tip jar wasn't light. She shared with her employees, and I wanted to make sure she was taken care of.

This dance started when the place opened, and I came in. She wanted to give me change, and I told her I was just putting it in the tip jar, and she should do the same. After a month of going back and forth with it, she finally gave up, putting whatever change leftover in the jar.

I felt it was a win on my end.

If anyone else checked me out, they did the same thing as Indie.

"I'll get Marley to help you."

This gesture was a surprise. I'd thought for sure she'd want to see me drop the five large coffees and burn myself to shit in retaliation.

She stepped around the corner and called out for her brother who came from behind the glass.

"Can you help him to his car please?" Indie asked him.

"He should just make a few trips," Marley growled as he saw it was me needing the help. Yeah, no love lost there. That was what happened when you broke someone's baby sister's heart irrevocably.

He lifted the boxes and waited for me to get the coffees in the little cardboard carrying case.

"Thanks, man. I appreciate it." I turned to Indie. "Thanks." She said nothing, just nodded.

What I wouldn't give for her beautiful smile to smile for me, at me, or something with me once again.

Marley was ... well, Marley. True to his name, he was high as a kite most of the time. On what exactly, I didn't know, but probably weed. Longer hair in the back brushed his shoulders. It was the beard I didn't understand.

It was long and bushy, but he tied it in a ponytail right at the base of his chin. At first, I thought it was because he worked here and was trying to keep hair out of the food. Then I'd seen him out exactly the same way. To each their own.

Marley held the door open as I walked through and led him to the Tahoe.

"You know she's never going to take you back, right?" Marley stated as I bleeped the locks and carefully opened the passenger side door. This was a bit out of the blue. He hadn't said anything to me about his sister in years. Then again, our time together was very limited, and he'd never been given a face to face opportunity like this.

Indie set me up wide for this one. Couldn't blame her, though.

"You come in every mornin' flashin' all that cash like some biker big shot. Givin' more than you should just to what, buy her? That shit doesn't work on her. She's not for fuckin' sale. You should already know this," he continued, standing next to the passenger side door.

I set the coffees down on the floorboard in a way they wouldn't tip over, then reached for the boxes. "Who said I wanted to start shit up with her?" Because I knew no one had. That bridge burned and was ash that was swept away with the wind. Nothing but time rewinding back to high school and different choices made would allow her to want anything to do with me, besides my money for her baked stuff. Since I couldn't change time, I had to deal with the fallout.

"Because a blind man could see right through you. How you look at her now like she's your last meal and you're a starving man. Like she's everything you always wanted—the sun, moon, and fucking stars. Well, let me tell you that meal is dead and gone to you. You're a pitch black sky with no rays of light. She fuckin' hates your ass."

She did. I knew it down to my shattered soul. And as much as I didn't want to care, that I didn't want it to bother me, it did and it pissed me off. She had been under my skin since the time we first saw each other in high school. Never had she made her way out. At this rate, she never would. She was an unseen tattoo carved into my soul that I felt every time I'd thought about her.

"Just came to get my family some donuts and coffee and support our local businesses." I set the boxes down on the seat and turned to Marley, the look of disgust on his face.

"Right, just keep it that way. She doesn't want you. Don't forget it."

Before I could say anything or punch him in the face, he turned and walked back into the store.

Motherfucker.

Slamming the door, I went around to the driver's side, jumping in and turning over the engine.

Nothing Marley said was a lie. Didn't mean I had to like that shit. It was well over time to let it go. To let her go.

When she left Sumner immediately after graduating, those ties should've been cut then. But they weren't. It was as if they followed her everywhere she went, connecting us. And when she came back to town, it was a kick in the gut because those ties were only reinforced.

Seeing her everyday made them tighter. I was so fucked when it came to Indie.

Sure, I could go out and fuck any woman. But Indie, she was the only one I'd ever truly loved. The only one who meant something when we had sex. The only one I'd wanted to call mine, but life got in the way.

"Fuck me," I grumbled, shaking my head and

unable to clear my thoughts of her. She was always there. Always lurking.

Driving to my folks' place didn't take long, and I pulled into the driveway and killed the engine. Sucking in a deep breath, I pushed all the thoughts of Indie down and prepared for this not so fun conversation ahead of me.

My father tended to blow up at the mention of Nick because of the shit he pulled in the past. No, not just the Princess thing. There was a huge list of his indiscretions that my father could recite by memory. Which now that I thought about it was probably another reason Nick contacted Raid instead.

Raid wanted me to come and take some of the heat my father had to dish. Not a problem. Plus, I had those kickass lemon bars. No one could resist those. It'd be fine.

My brother pulled up behind me on his Harley just in the nick of time to help me carry in shit.

I hopped out of the SUV as Raid swung his leg off the bike. "Where's your bike?" he asked, knowing I'd rather be on my bike than any four-walled vehicle.

He started pulling things from his saddlebags. Stacks of papers and folders, no doubt still investigating Nick's shit. Lord knew what he found now, but from the look on his serious face, it wouldn't be great.

"Clubhouse. Got some shit to hopefully ease Dad enough so that he doesn't blow the fuckin' roof off the house and piss Mom off. Get over here and help." I nodded to the passenger side door.

Meeting with parents could go good. Or

extremely bad. Depended on the day. And with this topic, there weren't many positives.

A wide smile came across Raid's face.

"What?"

He nodded to the boxes with the bakery logo on it. "You're sure a fuckin' glutton for punishment."

I looked down at the box then back up at my brother. "Shut the fuck up."

He laughed full-out and carried the coffee holder while I grabbed the large boxes. Of course Raid knew everything.

The sound of a motorcycle coming from around the corner had our attention as we turned to it. My gut tightened as Uncle Breaker and Aunt Shaina pulled into the drive.

"Fuck me. Dad knows it's Nick," I concluded with their arrival.

Raid nodded. "Yep. Reinforcements."

"He probably already knows everything," I said as Raid shook his head.

"Doubt that..."

The hairs on my arm stood to attention. "Maybe we should call the fire department and let them know there's about to be an explosion."

Raid shook his head with a small smile as we moved toward the door.

Aunt Shaina climbed off the motorcycle with Uncle Breaker following. They took off their helmets and came our way. Aunt Shaina's smile was so wide she looked as though she'd burst. That was her, though. Happy. Fun. Loving.

Uncle Breaker lifted his chin, and I followed suit. Aunt Shaina went in for a hug but that was impossible with my hands full. I turned my head to the side and kissed her on the cheek.

"Oh, you boys." She glowed.

"Let's get this shit done." Uncle Breaker was already pissed off. Sounded like a great morning if you asked me. Four pissed off hot heads at your service.

Uncle Breaker held the door open for all of us to enter, then brought up the rear and followed us in.

"My babies!" my mother cried, coming through the kitchen, into the living room, and to the doorway.

"Ma, not babies anymore. Think you'd know that by now," Raid said, earning him a slap on the shoulder.

"None of that nonsense. You'll be my babies until my last breath."

That was an uneasy thought. One I washed from my brain.

Her hands went on either side of Raid's head and kissed his forehead. Something that he had to bend down for because there was no way in hell she'd be able to reach him. We were tall motherfuckers.

Once she let him go, it was my turn, and she did the same to me. "Hey, Mom. How are ya?" I asked, kissing her on the cheek when she was done with me.

"Great now that my boys are home." She reached for the boxes. "Give me those," she demanded, but I held them away from her.

I wasn't a fucking moron. Mom was gold in this

house and didn't do any unnecessary work according to our father. That meant carrying boxes the ten feet from the front door to the kitchen.

"Nope. I got them." I sidestepped her and moved toward the kitchen where my dad happened to be.

"Hey, old man," I teased, sitting down the large boxes.

My father came up to me without a single word and socked me in the stomach. It wasn't hard and didn't make me gasp for breath, but it got the point across. "Call me old again and I'll break your body."

"So touchy. You forget to get laid this morning?" I taunted, tightening my abs in case he decided to go in for another.

"Don't you worry about me. Getting laid is always a top priority in this house." He wrapped his arms around me in a tight hug. I returned the gesture and slapped the man on his back a few times.

We broke apart, and a smirk graced his face. I liked my parents happy, so sue me. I didn't really want to hear about them fucking, but it came with the territory.

After greetings went around and everyone devoured coffee and Fallon's treats, my dad asked us all to sit around the table.

The house we grew up in was modest. Three bedrooms, two baths, and a huge deck off the back of the house. This place was all Raid and I knew except for the clubhouse. Mom made it a home and always said a bigger house was more for her to clean. Which was a line of shit because Dad hired a company to come in and clean. See, Mom was queen here. Everyone bowed. Dad made it that way.

The table in the dining area was large and fit all of us comfortably as we took our seats.

"Let's do this," my dad ordered, and shit was about to get dirty.

CHAPTER FOUR
Indie

THAT MAN.

Every damn morning, he came in for coffee.

Every damn morning, he left a huge tip in the jar for us.

Every damn morning, I wanted to smack him upside the head, then tell him thank you for the extra.

Except, I didn't.

Even after all these years Ax Monroe still made my heart rate speed up. Only now it was from rage. An anger so harsh that I knew it wasn't healthy for me.

I should be over it, but deep inside my soul I just couldn't let it go. I wanted to. Damn, did I want to. It would make life so much easier, but it was there every day.

GramO always said, "There was a thin line

between love and hate." Then she told me that was what Ax was to me. Even though she was always right, I so wanted to doubt her.

I was not a fish about to get on some man's hook.

Something inside of me just wouldn't shake it or him. No matter the hurt he caused me, he was there like a scar on my heart always bleeding. Moving away from Sumner didn't help erase him from my memories. Instead, it made me remember him more if that was possible. I hated being away from my family, and he would not keep me from being with them, so I came back.

First time I saw him when I returned was like my heart stopped then caught fire. It was pain and sorrow. Then it turned to rage and anger. I could deal better with the latter than the former.

It'd been years. Years. How this man had kept some type of control over me, I did not know. Maybe if I figured that out it would be a start to ending it. To moving on fully with my life. To forget about the past and start living again.

What I needed was my mom to come and sage me out. Maybe this time it would erase all negativity, and I could ignore the hundreds of times it hadn't. She always had this way of cleansing the aura around people. She had a gift. Unfortunately, when it came to Ax, she had troubles with those gifts.

All this inner turmoil sucked and sent me in a bit of a downturn.

I thought it was because we never actually had closure. Maybe? Hell I didn't even know anymore.

Ahhhhh!! I needed to scream it out.

"Stop it. No one brings you down," I murmured to myself when not a soul was around.

A prickle hit me and slithered down my back. Someone was watching me. I hated that feeling. It always took me back to a time I never wanted to revisit. A time that taught me to always watch my surroundings. Here, though, I felt safe, and this feeling was unwanted.

Turning, I released a breath of air I didn't know I was holding as my eyes landed on a very attractive man with blond hair neatly styled, wearing a navy polo shirt and khakis who was sitting at a table by the window looking at me. A smile came to my lips as I moved around the counter.

"Hey, Blaine. What are you doin' here? Thought you had to work?" I asked him as I got closer.

He pulled me into his arms and wrapped me up in them. "Had to come see my girl and see how her day's goin."

I squeezed him tightly and pulled back. "Friends, remember, Blaine? You said you could do friends."

Blaine and I met several months ago at a bar here in Sumner called Bimbo's. I was out with a friend when we met. Our eyes connected across the room, and we didn't leave each other's side the entire night.

"I can want my friend to have a good day," he retorted as I pulled away and looked up at him.

"A text would've fit the bill. Now you've gotta drive all the way back to Dawson." He lived about an hour away, which was another reason why I wanted to just be friends.

"I've got the day off actually and wanted to take you to dinner tonight. You up for it?"

Dinner. Okay. "Sure. I don't get done until around seven."

"Not a problem."

"Indie! Get back here!" My sister Meadow finally made her appearance at work and was already yelling.

"I've gotta go. Pick me up here at seven. Okay?"

He pulled me into his arms again and kissed the top of my head. "I won't be late."

We disentangled ourselves from one another and stepped back. "I'll be here."

Blaine's eyes danced and I had this strange feeling that he was going to kiss me.

Moving quickly, I stepped back. "I've gotta run. See ya later." I practically ran to the back where my sister was, my heart beating hard.

Meadow was standing by one of the large stainless-steel tables in the kitchen, looking down at a clipboard and paying me no mind as I got my heart to slow down. "All the cardboard hasn't come in yet. I put that order in weeks ago," she said.

We used the cardboard circles, rectangles, squares and anything else we needed to put under the cakes for stability. Even had PVC pipes to help with that task too. Cardboard was a priority. Not top priority, but it was up there.

"Call Mario and see what the holdup is."

She rolled her eyes at me, looking exasperated. "You don't think I've tried? That man only wants to talk to you."

"Just because he wants in my pants. Not. Gonna. Happen," I responded, meaning every single word. Mario owned a warehouse called Surplus just on the outside of Sumner that sold everything. I don't say that lightly.

You needed lights? No problem. He had them. You needed saws? He had that too. What his affiliation was in life, I didn't know or want to know. I just needed the supplies at a decent price, and he said he'd deliver—double bonus.

"I've gotta get started on the Anderson cake, and then I'll call him."

Meadow tapped her pen on the clipboard and looked down at it, her pen stopping. "Is that the dinosaur?"

"Yep. The 3D, big as hell, they probably won't be able to get it through the door dinosaur." This was no stretch of the imagination. The thing was large.

Meadow started chuckling. "Have at it. I'll be in the front."

"How are the little ones?" I asked her before she made it too far away from me.

"Ornery and missing their Aunty Indie."

It was my turn to chuckle. "I'll get them, feed them all sugar, and bring them back to you wound tighter than the skirts Luna wears."

This had us both in fits of laughter. Luna was the oldest sister who got the stuffy gene in the family.

Business skirts and blazers were all she wore. She had a job in Atlanta as an accountant, and yes she did our books too. Told you I didn't do numbers.

But the skirts she wore were so tight, I was surprised she could sit down in them without splitting the seams. Somehow, she managed. It was a running joke with the entire family.

Meadow's continued laughter could be heard easily as she walked to the front of the store.

"So was that Blaine who just left?" she asked me, being her nosy ass self.

"Yeah. We're going to dinner tonight."

Meadow put the clipboard under her arm and rubbed her hands together like she was coming up with some mysterious plan. Who the hell did she think she was? The Wizard of Oz or something?

There was no yellow brick road in these parts.

"That is so exciting!" she exclaimed. "You need to get laid."

This had my head snapping to her. "Could you say that just a bit louder? I don't think the customers upstairs heard you," I snarked.

She put her hands over her mouth in a megaphone style and sucked in a deep breath. Before she could yell it, I wrapped my hand around her mouth so only muffled noises could be heard.

Meadow was laughing.

"Stop it. I don't need everyone knowing shit. You know how small Sumner is."

I released my sister as she turned from me. "Don't we know that. I'll be up front."

Moving over to the office where we had standing orders, I pulled out the file marked "Anderson" and grabbed a clipboard, *yes we had a serious thing for clipboards around here,* and made my way back out to the table, opening it on the way and clipping what I needed to the board.

It was little Scout Anderson's sixth birthday, and he wanted a dinosaur. He wanted it to be about eight feet tall and from his little arms going around in a circle like the size of a table. Thanks, but that wasn't feasible. It would be pretty awesome, but it needed to fit through the doors.

Instead, I talked the kiddo around to a large dinosaur with its head climbing out of a cage with his hands tearing at the chains opening for him to get out. Pretty much a top view of the dinosaur tearing itself out of confinement. It was definitely more doable than an eight-foot replica of a T-Rex.

While I loved baking all the sweets in the bakery, this right here, designing and crafting a cake to make it look alive, 3D, and elaborate was my passion. It was what made my passion into a business. Just like GramO said.

Excitement hit me as I went over the sketches I'd made, another passion of mine. It was go time, and I was ready to work. The sheet of paper by the sketches had a list of supplies I'd need.

Getting busy, I easily fell into the zone, blocking out everything and every sound around me. Molding and sculpting the cake was awesome. I could see it in my head and started to carve off pieces to round certain areas. The image to me was so vivid, and full-out joy filled me.

"Know you hate to be bothered when you're in the zone, but someone wants to talk to you," Meadow called from behind me a few hours later. I'd just gotten all the cake formed of the dinosaur's head and was thinking of working on the hands next. Did I mention when I was in the zone I lost track of time too? Well, I did.

"Who?" I asked as I turned around seeing Blaine there, a wide smile across his lips. I looked over at the clock on the wall as it read a quarter to seven.

"Shit. I'm so sorry. I got busy..." I held up my cake covered hands. Hell, I probably had it in my hair and on my face at this point of the process.

"You lost track of time. It's fine," he stated with a grin on his face, holding up a plastic bag. "I thought you would, so I brought dinner."

Wow. The forethought was impressive even if I had long ago sworn off giving in to a man easily ever again. I grabbed a towel off the table and wiped my hands off as I rose from the stool I'd been sitting on, feeling my tight muscles. Yeah, I'd been sitting way too long.

"That's so sweet!" my sister said with a wide smile.

My eyes went to my sister. "You can go now."

"Right. Everything is cleaned up. I'll lock the door behind me."

"Thank you." She stared at me a beat, winked, and turned to the door.

If she thought I would screw this man back here

in my sanitized area of cakes, she had another thing coming. That didn't work for me one bit. Not that I was going to screw Blaine or anything, but it was the thought.

"What are ya workin' on?" He nodded to the sculpted cake behind me. On instinct I turned to the side and admired my work. Getting the cake just right was important. Just like any other structure, the base was always important to the stability of the piece. I needed to focus on that next and not the hands.

"Dinosaur. Once the fondant covers the cake it'll look more like a head."

He turned his head this way and that, inspecting my work. Part of me felt a little shy with him measuring my cake. I loved what I did, and I didn't need anyone telling me I sucked. But Blaine wouldn't do that. Nothing in the past few months should lead me to believe he'd tell me I was a horrible baker. Those damn insecurities again. *Thanks, Axhole!* I shook my head. Now was not the time to be thinking about him.

"I can see it. You're very talented."

This had me smiling with relief. Had to admit, I liked hearing the compliment from him. I'd texted him pictures of my cakes, but he'd never come in the back like this. It was nice to share this part of my life with him.

"Thank you. Why don't we sit over there where cake isn't everywhere?" I pointed to the clean table only a few feet away. It had stools around it, but I'd sat on a stool long enough today, so I grabbed a chair.

"I would've gotten that for you." Blaine told me as he pulled out Mexican from the white bag, the smell making my stomach growl. He smiled. "Knew you like burritos and rice."

"I'm starving. I haven't eaten since breakfast. Once I get in the zone, I stay there until something pulls me out."

He handed me a wrapped up greasy goodness. I took it and opened it. Truthfully, I didn't care if it had beans in it, which weren't my favorite, because I was so hungry. Once Blaine got his food out and sat down, I took a huge bite and groaned loudly.

Blaine chuckled. "Good?" he asked.

I opened my eyes, not realizing I'd shut them, and felt a blush creep my cheeks. Yes, Blaine and I had been talking for a couple of months now, but that didn't mean I knew him really, and I felt a little shy at the noises I made.

We hadn't made it anywhere near moaning in our relationship. A kiss maybe, but moaning in pleasure, not so much.

"Very. Thank you for bringing food here. It was very thoughtful of you." More than thoughtful.

He shook his head. "Not a problem. You told me how you get when you're working, and I selfishly wanted to spend time with you, so I brought food to you."

Little butterflies flitted in my stomach. Yeah. I was twenty-seven and I was getting butterflies. It was sweet, him knowing that information about me and going above and beyond to make sure I ate. It'd been a long time since someone thought of me in such a way.

"I appreciate it. So what made you come to town today? Not that I'm complaining." I smiled at my food as he gave me one in return.

"My boss is an asshole, so I called in sick and drove here."

"What happened?"

He waved his arm in dismissal. "Nothing too bad. Just putting more work on me than I can do in one day. Got fed up and needed a break."

"Where do you work again?"

"Over at Georgia State Bank in Dawson."

I nodded and took another bite and wiped my mouth with a napkin. "That's the thing with owning your own business. You don't have to answer to anyone but yourself. And that side of me can be a bitch sometimes."

He full-out laughed. "What does she bitch about?"

"Everything. The floors didn't get cleaned good enough, the cake fell, the cupcakes were put in the cooler without any frosting; you know, all that fun stuff."

"Sounds like a royal pain for you."

"She is. She tried to get me to do math, but I refused. No math here," I teased, making him laugh deep which egged me on. "I mean, come on; cups I'm great with, but balancing all the books? No thank you."

"Math is a part of life unfortunately, but it's how I

make my living. Or writing loans documents. None of which is fun or exciting."

Swallowing down my bite, I liked the banter between us. "Which is why my sister does it for me. Then I can create, bake, and have fun. It was the point of me starting the business in the first place."

"I admire that. Unfortunately for me I don't have a talent I'm great at to open my own place. Part of the working force I am."

I swiped the napkin across my face. "I realize I'm lucky. Very lucky actually. If I didn't have my family here to help and support me, I'm not sure I'd have made it. They've been a huge part of my ability to make this bakery the success it is today."

"I love how close you are with your family."

A smile came across my lips. "We are. How about you? Are you close with yours?"

It had been a curiosity of mine for a while, but I never had an opportunity like this to ask him.

His head shook. "Some distant cousins, but no one I'm close with."

This shocked me. "Your parents? Siblings?"

"Don't have a clue who my dad is. Mom passed about six years ago in a car accident. I only had a brother, but he's gone too."

My heart broke for the man. I put my food down, cleaned off my hand, and put it on top of his, giving him a squeeze. "I'm so sorry. That had to be hard."

He turned his hand around and held mine just the same. The touch didn't feel intimate, but it did feel powerful as if he was telling me something he had trouble expressing.

Blaine's smile felt a bit forced, but it was there all the same. "Thanks. It has been, but I'm good."

I tried pulling my hand away after giving his another squeeze, but he held it tight, and my eyes shot up to his.

"Give me one more minute," he asked low, and I could feel the pain coming from him. Therefore we kept our hands together.

Once he released me, I teased, "Not that I mind holding your hand and all, but this burrito is screaming my name."

He chuckled. "Please eat."

I dug back in as did he. At the last bite, he asked, "Good? Are you full?"

My hands crumbled up the paper and tossed it to the table. I grabbed my stomach, feeling how full it was. "Now I'm gonna have to clean up and get home so I can sleep." The fatigue of the day was officially starting to pull me under.

"Let me help," Blaine responded, getting up grabbing all the garbage and tossing it in the trash.

"Thanks."

He looked over at the cake a bit puzzled. "So, what do we have to do here?"

On a smile, I got up and moved over to the cart we had on wheels. "We put this wax paper over the top of it." I handed him the box that was on the side of the dino. "Then we put it on here and roll it into the fridge. The rest of this I'll put in one of the tubs I have, and Marley will take care of it later."

"Sounds good to me."

Everyone had left for the day, and I had to admit that normally I'd clean all my stuff up before I left, but I was exhausted and needed sleep. Marley would bitch about it tomorrow, but he'd get over it.

"There. You ready to head out?" Blaine asked as I looked over all the tables. We were able to clean it up pretty well.

"Yeah. Let me grab my bag."

After moving into the office, grabbing my bag and pulling out my keys, I moved to the front of the building. "Let me check all the locks and set the alarm. I'll meet you at the back door."

"Sounds good." He went to the back and me to the front.

Blaine was a very nice man. He'd always shown me respect, moving very slow with me. Was it horrible that part of me wished he'd just kiss me and not let me breathe?

Only one man had ever done that to me. I shook my head and checked all the locks, moving to the security panel and setting the alarm.

"Let's go. We have a minute before the alarm goes off, and all of Sumner will be here watching."

He smiled. "Let's go then." Blaine held the door open for me, then shut it when we were out. Locking it, I turned to him as he grabbed my hand and pulled me to my car.

"Thank you for having dinner with me," he said

with my back against the car and him standing so close to me. So close I could feel his breath on my lips.

"Thank you for bringing it to me."

His hand came to my neck, and my eyes closed with thoughts of another man touching me this exact same way. When his lips touched mine, they were so gentle, kind and slow.

It was nice.

Unfortunately, nice needed to be more.

When he leaned back and smiled, I did so as well, but I didn't feel that smile at all.

"Thank you. Get home safe," Blaine told me as he opened the car door for me, and I slid in. "Sleep well," he said, shutting the door and stepping back from the car.

Then he turned and walked away.

All the while confusion mottled my brain. I needed more. Most people would be thankful for a guy like Blaine. Me? I just needed more.

My head fell to my steering wheel. *Pull your shit together, Indie.*

Sucking in a deep breath, I sat up, turned the car on, and headed home. When my head hit the pillow, all I could see were blue eyes that were not Blaine's.

CHAPTER FIVE

Ax

SIX HOURS EARLIER

"Fuckin' knew it," my father, Buzz, said from his spot at the kitchen table where we were having our meeting. Considering my father was smart as fuck, I wasn't surprised he already knew.

He'd told me a long time ago that normally it was every two or three years Nick did something stupid and would come to my father and Uncle Breaker to ask for help.

They'd helped him so many times, but judging by my father's face, he was officially done with Nick's bullshit. Nick was his brother, but enough was enough.

"It's deeper," my brother, Raid, said pulling out some papers from the pile he brought in the house. Raid got the tech savviness that came from our father. While Micah and Dryerson came in with all their experience from the service, Raid got it from dad. And he was damn good.

"How much deeper can you get than fuckin' with Old Red?" Uncle Breaker asked.

"He's the loan shark?" Aunt Shaina asked. Her and mom were in on this conversation. It wasn't club business per say. But it was family. The lines with ol' ladies and knowledge with the club had begun to blur over the years. Considering they were normally involved in the ups and downs, it was difficult to keep them out of it.

We still kept them out of the extra business end of our club. That was strictly for the brothers, and if we went down, no way our women would.

"Yeah. No one you wanna fuck with," Uncle Breaker responded, putting his arm around her shoulders and pulling her into him.

"Raiden," my father warned, wanting him to get on with it. Truth be told, I wanted the same thing. Just get it over with already.

"Right," Raid started. "It's more money than I initially thought. He's up to a little over half a million."

"You've gotta be shittin' me," our father said, slamming his hand on the table, causing the glasses and coffee cups to shake. My mother jumped as if she was going to grab each one of them to stop them from spilling. It must be a mom thing considering it happened all the time, and Aunt Shaina did the same.

"'Fraid not," Raid continued. "His ass is dead if he doesn't come up with the cake."

"Let him fuckin' rot," I announced, and eyes came my way.

Honestly, between all of us, coming up with the cash wasn't an issue. With the four of us contributing, half a million was a drop in the bucket. We'd turn it around in a month or two and have our rainy day funds restocked.

This was principal.

Hang the fucker by his balls, no more bailouts. True, the man was blood, but we knew family didn't always come from blood. Family was the people around you, that you gave a shit about. You chose them. Genetics only got you so far.

Nick was a piece of shit. We'd known it for years, and I was sick of it. My uncle and father didn't need to be putting up with Nick's shit anymore. Hell, we all were at the end of our rope apparently. He was a fucking old man and should be able to handle his own messes. Yet here he was acting like a child, begging for help.

"He didn't tell you why he wanted to talk exactly?" my dad asked Raid, who shook his head.

"No. Just that he wanted to have a meeting. I told him no, but he's been blowin' up my fuckin' phone, and I finally blocked his ass."

A chuckle escaped me. Raid didn't play. No doubt in my mind if Nick stood in front of him, he'd have a missing tooth from Raid's fist. Family or not. He wasn't one to piss off. Hell, none of us were.

My father pulled out his phone, hit the screen, then set it in the middle of the table. It began ringing, and we could hear because he put it on speakerphone.

This was going to be entertaining.

"Brother!" Nick answered, way too fucking happy for my blood. He had a fucking bounty on him, and he was living it up, happy and without a care in the world? Dumbass. Complete and total dumbass.

"You wanted to talk. Talk," my father demanded, not giving any pleasantries. Yep, he was done.

"And hi to you too," Nick clipped back.

"Now is not the time to be fuckin' around," Breaker added.

"Other brother!" Nick cheered again.

The growl could be heard in my father's voice. "Talk now, or I hang up and we don't answer when you call again."

"Right... Right..." He stuttered a bit. "Want a meeting with the club. Can you set that up?"

My father leaned into his arms resting on the table, his pulse thumping in that vein on his neck that always came out when he was seriously pissed. Yep, he was pissed. "First of all. You do not call my boys about this shit and put them in the middle of your fucked up messes. Second. Who the fuck do you think you are to demand a meeting with the club? You were here, you'd have two black eyes, motherfucker."

"Calm down," Nick tried.

"Calm down? Are you fuckin' kiddin' me?" Uncle

Breaker said. "You think for one second that we're gonna set up a meeting with the brothers for you, you've lost your fuckin' mind."

"But I want to join." Nick started. My head was about to explode. Four testosterone-filled men in one room talking about shit they didn't want to... Yeah, there'd be a lot of fireworks. No way he was even coming here, let alone joining

"You're not fuckin' joining. You're out. It was voted. Once voted, that's the final say. How many fuckin' times do I have to tell ya?" my father growled. "Obviously a fuckin' million since you can't get it through that thick skull of yours."

"I'm better. I won't go near that woman. Swear it!"

Uncle Breaker cut in. "See? That right there tells me you have no idea what the club is about or what it stands for. And I'm not educatin' ya. Tell us what mess you're in."

"Me..." He dragged out the sound for much longer than needed for some reason. "I'm good. I just..." He paused. "Just..."

"Would you spit it the fuck out, Nick!" My father's voice rose a few octaves.

"Need a job," he said, surprising me. The shit he was in—no job was going to pay him what he needed.

"So get one. You're a fuckin' electrician," Uncle Breaker said.

"No, need a big job. One where I can earn some serious money. You know, a job for the club."

My father sat back in his chair. "So, you're in half a mill to Old Red, huh?"

"Wha—" Nick started.

"You don't think my boys know what the fuck they're doin'? Raid had the info before you hung up the fuckin' phone, dumbass."

"If you think the club is gonna give you a half a mill job, you're out of your mind. They won't give you a fuckin' penny for anything," Uncle Breaker added.

"This is my last hope." Nick started talking fast. "I gotta get this money to Old Red or he's gonna kill me. You don't want me dead, right?"

Gaslighting... I hated that shit, and Nick was trying his damnedest to put it on all of us. Not going to happen.

"I don't give a shit," I responded, and my mother gave me a look. One I couldn't read, but it was the truth. I had my family, and he was so far out of the circle that if he disappeared, he wouldn't be missed.

"You say anythin' to Old Red about the club?" Raid asked, and the room went still.

Yeah. This was a very important question that needed answering like yesterday.

Nick said nothing. Dead quiet on the other end.

My hands balled into fists when the silence went too long.

"Answer!" Uncle Breaker ordered.

"I—" He broke off once again.

"If I call Old Red and he tells me you said a single word about the club, I'll come kill ya myself," my father stated matter-of-factly. "You won't have to worry about payin' it back. You'll be six feet under."

"Great way to treat your brother..." Nick grumbled.

"Are you fuckin' kiddin' me!" My father's fist came down hard on the table. This time we all reached for our cups and glass, but some of us were too late, and shit spilled everywhere.

Without a word, my mom got up and brought back some towels. Raid and I took them and began to clean the mess up. Remember. Mom was queen here. We cleaned; she did not.

She gave me a soft smile which warmed my heart. Loved that woman.

"What did you tell Old Red?" Breaker tried keeping the focus on the information while my father wanted to punch something, namely Nick, hard.

"I didn't..." Nick trailed off.

"I'm callin' his ass," my father stated. "One fuckin' word, and there's no place on this fuckin' earth you can hide. I'll find ya, and I'll take the money out of your skin."

"I didn't mean to. It just came out!" Nick practically cried over the phone. Yeah, this fucker would be dead.

"The club isn't givin' you shit. No one at this table will give you shit. You fly on this one solo, and you will pay for even sayin' my club's name to Old Red." My father reached over and punched off the call.

Immediately the phone started ringing again. My father looked at it, hit some buttons, and the ringing stopped. Breaker's started, and he did the same thing as his brother: blocking Nick. Then mine. I blocked him too.

"What do we do?" my mother, Bella the Beautiful, I loved to tease her, asked the table.

"First, we gotta take it to the club." My father rubbed a hand over his face. "Cruz will either call Old Red himself or have one of us do it." He pointed between himself and Uncle Breaker. "Gotta find out how deep this is gonna affect the club."

Uncle Breaker rubbed his hands down his face. "You know he told Old Red we'd fork up the money, and that shit ain't happenin'."

"Yeah, but if Old Red is expectin' it from us, what the fuck are we gonna do? Old Red doesn't fuck around," I stated.

"Let's get to the clubhouse and sit down with Cruz. Then we go from there," my father said, getting up from his chair. "You two don't need to be there. It's our fucking mess to take care of."

"You'll let us know, though, if there's something we can do, right?" Raid asked, getting up from the table.

"Yep. Sure. Cruz will call church, and you can find out what we're gonna have to do then."

I rose from my chair and gave my father and uncle a chin lift. "You need anything, call me."

Leaning over to my mom, I kissed her cheek. "Gotta run. Got shit to do."

My father walked over, putting his hand on my shoulder and squeezing. "Thank you, son." He then slapped Raid's shoulder, saying the same. "Now get to work."

On a chuckle, Raid and I headed to the club-house. We had a new supplier and needed to prep for the delivery.

Cruz was going to be pissed about Nick. But Ravage had Ravage's back. Nick would be swinging with a noose around his neck.

CHAPTER SIX
Indie

'This is great," Blaine said after chewing and swallowing the peanut butter bar I freshly made this morning, considering I knew he'd be here and needed to make sure everything was ready for the bakery to open.

I kept the baked goods on a bit of a rotation and would make several servings of each, but once the treat was gone, there was no more for the rest of the day. It was the only way that I could keep all the customers happy. And keep demand up.

There was no way I'd be able to make every single treat I wanted to every day. It just wasn't feasible. Instead, I started doing this rotation, and it had been doing very well.

The morning rush of people strode in and out, patrons saying hi to me every time.

"Thanks." While I knew my pastries were delicious, the compliments still embarrassed me a bit. Or maybe it was just him. His compliments made me happy.

"What do you like best here?" he asked me.

We were sitting off to the side where the big window was letting all the sunlight from the day in. It was warm and semi-private.

"Gingerdoodles. My GramO's recipe, and it's the best."

"You have any up there?" He nodded to the glass cabinet.

"Nope. Haven't had them up there in a while. I like to only make them when GramO can come and do it with me."

"I know your GramO means a lot to you."

"Yeah. She does."

"How'd the dinosaur go last night."

"Great! There's still a lot of work to be done, but the green fondant makes it look like a dino. I can show ya later." I took a sip of my caramel macchiato and set the cup down to the table. The plan in the beginning was to use actual mugs, but the dishes became too much and keeping ahead of them drove me nuts. Paper it was.

The customers liked it, and that was what mattered.

"I'd like that."

"After you're done then." I pointed to his double chocolate covered in chocolate donut. They were seriously good.

People came by the table to say hi, so our conversation was interrupted pretty much every minute.

"Ms. Popular here," he teased when we had a break in the pleasantries.

"They all know me, or at least that I own the place. And we're friendly. It's the way I designed it to be."

The bell over the door went, my eyes lifting to it on instinct to see Ax striding in. Dark denim jeans, black T-shirt, leather jacket and his black baseball hat turned backward. Dangerous. That was what he looked like and what he was. And fuck me hotter than hell itself. Life was not fair one bit.

He searched the counter and behind to the work station. Not finding what he was looking for, he turned and his eyes landed on mine.

Instantly I felt the heat that tingled up my spine just from his intenseness. Just as if he could see directly down into my soul without my permission. Like he knew all my dreams and would pull them out one at a time. I fucking hated that shit. He had no right to have this hold on me, and inside I tried shutting it down tight.

Ax's eyes shifted to the man sitting across from me who was looking out the window at something. A snarl came to his lip.

Why was that sexy? Why? Why? Why? Snarling should not be attractive in a man. *Tell that to my body.*

I hated this man. Hated him. He was a dick. Would always be a dick, yet here my body was on fire and my heart rate picked up.

"What..." Blaine asked, then turned and followed my gaze.

Ax's stare, though, never left me. I was a fly to his spider web, and I couldn't take my eyes off of him. My throat got a bit dry, and I swallowed, hoping to relieve some of it, but it didn't help.

"You know him?" Blaine asked, turning back to me.

It took everything in my power to put my focus back on Blaine, but somehow I dug down deep and pulled it off. "A regular. Comes in every day."

"Doesn't appear you like him that much," Blaine said, being observant.

"Who wouldn't like money in their register? It's all good." I tried shoving it off.

While I could feel Ax's stare boring into me, I didn't turn away from Blaine. He was who I was with in this moment, and I needed to stick to it. No matter how much I wanted to turn back to Ax. To catch his gaze once again and get the swarm of butterflies in my stomach. Yes, he gave me a swarm, while Blaine just gave me some flitters. Like I said—life wasn't fair.

Lord save me, it was so hard. I heard his voice order. The register taking his money. The extra clinking in the tip jar. His bootsteps walking right by me. The door opening and bell jingling.

When I heard the bike roar to life, I felt as though I could breathe again.

What was I thinking. Bad idea, Indie. Bad. You did nothing but make yourself crazy.

"Indie, we need you!" Meadow called from behind the counter. The look on her face was one of panic. That was never a good thing. But a distraction from Ax was always welcome.

"Sorry. I've gotta go. Text me when you get back home," I told Blaine, getting up from the chair and taking the cup of coffee.

"Can I see you tomorrow?" he asked quickly.

"I thought you were going back home? Surely you don't want to drive all that way back here."

He bit his bottom lip. "True. Maybe I'll take tomorrow off."

I quirked my brow. "That pissed at your boss?"

"Nope. Tomorrow would be just for you."

I felt the heat crawl up my neck. Why did he have to say such nice things to me?

"Text me when you get home, and we'll talk about it. Deal?"

"Deal." He got up from his chair and wrapped me up in his arms, hugging me tightly. "Hate I live so far away."

At the moment, so did I.

I pulled away. "Talk to you later. Okay?"

"Later." I turned and made my way to Meadow, hearing his feet on the floor and out the door.

"What's wrong?" I asked, dropping my cup in the garbage and going straight to the sink to wash my hands.

"Don't be mad," she started, and I became alarmed.

"If the dino cake is…"

She shook her head quickly. "No, but we had an order come in this morning for two flat sheet cakes. Marley burned both of them."

My shoulders fell. "Seriously?"

She smiled. "Nope. Just could see you wanted to be done with Blaine, so I gave you an out, and you took it." She shrugged. "I'm always there for ya, babe."

I pulled her in my arms and hugged her tight. "Thank you. I like him, it's just…" I trailed off, not finishing.

"Him. I know."

I pulled back from her and stared in her eyes. She did know. It was there plain as day. Fuck. I thought I'd hid it well. "Let's not go there. Okay?"

"Love you. Now get the dino done."

"Okay, drill sergeant," I teased. "Love you too."

Making my way to the back, the bell over the door went off. "Welcome!" I called out and turned to the door. My breath caught as shock hit me like a sledge-hammer. Walking into the shop was Bella, Ax's mom.

Holy shit. It had been a while since she'd come here, and each time she got the same reaction from me.

Her smile was warm as always. She had never showed me anything but respect and kindness over the years.

We saw each other occasionally when she came in, but every single time she did my heart hurt. Part of me missed her. As crazy as that sounded, when I wept for Ax, I wept for her too. She'd taken on the role of second mom so easily, always being there to talk to.

The more I thought about it over time, I'd come to the conclusion that she was just a person I connected to at a young age. Her not being in my life the same way as before hurt, but like everything else to do with Ax Monroe, I pushed it down deep. It was how it had to be for what little sanity I had left.

Grabbing a towel, I wiped my hands and came to the counter. "Mrs. Monroe, how are you?"

She smiled then shook her head. "Young lady, you call me Mrs. Monroe one more time, and I'm feedin' ya to the fishes."

This had me bursting out laughing. We had a running joke. One that came so naturally that I didn't even realize I said it until it came from my lips.

"But you are," I challenged.

"True, but no one calls me that. Makes me feel old," she replied on a dazzling smile.

She was nowhere near the 'old' she thought. Whatever she'd been doing to her skin over the years, I needed to find out and steal the idea. It was so creamy and smooth. There was no way she had any foundation on, just her eyes popping with mascara.

Natural beauty. That was what she had, and she'd passed it along to her boys. They had her dark hair while they got the twin gene from their father.

"You know you're not old one bit."

The woman standing next to her was just as breathtaking as Bella. I'd seen her around town and knew her name, but really didn't know her. "Hi, Tanner. Nice to meet you."

Her hand went on her jetted out hip. "What the hell? How come I get the Tanner?"

At first I thought she was serious, and my heart stopped, thinking I'd been disrespectful. She must've seen the look on my face because she burst out laughing. "Joking! Just joking!"

Only then did I let out a breath. Not only was this Ax's mom and her friend, but these were ol' ladies in the Ravage Motorcycle Club. If anyone messed with these two, their husbands would go crazy. And Tanner's man, Rhys—holy hell. Met him one time, and I pissed my pants.

No. Literally, I had to run to the bathroom in Ax's parents' house because I was leaking. He was one scary motherfucker!

"What can I do for ya?" I asked leaning into the glass case.

"My little girl is turning sixteen," Tanner said. "And I was hoping you could help me out with a cake."

My head nodded automatically. "Yep. That I can do. When do you need it by?"

Tanner winced. "That's the thing. I need it Saturday."

Shit. Saturday would only give me four days to get it done, and I still had to finish the dino.

"What do you want exactly?" I asked hesitantly.

"A Barbie car," Tanner said with a wide grin on her face. "Hot pink convertible driving down the road with my girl sitting in the driver's seat."

That could be fun to make, but time. "I..."

Tanner held up one finger. "And four Harley's following behind her on the road."

A laugh bubbled out from my lips. Oh my, her little girl was in trouble. License or not, she wasn't going to get much privacy.

Stopping myself from laughing, I told Tanner honestly. "I don't know if I can get it perfect in that amount of time." I took a lot of pride in my work and wanted it to be perfect.

Bella leaned in closer and asked, "How about we pay double? Could you get it in then?"

"It's not about money. While I'm grateful for it, I just don't know. One sec." I moved to the back and grabbed the order form clipboard we had hanging on the wall. We had some steady orders and two flat cakes with nothing too elaborate due.

If I moved some things around, I could get the two flat ones done with ease in a couple of hours. The dinosaur was really close to being finished.

I'd have to bust my ass to get this cake the way I'd want it.

But this was Bella. I really couldn't say no to her. There'd be some long nights, but I could do it.

Walking back to the couple, I smiled wide. "Of course. I'll get right on it."

"Seriously? You'll be able to do it?" Tanner asked excitedly.

"Yeah." I wasn't going to tell them I'd probably be up until midnight and up at five for the next few days, but I'd make this work.

"Perfect. Saturday at the clubhouse. We need you to bring it there. Do you know where that is?"

My stomach fell to my feet. The clubhouse. I'd been there once, and it wasn't the best experience.

"YEAH. I know where it is. What time?" I asked, not wanting to go anywhere near that place in fear of seeing her son, but I'd walk through hot coals for Bella.

"Can you have it set up by three? We're surprising her with a party."

"What's her name?"

"Mazie. The big sixteen. Her father is losing his shit." She laughed as if this were a good thing. To me, I'd want to run for the hills.

"Okay, let's sit down for a minute and you tell me what you're thinking, and I'll see what I can draw up."

"You draw all of your cakes?" Bella asked. She didn't know much about my life now it seemed. Understandable.

"Yes. Every one of them. I have a book."

"Let's see it!" Bella said as she and Tanner took a seat at the table.

I went and pulled out my huge binder and brought it out to the table.

That was how I ended up sitting with my ex's mom and her friend, gabbing and creating a kickass Barbie car.

Now, to get it done and to the clubhouse on time. Lord, please do not let Ax be there when I deliver it.

CHAPTER SEVEN

THE BASS OF THE MUSIC BLARED IN STUDIO X, EACH thump bringing the pulse of the club higher and higher. Ravage had many business avenues, and the strip club brought in a lot of clean cash. We needed legal sides of Ravage business to combat the illegal. Money laundering, cleaning, filtering funds—didn't much give a shit how one chose to view it—this was the way we balanced our lives in the club.

Princess ran the show here at Studio X, but lately many of the ol' ladies were working in one way or another as well.

Princess was a stickler for everything. How the place was run. Expectation of the girls. Expectations of employees. Expectations for the customers.

And that was where we came in...

Raid and I drew the lucky as fuck straw and got this gig. Keeping assholes away from the entertainment wasn't difficult. Had to admit, the job was fun. It was usually the booze that gave the patrons more courage to stand up and play grab ass with the girls.

Not here. That shit didn't fly. Hands stayed to themselves unless they went to the back for a private show. Only the girls who wanted to offer private shows did. Those who didn't, didn't. No one here was forced to do anything they didn't want. And there were limits in the private shows on touching as well. Money bought certain things, but not everything.

It was how Princess had such a loyal group of girls working for her. Each girl knew they had protection, not only from her but us. No one fucked with them. No one. They worked for Ravage, and that came with huge benefits.

Not to mention, for us, having pussy on tap wasn't a bad thing at all. Bottom line with that was it was all consensual.

The place was filled to the brim. Not a single seat empty even around the bar with a few hanging out around the red walls.

Studio X had a state of the art sound system and lighting. Both were going full bore.

The large stage was located against the back wall. There were four poles on the stage in various places. Three girls were currently on the stage, each in their own space, dancing enticingly and getting the attention from the men with praise. Money flew to the dancers' feet and that was what they were there for.

Old as time, pussy always sold. Magazines. Porn. Dancers. There was always money in that shit.

Currently, Ravage only dealt with the dancers and what was done in the private rooms. At one point we had a set of girls we took care of, but over time, that was weeded out.

We wanted to keep this side completely legal.

"Alright, Studio Xers!" DJ Joker yelled into the microphone, catching attention as the lights went down. "Let's hear some noise for Glimmer!" His voice trailed off as the beat changed and a buxom blonde became illuminated by lights in the center of the stage.

Her back and high heeled foot rested against the pole, arms raised above her head, and breasts tilted out. The perfect silhouette.

Glimmer was covered in a very sheer gown type thing with sexy hot pink bra and panties.

Yeah, she had the entire room on their feet.

She'd been one of the primo dancers here for a while, and the entire mood in the room changed when she appeared. My attention went right over to Raid who was on the other side of the club and nodded at me.

Eyes now to the crowd, we moved closer to the stage. Craziness always happened, but it had gone too far at times too. That was when we had to step in.

I was on the left and Raid was on the right, our arms crossed over our chest, watching and waiting. Nelson, another bouncer, was sitting in a chair in front of the stage. Three men ready and waiting to jump in if needed.

The woman was hot as fuck and deserved every

dollar thrown up on the stage. It might have been the reason she didn't do any private dances in the back. Or it could have been she was one of the shiest women I'd ever met.

How she turned into a sex kitten on the stage and all that innocence vanished was crazy to me. She'd never hit on me once but had always been polite. I'd never had her, but I had no clue if anyone else had. If they had, it would be a surprise to me.

I could see her moving in my peripheral vision, but my sole focus was on the crowd starting to press in closer to the stage. One day, I had no doubt, that she would ensue a riot; I just hoped like fuck it wasn't tonight.

Or maybe I did.

Indie came to mind and her hatred for me. Yeah. Maybe I needed to punch something.

The man behind me made a reach for Glimmer, and I gripped his arm and pushed him back. "Back up, motherfucker."

She didn't allow people to put dollars in her G-string or touch her in any way.

Three minutes and twelve seconds seemed to take forever during her sets with the crowd so up and alert. When the last note played, the stage went dark, and I felt it before I saw it.

The man I had pushed back earlier leapt onto the stage.

Glimmer's scream was next.

Moving fast, I leapt onto the stage and gripped the motherfucker by the back of his shirt and put him in a headlock. Glimmer's frightened eyes came to mine as this asshole had her wrapped in his arms, hugging her like he had every right to touch her.

"Let go, motherfucker."

"I love you!" he yelled out, tipping her from side to side.

Gripping under his arms, I released his grip on Glimmer, and Raid was there to put her in his arms and rush her backstage.

Yeah, I needed a bit of a release. This motherfucker just gave it to me.

Knocking him to the ground, my knee went to his back and pressed him firmly to the stage as I pulled his arms behind his back. Reaching in my back pocket, I located a zip tie and put it around his wrists.

The man wasn't large; he just pissed me off and didn't follow the rules. That meant he needed to be taught a lesson.

The lights went up while I carried the man off the stage, and the money was cleared by two of the waitresses who I knew would race the money back to Glimmer when she was done.

"You are one stupid motherfucker," I growled and pulled him up to his feet. The dickhead was still calling out to Glimmer like she wanted to hear all the shit he could buy her. She didn't need shit from anyone. Considering she was already in the back, she wouldn't hear this motherfucker anyway.

Seeing everything was good with the club, just people being rowdy, I led this asshole to the backroom at the very end of the dark hall.

Kicking the door shut, I threw the man to the floor.

Seconds later Raid burst through the door and slammed it so hard it shook the walls. His face was a mask of fury.

"Is she okay?" I asked, trying to get a read on my brother. He was as angry as I was, but it was on a different level. Bad day? Or was she hurt in some way.

"She'll be fine," he replied, stalking to the man and picking him up by the shirt, his feet dangling as they didn't touch the floor. "No thanks to you, motherfucker." Raid's fist connected with the man's gut, and he fell back to the floor groaning.

The man on the floor pleaded as I came behind him and picked him up once again. "See, you've really pissed him off, and he doesn't get pissed off. So what do you think he is going to do with you??" I taunted.

Taking out my knife, I cut the ties holding his arms behind him. Once released, he tried to get out of the headlock I had him in. Throwing down the knife, I punched him hard in his right side.

He fell to his knees, and Raid punched him in the jaw and he crumbled to the floor.

"You're no longer welcomed here. You come near here or Glimmer again, and I'll beat you until you're dead. Do you understand me?"

The man had tears rolling down his face. Reaching down, I pulled out his wallet and pulled out the cash and his ID. "Rodger Anvil. I know where you live." I pulled out a picture of him, a woman and two children. "And I know who your family is. I don't want to hear or see you again. Do you understand?"

"I get it." He practically cried.

"You will," Raid growled, and we started to teach him he wasn't welcome back to Studio X or anywhere the Ravage MC were.

CHAPTER EIGHT
Indie

"REALLY, I CAN'T. I HAVE A LOT TO FINISH ON THIS cake and only one more day to do it," I told Blaine, holding the phone between my ear and shoulder. I was knee deep in cake and fondant.

He wanted us to go on a date, but there was so much for me to finish.

Tanner's cake along with the few other orders came first. Blaine was wonderful, but time was too precious at the moment. Each tick of the clock was one second I didn't have to complete the project. Needless to say, I wanted it to be perfect, and I'd bust my ass to get it that way.

"You sure?" He tried once more.

I sighed deep, hating that I was brushing him off but needing to do so all the same. "I'm sorry, Blaine. Once I get caught up we can."

"It makes me happy that you love what you do."

The comment made me stop for a moment. "Umm ... thank you?" I really didn't know what to say to this. I guessed it was because it had been a long time since anyone had said it.

"You'll text me later?" he responded, the edge of hope in his voice.

"I will. I've gotta run."

"Bye, Indie." My eyes closed at the disappointment in his tone.

"Bye." I dropped the phone with a clatter to the table and used my knuckle to hang it up.

Turning back to the cake, I put my entire focus on this sixteen-year-old's birthday. It was a bit bigger than I thought it would be, and I had to ponder how I was going to get this inside the clubhouse. There was no way I'd be able to pick it up myself which, was something I should've thought about before going nuts.

I wanted to impress Bella. Stupid, sure, but that didn't mean it wasn't true.

Diving back into it, I was in the zone once again.

So much so that when my sister, Meadow, touched my shoulder, I jumped and gasped at the same time.

Inspecting the cake instantly, I didn't see any damage. Thank God. Time wasn't on my side and if she... "You're lucky you didn't hurt the cake!" I might have yelled that. Okay, I did. Too many hours went into putting this cake together to have it ruined now. There was already enough stress on getting to the clubhouse.

"It's fine, but you're not," she said, lifting her brows in that knowing way she did with her kids all the time. The mom brow. It wasn't sexy or fun. It was a "get your fucking shit together" way.

This grabbed my attention from evaluating every inch of the cake just in case. "What?"

It was then that I looked around the bakery only to find no one and utter silence. No light came through the windows either.

"It's after ten. You haven't eaten much today, and you're exhausted." And there was the mom tone to match the mom brow. Great.

"Ten? Where did the day go?" I asked, not really expecting an answer.

"Yes. It's time to go home, Indie," my sister ordered. I really didn't like being bossed around, but my stomach took that chance to grumble. She was right. The fatigue caught up to me like my sister flipped a switch inside me saying, "It's time to collapse now, Indie."

Wiping my hand on a towel, I responded, "Fine. Let me clean up."

Meadow grabbed my shoulders, halting my actions, and I stilled. "I'll clean up. You go home."

"Who has the kids?" I asked, knowing she had to be home for her family.

"Their father."

"Are you sure you don't want to go home?"

We both burst out laughing. Her husband Devon tried so hard, but with those two kiddos he was a pushover. "Yes."

"Thank you, baby sister," I said, wrapping my arms around my sister and feeling it returned.

When we pulled away, I smiled wide. "Now when you go home you'll be sweet."

"Working here is killer on my clothes," she responded, looking down at her shirt. She wasn't wrong. Pretty much everything I wore always had some type of baked good on me at one time or another.

"Shout it out!" I responded to Meadow's laugh.

Getting my things, I checked the front door to make sure it was locked. It was, of course. My sister wouldn't forget something like that. The bakery was clean, and all the tables and chairs where they should be.

I loved that I could count on her. Leaving the lights on, I called out goodbye to my sister and went out the back entrance, locking the door behind me as it closed.

The night was beautiful with the moon shining bright. Exhaustion hit me as I made it to my car. Stopping briefly, my brow furrowed. A sheet of paper lay beneath my windshield wiper which was not there when I parked earlier.

That uneasy feeling came over me again. The one that sent shivers up my spine and told me I wasn't alone.

I did not go around my car and grab it. Instead, I got in my car and locked the doors, ignoring it completely.

I listened to true crime stories sometimes, and

from that I learned this trick to get you to stop so they could nab you. So if my senses were right, I wasn't going to give anyone the chance to do just that. Starting the vehicle, I pulled out and looked around to see someone.

Only darkness stared back at me. The more I scanned, the more I saw nothing. But I still couldn't shake the feeling.

It wasn't until I got into my garage and the door was shut securely that I got out of the car. Shutting the door and moving to the paper, I picked up the note.

Opening it...

TICK TOCK GOES THE CLOCK.
    As it moves, I will not stop.
    Have no fear.
    My darling dear.
    I will make him disappear.

AIR CHOKED my throat as my hand started to shake. This couldn't be happening again. I wouldn't let this happen again.

CHAPTER NINE

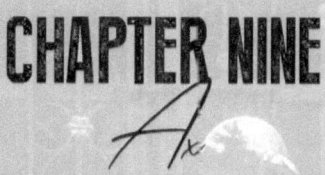

Ax

"You do realize your brother is fuckin' dead?" Cruz asked, but it wasn't really a question. It was a statement of fact. "Thought I made myself perfectly clear to that motherfucker years ago. His affiliation with this club—there is none."

"He's been told numerous times, brother. He just can't get it through his thick skull," my father responded.

I was sitting at the church table with Cruz, our President, GT, our Vice President, Uncle Breaker, Raid, and Dad. Dad told us to meet him here because he'd changed his mind, and we all needed to talk to our President about this fucked up situation.

It looked so fucking bad for all of us Monroes to have Nick putting the club's name on the line for his debts. Everything he did fell on our backs. Pissed didn't even come close to the feelings coursing through my body.

No one fucked with my club.

No one made me look like a fool to my brothers.

No one put my family at risk. No. One.

"His skull will be on my fuckin' mantle before this is over," Cruz growled.

Maybe I should feel something because the man in question was blood, but I was stone cold inside. I wanted the same damn thing. Ravage didn't get where it was today by letting shit like this slide, and Nick knew not to do it. He'd been warned over the years that he had nothing to do with Ravage. It was his choice to tell Old Red that he had the club's support. He had to pay the consequences for that.

"He knows we're pissed, but he still wants a meet. We could set it up, grab him, and make sure he doesn't breathe again," Raid suggested, and I felt my head nod.

"First, let's try to contact Old Red, see what we can do from there. We kill Nick and Red still wants his money, it doesn't solve our fuckin' problem," GT said his first words since the meeting started. "Got his number?" he asked.

Raid held up a piece of paper between his two fingers. "Here. Don't know if it's direct to him or his go-through, but it's all I could find. And I fuckin' searched hard for it. Man has his shit locked up tight. Don't know how people find him for money."

"That just shows how much pull Old Red has," I responded, feeling in my gut that this wasn't going to be good. Nick put us on the line. My gut was screaming it.

"Yeah. Fuckin' know that," Cruz growled through clenched teeth.

GT tossed a burner phone across the table to Raid. "Dial it, and put it on speaker." He ordered, and Raid did just that.

As it rang, we waited.

And waited.

"Yeah," a man's deep voice answered. From his tone, it appeared he was annoyed. We were too. Pot, meet kettle.

"Lookin' for Old Red. This him?" Cruz said as he led the conversation, and we just listened.

"Who the fuck wants to know?" the voice responded tersely.

"Cruz. President of the Ravage MC."

"Cruz. Don't know you," the voice responded.

"Is this Old Red?" Cruz asked again.

"Nope." The voice responded.

The tension grew in the room.

"You tell him to call me if he wants Nick." Cruz reached over and turned off the phone.

"Wants Nick?" my father asked.

"Couldn't say his money because I'm not givin' shit. Nick, though, I have no problem handing over after he's paid us for puttin' us in this shit."

Nick was dead. If he really did give our club's name, we'd be getting a call back and probably sooner than we thought.

"Show me everything," Cruz demanded, and Raid

started going through the details he found on this situation with Cruz and GT.

Raid laid out all the connections, where the money went, and how Nick got involved with Old Red. It was a fucking mess, but Raid did his homework. From the look on Cruz's face, he respected all the work that he had put into unraveling the facts.

Now, we waited to see if Old Red would call back, and when he did, what did it mean to the Ravage MC.

This was where I struggled.

Patience.

There wasn't much in life worth the wait.

In fact, the only thing I had ever truly treasured waiting for was that first taste of Indie's pussy. She was worth anything and everything. Yet, young and dumb, I tossed her aside like nothing mattered when it all was absolutely tied to my fucking soul.

"Are you sure you want this?" I asked her, looking down at the most beautiful girl I'd ever seen. Her hair was spread across the blanket, the sun glistening on her hair.

"Yes. I want this. I want you."

"I love you, Indie."

"I love you, Ax."

Slowly, I pressed inside her. She closed her eyes and a furrow went to her brow just as my cock met the barrier inside of her. "Are you okay?"

She nodded. "Yes. Do it, Ax."

Not wanting to draw out the pain, I pressed in hard. Indie's back arched, and she swallowed deeply.

I loved her. Having this part of her... I'd never let her go.

Adrenaline built inside me with every passing moment. Yeah, Nick was going to pay for this shit. Not because waiting on the powerhouse that was Old Red drove me insane, but because idle time left me all fucked up inside about her.

My only regret.

Yeah, I was raised Ravage. We lived life on the edge, walking the line.

No regrets.

Yep, I believed that shit about everything.

Once the word was spoken, it couldn't be retracted. Once the day was over, there wasn't some rewind button to take me back. So live free in the moment taking chances and not fucking looking back.

Except long ago, I tied my fucking soul to a woman only to lose my ever-loving fucking mind and made her hate me.

My one regret.

Indie Fallon hated me as much as she dared to once love me. I did it.

I asked for it, no fuck that—I demanded it.

No regrets ... I had only one

And more than that, no amount of waiting would change the way she felt.

A level of hate, mistrust, and disloyalty I fucking earned.

I could be patient for even the mere hope Indie would give me her soft smile once again, but for a motherfucker like Old Red, yeah, waiting wasn't really a thing for any of us.

Yet, because my fuckface uncle dragged us into this shit, we had to wait.

Nick, the piece of shit who shared my blood was going to pay for this shit. No doubt about that, and I wouldn't be left with a single regret for it either.

CHAPTER TEN

Indie

I sat back in the driver's seat of the bakery van, thinking of the note and trying to forget it at the same time.

Except it wouldn't leave my brain, just spun on and on as worry and dread seeped into every pore of my skin.

Sleep evaded me all night. After tossing and turning forever, I finally got up and watched some mindless television with Gizmo, my pup at my side, wondering what the hell I was doing up.

The "set it and forget it" infomercial had been on a never-ending loop. At some point I passed out, only to be woken by my alarm what felt like minutes later.

The negative of having your own business meant there was no one else to cover for you ninety percent of the time.

I had the Barbie car and four Harleys strapped

into the back of the van so they didn't move an inch, and that was the only thing I needed to concentrate on right now. The cake turned out even better than I sketched out and imagined in my head. Tanner gave me a picture of Mazie, and I was able to create her with fondant and some rice crispy treats, which was easier to mold. I couldn't have made it any closer to her. It was a damn good job down to the airbrushed rosy cheeks she'd have from driving in the wind.

For the bikers, I may or may not have made one to represent Ax with the skull ring he often wore and his dark hair curling out from his helmet. But if anyone were to ask me, I'd never tell a soul how much detail I put into it. It was for me and me alone. A little secret temptation I couldn't resist no matter how hard I tried.

Hopefully everyone else didn't notice it.

I'd assemble this monster when I got to the clubhouse. There would be some finishing touches I'd need to make to allow the piece to flow, considering I had to break it down into two parts, but I had all the supplies I'd need with me.

The heaviest piece was the car sitting on the road. That had to be one piece because splitting it would ruin the entire cake. So I went with the path of least resistance.

The other section just had road and grass. I'd place the Harleys, created by tongue depressors and rice crispies as well, on it after it was set on the table. They would slide into the cake with dowel rods to hold them in tight.

All of it was edible, except the frame that is. Marley made a wooden structure to hold the weight. Another reason I wanted Marley around, he was great at creating the sturdy bases for my cakes. Personally, I could make them, but I'd rather be creating.

When I'd called Tanner and told her about the size and weight of this cake, so she'd have some place sturdy to put it, she announced she was sending Booker, Deke, Green and Ryker here to help lift it into my van. Then we'd go to the club, and they'd lift it to where it needed to go.

One, I appreciated the help more than she could know. I was going to call in Marley, my brother-in-law, and Cody to come and help, but Tanner saved me the trouble of that task. Two, I was so happy that Ax wasn't on that list of helpers.

That was why I was currently meshed between four Harleys. Two in front and two behind, following me down the road. It was like I had a million dollars in the van, instead of a cake that they'd be eating later on, and they were guarding it like a state secret.

I had to admit, it did make me feel safe nestled between them. Somehow, I knew that no matter what would happen, these four men would protect me, and it didn't have anything to do with cake. It was a strange thought; that was for sure.

As we got closer to the clubhouse, an uneasy feeling slithered down my spine. This compound was not on my top ten favorite places to be list. It was more on the never wanting to be there again list.

Some memories sucked ass, and they raced through me all at once.

There was a time I loved the thought of spending a Friday night here. My heart, my soul, and the depths of who I thought I would be were ripped from me in this very space so long ago. Yet, it remained vividly in my mind.

I found it to be a blessing.

Took some time for me to get there, but yeah, Ax ending it how he did taught me a hard but necessary lesson.

Trust no one with your faith, your future, or your heart.

Keep the walls up.

Have fun, but never let anyone see your pain, your insecurities, or your weaknesses.

Sucking in a deep breath, I forced the memories that wanted to invade me back down to the recesses of my soul.

Now wasn't the time; hell, never was too soon for that. It needed to stay buried, and I wished I had the strength to keep it there forever. Alas, I didn't.

The bikes in front honked as we approached, and the tall steel gate opened with a ratchet sound. It looked as though it could take a hell of a beating and still keep everyone out.

Entering the clubhouse was a sight to behold. The area was so much larger than it appeared on the outside. On the left was the clubhouse, and next to that was a huge blocked structure that held rooms for its members. Was it members? I forgot what Ax told me.

Off in the distance to the right was Banner Automotive that had a separate entrance. In the parking lot, bikes and vehicles were parked and next to the clubhouse was a wide open space with picnic tables, a fire pit and tons of chairs.

Currently, only a few people were out and their eyes were on us as we came into the place. As protective as they were about the cake, this didn't surprise me one bit. They'd want to know who was on their turf.

Did I just give a football reference to bikers? Lord save me.

The bikes pulled off straight then to the left and parked. Deke motioned me to pull into an open area close to where the clubhouse was. Backing in slowly, I saw the door and it was big, which was good. This monster needed its space, and I just hoped everything went smoothly.

Shoving the gear shift into park, I unbuckled, shut down the van, and got out.

Closing the door, I jumped when I saw the men so close to the van already. They were like ninjas, being all quiet and sneaking up on me. I held my chest and gasped. "How about not sneaking up on me with your mouse shoes?"

Ryker burst out laughing. "Mouse shoes? Seriously?"

"Been called a lot of shit, but never told I had mouse shoes." Deke grunted with a tip of his lip. He seemed to be the most serious of the four with me. Not Rhys serious, but a close second. He did have the same intensity though which was a bit scary.

"Y'all are so quiet. One minute you're not there. The next 'poof,' you are." I shook my head.

"Yeah, we poofed to you," Ryker said, laughing harder, and seeing Deke actually laugh made him not so scary; at least for the moment.

"Can we get this monster out of the van? I still have some work to do on it, and I want it done before the party starts," I told them, feeling myself smile as well. These guys were something else.

"Sure thing, boss." Green mock saluted, making me chuckle.

These guys were funny.

I opened the back of the van and quickly inspected the cake. Luckily nothing had moved on the drive. That was always my biggest worry when traveling with cakes I'd spent hours on. One curve too fast or a pothole in the road could mean disaster quickly. It was why I drove much slower when it came to the cakes.

"Let's get this motherfucker inside," Booker said with a bit of snark to his tone. Not sure where that was coming from, but it was also none of my business. Just hoped I didn't piss the kid off.

There was no way I could've gotten this cake into the clubhouse by myself. It was so heavy even these three huge men were straining. *Maybe a little bit smaller next time.*

"Hey there." A woman with straight black hair

with red streaks down the sides came up as the men stepped into the clubhouse.

"Hey. I'm Indie," I introduced.

She gave a soft smile. "Princess."

"Nice to meet ya." I left out the again because years ago we'd met briefly, but this woman wasn't someone you forgot. She had this aura around her that expelled power. If I had to bet, she did not get pushed around by anyone and wasn't someone to mess with.

"While I'd love for you two to talk like hens all fuckin' night," Booker growled, "can we set this damn thing down?"

I looked over my shoulder to see the men had the heavy load. Deke, Ryker, and Green didn't look to be strained one bit. Their muscles—and I mean muscles —flexed, but nothing like Booker's.

Booker had sweat on his brow, and his arms were shaking just a bit. He was younger than the other three; that was for sure. How much, I wasn't certain. He was lean with dark hair and was Ax's cousin.

Deke was a hunk of a man. He looked like a fighter or, at least, someone no one wanted to mess with. He had high cheekbones, blondish brown hair, and eyes as blue as crystal.

Ryker was a smartass, and I liked him because of it. Not to say he wouldn't rip someone's head off in a second, though. He had tattoos on his neck with dark hair and eyes. A heady combination.

Green was quieter than the rest, which meant I didn't know how to read him. Those were the ones you really needed to look out for. He had blondish brown hair and tattoos down both arms.

Pretty much hot as hell. *Want to join the Ravage MC? Please check the hot box. Done? Now you may enter.*

"Over here, smartass," Princess said with a wave of her hand, motioning us near the side wall where a large wooden structure stood on the ground. It looked like they'd made it just for the cake, which was nice of them. They took the weight of the cake seriously.

I held my breath and clinched my butt cheeks, hoping like hell these four men were going to set down this car without it cracking.

As soon as it was down, I exhaled. It had happened many times when I'd gotten a cake to the destination perfectly. Go to set it down and bam—I was trying to fix the damage on the fly.

Now I could get to work.

"We'll be back," the guys said as they went out to get the second piece.

"Damn, woman. This is awesome," Princess commented, coming up to the cake. "Tanner has Mazie out or she'd be here for ya."

"Thanks. And no problem. I'm planning to do the final touches and then leaving." I smiled wide.

"You should stay," Princess offered. This wasn't abnormal. Nine times out of ten when I delivered a cake, they asked me to stay. I didn't, but it was a nice gesture.

"Thanks, but I need to go," I responded.

The guys came in with the second piece, and

Booker wasn't struggling as much with this one. They set it down. "I'll go get my kit."

"I'll grab it," Green, the quiet one, answered.

"Thanks," I replied, waiting for Green to come with my kit so I could get busy.

"So you and Ax I hear..."

My eyes shot to Princess. *What? How did she know about that?* She smiled, and my face must've given her a hell of a look. "Bella told us. High school is hard for these boys."

I scoffed. "Not for Ax; it's ancient history." He was in a class of his own in high school. Ruled the place and could do anything he wanted to. Took advantage of it at every turn as well.

"That's the reason he comes into your bakery every morning?" she asked as Green walked in with my box and a smile.

How the hell did this woman know this part, and what was she insinuating? Whatever it was, she was wrong.

"We have good coffee. You should come in some-time," I told her on a shrug. No way I was giving any thought to why Ax would be there every morning.

"Sassy, I like that."

Her words were strange in the sense that she 'liked' me. But it was better for her to like me than to be on her bad side.

"I'll let you do your thing. People will start filterin' in soon. They should leave ya alone," she told me, letting the Ax thing go which relieved me.

"Thanks."

Princess took off with the four men, and I was left alone with my cake.

Now this. This was normal. This was centering.

Now to just get it done before Ax decided to come. That would be a disaster.

Do my job and get going. No entanglements from the past.

Business was life, and I was doing this for my business ... right?

CHAPTER ELEVEN

Ax

SHE'S HERE, WAS MY FIRST THOUGHT WHEN I SAW HER van with Fallon's Bakery splashed across the side along with her phone number. Why did having her phone number on the van rub me the wrong way? It did, though.

She was too easily accessible. It was her business, but still. That number staring back at me caused an alarm to blare inside of me.

"Holy shit. I haven't seen Indie in years," my brother Raid said, swinging off his bike. I followed, taking off my helmet and tossing it on my handle-bars. "Glad she came back."

"Why?" I asked as we moved toward the clubhouse.

"Sealed records when she was in Washington," he said vaguely, but it was enough to pique my interest.

I stopped and turned to my brother, needing to

know what the hell he was talking about. "What? Why the fuck haven't you said somethin' before now?"

My blood thumped through my veins. He told me everything; at least I thought he did. Yet he said nothing about Indie after she left my life. Even with her out of my life, that didn't mean I didn't care about her. I fucking cared way more than I probably should. But there it was, out on the table.

"Didn't think you were still into her," he answered on a shrug. "Checked her out when she got back to Sumner three years ago."

I grabbed Raid by his cut and pulled him closer. "You will tell me everything. I mean every. Fucking. Thing..."

While my thoughts envisioned Raid punching me in the face for touching him like this, my body was preparing for it. He did the complete opposite, though.

He laughed. Full out laughed right in my face, taking me completely off guard which I wasn't used to. The damn man knew too much.

Releasing him, I pushed him back. "Shut the fuck up. Let's go. She'll want to leave as soon as she's done assembling, so I don't have time for this shit right now. But you will tell me."

"I bet she's hot as fuck now. Back when you had her she was on her way, but now, I bet she's smokin'."

He was really itching for me to punch him in the eye. I felt my fist ball up, but when we opened the doors and Indie had her back to me, fussing with the cake, everything stopped. The anger and frustration with Raid disappeared.

She was in my space. My club. One place I never thought I'd see her again, yet here she was, and it was a beautiful sight.

My brother kept going, even though my feet were stuck to the floor like glue. He went right up to Indie and tapped her on the shoulder. She turned with a start, obviously focused on her work and not the world around her. Fuck, this woman turned me inside out.

It only took her a second before she recognized it wasn't me, and her smile widened.

"Hey, Raid," she responded, turning fully to him and tilting her head up to meet his gaze. It wasn't cold but wasn't completely open either.

My gut tightened.

He was my brother, my blood, and I wanted to massacre him for being that close to her.

"Ahhh, come here." Raid stepped closer and wrapped his arms around her, and red covered my eyes. She wrapped her arms around him and hugged him back, even with the initial hesitancy. I didn't give a fuck.

Fuck that shit.

Stepping closer didn't stop my brother one bit. I was pretty sure that it only egged him on because he pulled back and kissed her forehead. Yes, fucking. Kissed. Her. Forehead.

My eyes clouded red and steam mingling over, and it took superhuman strength to rein in the monster inside of me. Raid was my brother in more ways than blood but fuck me, murdering him was sounding better and better. When that monster was out, putting him back was difficult. But I needed him at times. That side was almost out of control. Raid knew this.

Raid turned to me, smiling like he could hear my thoughts, and Indie following suit. Her eyes met mine, and the warmth just on her face wiped away as if it was never there at all. Instead, a mask stared back at me.

Fucking hated that shit. That void in her expression and her contact with my brother was a fucking punch to the gut. This woman was tangling me up inside. Had for as long as I'd known her.

"Hey, Indie," I said while Raid put his arm around her shoulders and pulled her in tight to his side. She looked up at him, her lips tipping once again. She obviously liked where she was, which pissed me off. She needed to be with me, not fucking him.

"Hey," she said, coming back to me just for a moment, then back to Raid who, luckily, she released. But they were standing very close to each other. Closer than I wanted. Ever.

Not going to lie. I fucking hated that she was giving her undivided attention to him when she couldn't even stand to be in the same room with me. "Good to see ya, but I have to get the cake done," she told him, stepping further away from him. Her gaze moved between him and me. Lord only knew what was going through her mind.

"Stay for the party, and we'll talk," my brother responded, and my fists clenched. I was going to murder him. Slice him up into little pieces and feed him to the pigs out on Route 8.

"I'll see, but I need to get busy."

Raid leaned down to Indie's ear and said something that made her smile wide as he kissed her on the cheek, and then he walked by me with that fucking goofy grin on his damn face. He knew exactly what he was doing. Knew the button he was pushing and just kept pushing it harder and harder. Asshole.

His hand came to my shoulder. "Your turn."

"Better sleep with an eye open tonight," I growled at him and heard his chuckle as he walked away. That motherfucker. He'd get his. Tonight, tomorrow; didn't matter. It was coming.

Stepping up to the cake, I stayed out of her way as she grabbed a thing of icing and began to work. Each stroke she did complemented her work. The silence between us was deafening. Considering how the clubhouse was generally rocking, it should have been an impossible feat.

"You gonna say somethin'? Or just stand there starin'?" she asked boldly, not looking up from her work. Yes, she was ready to bring out the panther and take a swipe with her claws. It was as if I could see the predator right beneath the surface and fuck me—my cock hardened.

"Just lookin' at the cake. You're damn good at this."

She shifted the bag in her hands and squeezed out more icing. "That's why it's the job."

Snarky. This was going to go really well. The woman didn't want anything to do with me. Too bad I couldn't stay away. Too bad she was the drug I never wanted to stop.

"You got Mazie down to a T." And she did. The blonde hair was out behind her as if the wind was blowing it. Eyes and facial features were on point. She had real talent in this. I'd only seen cakes like this on that show my mom used to watch all the time. My dad, of course, didn't say a word and held her as it played. He did everything and anything for her.

"Thanks," she said quietly. "I've got a lot to finish. Is there something you need?"

"There are a lot of things I need," I said coolly.

She turned to face me with her brow tilted and almost a look of disgust on her face. *Great job, idiot.* "One of them is a beer." I turned to one of the mommas. "Go get one."

The momma smiled seductively. "Anything for you, Ax."

Two seconds later a bottle with the cap on was handed to me by one of the club mommas. I was surprised they were here today but Rainy was. "Here ya go, handsome." She ran her finger along my cheek. "Catch me later." She then walked away.

I watched Indie through these couple of seconds, and she was on fire. Her face was beat red, and anger laced every part of her. Her nose flared as she sucked in a deep breath. The icing in the bag she held started to come out, and a glob hit the floor.

Her gaze went to the floor. "Shit."

"Come on. She was just helpin', so I didn't have to leave ya."

"Oh, she is happy to help you, Ax. And you are real good at leaving me; keep at it." Her glacial eyes locked on mine. "I'm sure you two will have a lovely night." She bit off the last word. "Now go away so I can work."

"You're here!" A female voice I knew all too well yelled over the music. Bella, my mother, brushed past me and cupped Indie's arms, then pulled her into a hug. "Thank you for doing this. You have no idea how you've made this day special."

Indie had to hold her arms out as not to get frosting on her or step in it on the floor.

Mom pulled away, smiling wide at Indie. She'd always loved that girl. My mother took it harder than I had when Indie disappeared from my life. Or, at least, a close second. She'd kept in touch with her but wasn't as close, but she never really let Indie go.

My mom released Indie and came to me, wrapping her arms around my stomach. I leaned down for the kiss on the cheek she loved to give her boys. "How's my boy?"

"Good," I replied as her eyes kept moving between Indie and me. She could probably feel the vibe. It wasn't a good one. The tension could be suffocating.

"You botherin' this young lady, Ax?" my

mother asked me, her brow quirked. She was doing that mom thing where she was trying to worm her way into my head and know all my secrets. Sad thing was, she was actually good at it. Not that I'd admit that shit to her. I'd never hear the end of it.

"Nah. Just admirin' her work." I nodded to the cake, giving her my lame excuse she no doubt didn't believe one bit.

My mother then turned to the cake and gasped as she took it in, stepping away from me and growing closer to the cake in admiration "Oh my God. This is beautiful. So much more than I imagined. You have such a gift with this. I'm in awe."

A blush crept up Indie's cheeks which was sweet. "Thanks, Mrs. Monroe."

At that my mother turned, her eyes changing, "I told you to call me Bella. You call me Mrs. Monroe one more time and I'm gonna lock you and Ax in a room until you figure your shit out."

It was Indie's turn to gasp, and her eyes went wide. Her hand went to her chest, squeezing the frosting bag and putting hot pink frosting all down the front of her. She didn't even flinch about it. "What? No we don't have anything to sort out." Indie shook her head adamantly.

Mom gave her the "mom look." You know, the one that would bring a man like me to his knees. She didn't pull it out often, but when she did, she meant business. She knew. Of course, she fucking knew. She wouldn't be my mother if she didn't. After all these years Indie had been out of my life, my mom fucking knew. Dammit.

"You do, but that's for another time." She turned back to Indie. "You keep up the Mrs. shit and it'll be sooner than you're both ready for."

Her words hit me in the gut. Both ready for? What the hell did that mean? And she really wanted to lock us in a room together? She had a plan. What that plan was, I had no idea, but it was there, forming in her brain. She was planning on sticking her damn hands in this mess, and she needed to stay out of it.

This didn't sound good on either end.

"We're cool, Ma. Just seeing her creation. She's very talented."

She huffed. "Yes, but whatever. I'll deal with that later." Mom kissed Indie on her cheek and took off to the kitchen, dismissing me. No doubt I'd be getting an earful later.

"Ummm ... is she serious?" Indie asked me, watching Mom leave.

"Do you remember anything about Mom?" I asked, knowing the answer.

"Of course," she clipped back.

"Calm down." Indie closed her eyes and breathed in deep. She opened them again and reined in the panther for a moment. "Mom has become way involved with her boys' lives. Or as much as we'll let her. So yes, she's serious. Not sure what she's thinkin', but she's stirring up a plan. That I do know."

"We have nothing to work out. What's done is done," Indie commented, looking down at her hand

and seeing the bag of icing. Then her apron. "Shit. I need to get this done. You need to go."

Indie turned her back to me, slipped off her apron, and used it to clean up the floor. It was so fast I didn't have a chance to help. Then she started on the cake once again, giving me another dismissal. That shit was getting old.

She had a shirt on that hung off her shoulder, showing her creamy skin, the bra exposed. Beautiful hair up in a ponytail, and her long neck was a temptation I couldn't resist.

Slowly I moved up behind her. She must've not heard me because she kept busy. Leaning down, I brushed my lips across the collar of her neck, sending a bolt of lust down me. Indie's body stilled then shivered.

Before she could turn around, I was gone, the taste of her buzzing my lips.

She would forever be the drug I couldn't stop craving.

CHAPTER TWELVE
Indie

I FELT IT. SO LIGHT IT FELT LIKE A FEATHER TICKLING my skin. It was his lips. I knew it was. Not his fingers or nose. It was definitely his lips.

When I swung around, he was in the thrash of people in the clubhouse, blending in until he was nowhere in sight.

Turning back to the cake, I felt my hands tremble as the butterflies in my stomach fluttered to flight. My skin was already hot, but a pickle now came with it.

Six years. Six years since I'd felt his lips on me. It wasn't something I could forget. It took me back to a time when his kisses were my whole world.

"Ax, what are you doing?" I slapped him on the arm and pulled back. "We're in the middle of the hallway."

"Don't give a fuck. Need a taste of you to get me through the rest of today," he growled low, and wetness pooled between my legs.

His lips touched the skin of my neck, running up and then down. God I loved him. So much it hurt sometimes.

My head tilted, giving him more access. With that, he grabbed my hips and pulled me against his hard erection. It was my turn to groan.

"This isn't a porn studio," Mr. Baker yelled from the science room door. "Move it along."

We pulled away, looking in the teacher's direction. "Shit," I said low so only Ax could hear.

"Move along, Mr. Baker," Ax said to chuckles in the hallway. "My girl. My school." He wrapped his arm around my shoulders and pulled me down the hallway.

Snapping back to the present, I shook my head, hoping to clear it. God, I loved the way he took charge of things and didn't take any shit from anyone. He'd always been on his own playing field. It made me feel powerful when I was with him. That out of everyone in our school, he chose me. When it ended, that power vanished and humiliation took its place. It took years for me to get that power back. I fought for it and didn't want to go back there.

While the shake of my head didn't work to clear the thoughts of Ax Monroe, I had a job to finish. The sooner that was done, the sooner I'd be out of here. And the sooner I'd be away from Ax and all his manly alphaness.

Several people came to look at the cake while I worked, but only one stopped to talk to me. Buzz, Ax's father. "Thanks for doin' this for the club."

The deep voice had me stopping and turning to the man. He was handsome with blond hair and a great smile when he showed it. He was a twin just like his boys, Ax and Raid. He'd always been nice, but distant to me. Cordial but never asking me any real questions.

I never knew if that was because he didn't like me too much or if he knew I'd just be another notch on Ax's bedpost. From his good looks, he probably knew the game his boys played in high school.

I wish I'd have known...

I shrugged and twisted the piping bag to do the final touches on connecting the roads together. "Bella and Tanner asked. I wasn't gonna say no."

He smiled wide. The same smile his son had. Hell, both sons had. The one that didn't come out often but was now here on display. It turned his rugged features a bit softer which I didn't think was possible.

"It's appreciated. You need anything, you come find me."

I felt my mouth open to respond, but nothing came out for a moment. Stunned, maybe. Hell if I knew, but I took his kindness. "Thanks."

Buzz lifted his chin like all the men here seemed to do before saying, "That one there looks like my boy." He tilted his head to the bikers. "Wonder how that happened?" Then he disappeared into the crowd. I swore I was going to have a heart attack if my heart kept beating out of my chest.

He noticed. Of all people, Ax's father did. Shit.

I hoped like hell he didn't relay that information to Ax. Not that I'd talk to Ax about anything.

Breathing in and out deep, I got to work and finished the masterpiece.

The cake was beautiful. Exactly, if not better, than I envisioned in my head and on the sketches I'd made. The hot pink convertible car was in front and the main focal point. Mazie sat in it with her hair blowing in the wind without a care in the world. Then the four bikers right on her tail trailed behind her. Yeah, the biker who looked like Ax. I had him tucked in the back, not as a standout display. Only someone looking for the features should have found them.

Sometimes I could be seriously stupid, but as a whole it was beautiful. Some of my best work to date. It needed to be captured and put in my book. It would be a huge addition to my work portfolio.

Grabbing my cell, I pulled it out and lined up the cake in its entirety.

I snapped a picture of the cake and the flash went off, making the dark space illuminate. It caught some of the women and bikers around me's attention.

My hand went up as I started to apologize, but two huge bikers started coming my way, their intense eyes boring into me. People got out of their way, not saying a word as they continued to approach.

Did I do something wrong? Because from the looks of these two, I fucked up more than just flashing my light in the club somewhere along the line.

My pulse picked up, and the hand my phone was in began to tremble. Yeah, I definitely did something wrong here because the fire glaring back at me was threatening to make me explode. Shit. Fear trickled down my spine.

I'd never met these two or seen them around. And judging by the venom in their eyes, I didn't want to meet them. Ever. Never ever.

"Why the fuck you takin' pictures? You know Mommas don't bring in phones period," the man on the right with dishwater blond hair said in a low tone.

While I didn't know that was a rule here in the club, I simply answered the truth. "I'm not a Momma." Yeah, I knew all about Mommas here in the club.

Ax made sure of that one. They were the women who hung around the clubhouse morning and night, ready to give whoever their assistance, either on their knees or back.

He tried to explain it to me that not everyone partook in the Mommas actions, but from experience I knew at least a few had.

"Why the fuck are you here?" The other one with dark almost midnight hair took one step forward, getting too close to me and invading my personal space. Terror. Yeah, that was what I felt. Pure terror through every cell in my body.

These men were going to hurt me. There was no doubt in my mind about it. How they'd hurt me, I didn't want to find out. I just wanted to get as far away as I could, but they didn't give me much room to move without having to touch them to escape. And no way would I touch them and give them a reason to touch me.

Instead, I took a step back and bumped hard into the table holding the cake. Shit! There had to be damage. I wanted to look back and make sure I didn't mess something up, but I couldn't take my eyes off the two men in front of me. No, I couldn't because they just took another step closer.

They were so close I could smell the beer on their breath. I was in serious trouble.

Before I could answer, not that me creating the cake would go over with these two, a hard body stepped between me and the men, pushing them back and out of my space. On instinct, I knew it was Ax by the size and shape of his body. Then of course the smell of him—sandalwood, musk, and well, Ax.

My hands lifted on instinct, gripping his leather and resting my head on his back, sucking in his scent. I'd missed it. It was a unique smell a woman never forgot. And here he was putting himself between me and danger.

"Back the fuck off," Ax growled so deep I felt it roll through his body. "She's off limits."

Off limits. That was a good thing. At least in this case. I really wanted to be off limits to these men. God, I hoped these two listened to Ax.

"Cone. Heavy," I heard Buzz, Ax's father say, his voice getting stronger the closer he got to us, but I didn't dare move from behind Ax. "Lay the fuck off. She's here to do the cake. She wants to take a picture of the fuckin' cake, she can take a fuckin' picture of it. You two need to back the fuck off."

There was the sound of a hand connecting with a shoulder, and I jumped unintentionally.

"You're fine. Nothin's gonna happen to you," Ax said without turning to me, but I felt those words to my soul.

"Sorry, man. Thought she was an outsider," the beefy man's voice said. And by the way, who the hell had names like Cone and Heavy? Apparently...them.

"Nah, she's Ax's," Buzz replied. "Come on." I then could hear footsteps walking away, but my body couldn't relax because of what Buzz said.

Ax's. Ax's? No way was I Ax's! Been there, done that, got the damn t-shirt... Not happening ever again, but I had to admit... If that meant those two not hurting me, I was grateful.

The man in question spoke. "You alright?" His voice snapped me out of my confusing thoughts, and I let go of his leather. He turned to me so close I could smell the beer on his breath. I could see the long length of his dark lashes. And those lips that touched me only a while ago.

"If I could keep my heart from jumping out of my chest, I'd be fine," I responded, putting my hand on my chest to keep the organ inside, like it would mysteriously help. When I did so, my hand brushed Ax's chest. Lord, please save me.

"No one touches you, Indie. No one. Ever." That gravelly voice of his was like a song. One that always had me in his trance. I remembered laying on his chest, just listening to him talk to me about his future plans ... our future plans. He'd always make me so calm, my eyes would flutter shut because I knew I was always safe with him. Or so I thought.

That snapped me back, and he was way too close and I had nowhere to go. I was already pressed against the table.

"Step back," I ordered, needing him and his aura to let me breathe.

His hand came up to the side of my face, his thumb touching my bottom lip. The nights that I'd dreamed of him doing this very move were too numerous to count. That face touch from him was one of the best memories I had of Ax. It wasn't some grand gesture or any words. It was a feeling. A touch that held more meaning any words could manage.

Staring into his blue eyes, I felt myself getting lost in the touch, in him. The gleam he gave me six years before shined brightly in them.

My racing heart began to crack and splinter. No. This couldn't happen.

"Back up," I ordered a lot stronger than I felt. Luckily, my voice didn't crack.

He leaned in to where he was a hairsbreadth to my lips. "We're gonna talk," he proclaimed.

"We have nothing to talk about. Now, I need to fix the cake those assholes made me damage before the birthday girl gets here."

Ax tilted his head to the side, his eyes going beyond me. "Looks good. Nothin' for ya to fix. Now we talk."

No. No. No. I wasn't talking to him. I wasn't having whatever this was in his head play out. Nope. Not me.

Turning around only put my ass right up against his dick. A dick, mind you, was as hard as a rock. Ax put his arms around me, and I tried to break free to no avail.

As hard as it was, I checked out the cake and pretended his strong arms weren't hugging me to his hard length and body. Nope, not here.

The cake looked pretty good. A couple of the bikers tilted just a bit, and I righted them. But all in all, not the damage I thought it would have. Great. Now I could leave; if I got the biker attached to me to let go, that was...

"Cake looks good. I'm going to leave," I told him over my shoulder and tried really hard to unlock his arms from mine.

He came closer, his lips against my cheeks. "Good. Then we can go talk."

"No. I have to clean up my stuff." There was icing, piping bags, and my entire kit spread out everywhere that needed to be put away.

Ax pulled away and let out a whistle that practically blew my eardrum out. Two men came running through the crowd, obviously hearing Ax over the thumping of the music.

"Clean this shit up. Then clean her tools, put them back in the kit, and put that in her van outside. Got me," he ordered. No, demanded.

"Yes, sir," they said in unison, and I saw the Prospect patches on their leather. Right, so these were the peons who took orders from the club in order to one day be part of the club.

It sounded like a sorority back in college. Each one pledging and doing stupid stuff to get in. Here, though, I had a feeling what they had to do was a bit more intense than shaving cream on a professor.

The two men got to work. Ax grabbed my hand and started to pull me. But I pulled back. I was not going somewhere we could 'talk.' Screw that. Nope. Us alone was not happening.

At my tug, he turned around and lifted his brow. Then he shrugged, and before I could say a word I was lifted, thrown over his shoulder into a fireman's hold, and we were strolling through the clubhouse.

"Ax!" I screamed. "Put me down!" I tried to wiggle out of his grasp. When the hard slap to my ass hit, everything inside me seized up. I could feel the wetness pooling between my legs, and it only made me fight more.

I hit his ass with my fists, yelling at him to let me go—which he did not. And not one single person stopped him.

The door to the clubhouse shut, and the cool air of the day hit.

"Brother?" I heard from beside me, and I lifted up to see Raid. Thank God.

"Raid, tell your brother to let me go now."

Ax's head shook. "Stay out of it."

Raid took in his brother and then took in me. When he took a beat too long, I yelled, "Raid!"

Raid's eyes came to mine. "It's time you two talk, and you know it."

"Talk? There's nothing to talk about!"

Pissed? No, try livid.

Ax didn't give his brother another thought and began his trek. No one stopped us this time. He carried me through the grassy area with people sitting on tables, just watching in amusement. Then through a door, up some stairs, which I hated to notice he did with ease, carrying me because he never bobbled me once.

He reached inside his pocket and pulled out a set of keys. Then the turning of a lock and a door creaking open filled my ears. Only two seconds later the door slammed closed and a lock was turned.

"If you think you're lockin' me in here, Mister, you have another thing coming!" When we went up the stairs, I admit I stopped kicking, but that was because I didn't want him to drop me.

Now.

This was a street fight. Nothing would be off limits. So I did what every women should do.

I kicked.

CHAPTER THIRTEEN

THE MORE SHE STRUGGLED, THE HARDER MY COCK GOT. And that slap to the ass? Yeah, I felt her body go completely still, and I could smell the arousal right under my nose. It took her a beat, but she went back to it.

Her yelling and screaming only made the grin on my face widen. Fuck, she did things to me no woman had ever done before. Parts inside of me that I thought were dead and gone long before.

Entering the room, I kicked the door shut, then slid her down my body. I felt every soft inch of her touch until she was on her feet, her full breasts feeling so damn good.

She glared up at me, probably thinking it would make me go away. Nope, only thought it was cute. That *she* was cute. Her heavy breathing only added to it.

"Let me go," she growled low, the vibration of her body doing nothing to tamp down my hard-on. Having her boxed in, there wasn't anywhere for her to go.

"We need to talk."

Fire blazed back at me as her head tipped up to me, our eyes connecting. "No. We really don't. I need to get my shit and get as far away from here and *you* as I can."

The feisty panther was coming out to play. I pressed her hips so close to mine that no way she didn't feel what she was doing to me. But her breath caught, telling me she felt it.

"Yes. We do."

Her eyes narrowed as she came to a conclusion. "You're not gonna let me go until you say what you need to say. Are you?"

A smile graced my face. She knew me better than most. "Nope. Not giving you an inch."

She huffed out deeply, her sweet taste filling my nose. "Fine. Talk. Get it out of your system, and I'm gone."

No. She wouldn't be gone. Seeing Cone and Heavy approach her like wild beasts, something inside me clicked, and all the pieces of the puzzles in my life started fitting together. Each going into its place inside me. Pieces that had been scattered for years, from going here to there.

She, Indigo was the one who made the puzzle complete. She had all the scattered pieces becoming whole.

Indie was mine. Had always been mine. She'd be mine forever. Convincing her of that was another story.

I felt a vulnerability in this moment that I wasn't used to, but I kept a tight hold on it, hoping it didn't come through my actions or words. She hated me. Wanted nothing to do with me. Even in this moment she couldn't wait to get away from me. I had a lot of work to do with her, and I'd do it. No matter how long it took.

I'd never shown my vulnerable side to anyone but Indie. She always had that part of me. Always would.

Indie's hands were on my chest with the intention of trying to push back, but I didn't release her; my arms wrapped around her tight. I liked her just the way she was, and with her skittering breathing I knew she was right here in the moment with me. The fire was becoming more sensual and needy, stirring in the air like the beginning of a tornado.

"I'm sorry." At my words, she stopped pushing, and her mouth fell open only to snap shut quickly. Guess I stunned her. Well, I stunned my damn self. It was something that should've been said years ago, but I never did. Why? Fuck if I knew, but it probably had to do with some fucked up pride thing.

"What?" she whispered.

"You heard me. Sorry I fucked us up. What we had up. I was young and dumb." Damn, she was so beautiful. The way her hair moved in little wisps around her face had me wanting to push them back, but I didn't release her. The way her lips were so full and wanting. She had a beauty no one compared to.

She swallowed deep. "Young and dumb. Yes. You were. Now let. Me. Go."

My head shook negative. "Can't do that. Did it then. Can't do it ever again."

"You have to," she said so quietly I didn't know if she meant to say it out loud. "Sorry doesn't fix this, Ax. What you did..."

My hands snaked up her back and clutched the back of her neck as I moved in closer, my lips coming so very close to hers they were only a breath away. "I know that. Doesn't mean I won't bust my ass every fuckin' day to make you understand and build us back up."

"You des..." She started to say, but I leaned down and fully took her mouth with every pent-up feeling I'd ever had of Indie pouring through it. Her lips were as soft as I remembered, and it didn't take but a second before she was kissing me back. Her hand slithered up my back to where she flipped my hat off, and her fingers went into my hair.

Fuck me, that felt good. The rough tugs only made me go deeper, wanting to consume her with everything in me.

She threw herself into the kiss wholeheartedly, taking from me and giving right back in return. God, it had been so long since I'd felt her against me. Since I had the taste of her sweetness devouring me just as I devoured her.

I was drowning.

I missed her. Fuck, did I miss her. Didn't realize how deeply until this moment. Or maybe I did with my trips to her bakery daily.

Six years, and it felt like yesterday. Like coming home.

Gripping her under her legs, I hoisted her up and pressed her back to the wall, then stuck my tongue inside and tasted everything she had to give.

Her ass had rounded over the time lost and was now the perfect peach for me to grab ahold of. Fucking perfect.

My cock pressed against her heat as her legs wrapped around me at just the right spot. She was on fire like a spider monkey rubbing up and down on me as her lips met my challenge head on.

Fuck, she was killing me. I needed to be inside her. Needed her to feel me. All of me.

Pulling away, my lips went to her ear as her breathing started coming out in haggard pants. "Rub that hot pussy on my cock." I trailed my tongue down the side of her neck, below her ear, and back up.

She groaned loudly, her head falling to my shoulder as she listened and followed my command.

"Fuck yeah. Right there. Your pussy is so wet for me. Isn't it?" I growled, but she didn't answer. "Wet and hot. Bet you're throbbing, the lips of your pussy ready to suck me in deep."

"Just shut up," she said between panted breaths.

"Not a fuckin' chance." Balancing her against the wall and with one of my arms, I slipped my hand between us, unbuttoned her jean shorts, and shoved my hand inside, feeling exactly what I was talking about.

"Fuck, I wanna lick every drop of this sweetness and make you scream." My fingers were so fucking slick.

"Then shut the fuck up and do it already." She pulled my hair hard, letting me know she was not messing around. Add in the small growl, and I was a goner.

Ask and you shall receive.

Attaching my lips to hers, I set her down on her feet only to rip off the shorts and whatever underwear she had on. The woman could've had granny panties on for all I cared, and I wouldn't know it because I didn't take the time to look.

Breaking away, I went down to my knees, lifted her legs and rested them on my shoulders. Looking up, her stark need flickered so brightly I was almost blinded. Being in front of her and looking up, she had no idea the power she had over me. That she'd always had over me.

Running my nose along her sensitive flesh, I inhaled in deep, loving her sweet smell. Not waiting another second, my tongue reached out and flicked her nub ever so gently with the tip.

She groaned, and I decided not to mess around as much as I wanted to play. That would have to be with round two.

Taking her pussy in my mouth deep, there were no playful licks. No gentle caresses. No taking, only giving.

This was fucking her hard with my mouth and tongue. I kissed it like it were her lips, my tongue moving in and out of her core, sucking every bit of her.

Her fingers came to the top of my head, threading through and pulling tight, hardening my cock even more. Damn thing was going to explode, and I couldn't fucking wait.

"Fuck!" she groaned, and I didn't relent. Over and over again, I kept eating everything she gave me. Each move of her hips, each nose, mouth and tongue touch built her up more and more. Her wetness filled me and covered my face. I didn't give one damn.

I loved every second of it.

Her legs quivered and her fingers pulled harder. She was about to come. She was right there. Her body was screaming it.

Taking her clit between my lips, I sucked hard, only to give a tiny bite to it, then back to sucking. Over and over again, mixing it up so she didn't know what was coming next.

She thrashed and moved her body up and down, feeling everything I was giving.

When her orgasm hit, I kept going riding her through the climax, but stopping just shy of her ending. I lifted her, her back skating up the wall as I reached down and unbuttoned my pants.

Fuck, this woman was beautiful. Her fiery eyes were glazed over in ecstasy, and I needed her. Needed her more than I needed anything.

I pulled out my cock, lined up, and slid deep

inside her. Indie's back arched on the wall, pushing her breasts into my face. Even clothed, I found her pebbled nipple and sucked hard. It wouldn't feel as good as bare, but beggars couldn't be choosers and all that nonsense.

"Ax!" Her screaming my name had my eyes connecting to hers. "Harder. Fuck me harder."

What control I had snapped hearing those words grace her beautiful lips.

"Get ready to ride."

Over and over, I thrust inside her, each of her noises getting louder. Her arms wrapped around my neck as she held on tight, her lips coming to my neck as she kissed and sucked.

I ground into her and circled my hips, hitting her clit. She threw back her head and hit the wall, screaming out in pleasure. It was no ordinary noise.

No, it was one I'd never heard from her before but fucking loved.

It had been too long since I'd been inside her, and I followed close behind.

My cock jerked and pulsed, and I reveled in Indie's heat as I spilled into her pussy, squeezing and milking every bit of come from me.

Moments later, or hours, fuck if I knew, our breathing was still coming hard, but I noticed the instant that Indie realized what she did because she pushed me hard, catching me a bit off guard as she fell to her feet.

"I cannot believe..." She grabbed the shorts and pulled them on, then slipping on her shoes. She moved so fucking fast and with me on my ass, boots on and jeans around my ankles, she had an edge.

Trying to get up. "Wait!" I called out to her, but she took off like a shot and slammed the door behind her. Getting up quickly, I pulled myself together, threw open the door, and took chase.

She wasn't getting away from me. Not now and not ever.

The heat was on.

CHAPTER FOURTEEN
Indie

MY TOMBSTONE WAS GOING TO READ *"STUPIDEST BITCH on the planet"* right across the top because that was me.

Alone with the man one time, and I screwed him against the wall. How fucked up was that?

I knew I only had moments for Ax to get himself together and come after me. Because I had no doubt he was coming. He kept talking all this I'm sorry shit. Well, bud, too little too late.

Carefully, I maneuvered down the stairs, quickly hanging onto the rail all the way down to the door. One mission: escape before I fell down the rabbit hole of stupid woman yet again.

What the hell was it about this man that I struggled to let go of? Seriously, it had been years and he still crawled under my skin like no one else.

"Indie!" Ax called, and my time was running out.

Pushing the door open, I ran straight through the grassy area like there was a demented dog on my tail. Oh wait. There was!

With the extra exertions, my energy was fading. With running the bakery all the time, I never ran. When the hell would I have time for that? But in this case it would've been nice, considering my legs felt like they were going to fall off.

When the big bulk stepped in front of me, I crashed hard and jarred my entire body. Shit, how hard was I running?

Looking up, I saw the same man I'd just screwed, only this one had a jagged scar across his brow. Raid.

"Let me go. I have to go," I pleaded, and it felt beneath me, but I couldn't do this. I didn't want to talk to Axton Monroe about anything. We fucked. It happened; lots of consenting adults had hookups. That was it. Now, I wanted to finish my walk of shame.

His eyes turned serious. "Are you hurt?"

"Indie!" Ax called as I turned my head to see him burst out the door and coming straight for me.

"He wants to talk feelings and shit. I don't want to talk feelings." I looked up to Raid. "So let me go. Please, Raid, I've never asked you for anything. Even after everything that happened I never did."

Raid's eyes roamed over me, then shifted over to Ax who I could feel at my back now. My body went taut.

"Brother. You fucked her? Seriously. How the fuck is that gonna solve anything?" Raid asked with a tone in his voice that surprised me and put me on edge, but I decided to look down at my feet.

One Monroe in front and one behind me. We were a fucking sandwich. My inside tingled at the thought, then I shut that thought down. No way in hell. Obviously, I had gone too long focused on work and not release.

I wasn't a whore. Hell, I wasn't even all that experienced, but here I went and fucked my ex against a wall like some lovesick idiot, and now—for the briefest of moments—I was thinking of having him again, only this time with his twin brother too! Seriously, someone commit my ass to one of those homes where I have constant supervision because I have lost my damn mind.

"This is between Indie and me, brother. You wanna let her go?" Ax asked.

"No," Raid challenged with an even tone that wasn't intended for an argument. "She wants to leave."

"Does it look like she's leavin', brother?" Ax clipped, his tone a sharp edge.

They were going to fight. I'd been around for these twin fights, and no way I wanted to be in the middle of one of their knockdown dragouts. I needed to get my shit together and get the fuck out of Dodge.

Swallowing down all the emotions knotted up inside me, I used the one reason I knew no one would disagree with. "I really have to get back to the bakery. Gotta close up and clean." That was a lie, but sue me! I wanted out of there. No, I needed out. More time between the Monroe boys meant more therapy later for my inner whore who had goosebumps simply by being in their presence. *Get a grip, girl, you've had your fill.*

Arms went around my stomach, and I was pulled backward into Ax's hard body. Raid took a step closer, and my breathing picked up. Oh my God ... this had to stop.

I'd just came twice, and my body was ready to go again. With brothers! No. No, no, no!

"I really..." Ax's lips came to my ear stopping my words.

"Told ya we needed to talk. Don't want ya leavin' yet."

My entire body shivered, but I burst out, "Told you we're not talking! Now both of you let me go before I start kicking nuts," I threatened, and both of them laughed.

Laughed. At. Me.

There was a little secret I kept in my arsenal. Before coming home, I took months of self-defense classes that turned into fighting lessons. It had been a while since I'd practiced which wasn't smart, but what the hell.

With my last stitch of energy, I went for it.

My foot slammed hard into Ax's shin. He had on steel-toed boots. So that wasn't an option. It caught him off guard, and he released me just enough that I could elbow him hard in the side.

At the same time, I thrust my body hard into

Raid, then spun. There were still hands on me, but I didn't give them a second to get a better grip.

I took off like a shot, and whoever had a hold of me released. Darting right to my van, Princess stood there, and I slid to a halt.

"I have to go." Fuck, what was it that Ravage always closed in together to protect their own! I was not Ravage and try as any of them might, I was not about to have a conversation with Ax. "I really need to go," I repeated, not wanting to be rude, because she'd probably kick my ass, but I really needed her to move.

"That was badass. I have some other tricks I can teach ya," she said on a smile, then crossed her arms and came to stand in front of me, just as two big bodies came stomping our way. "Go," she told me, and I didn't pause. Nope, I didn't need to ask her questions; I didn't need to hesitate. Princess Cruz was giving me what I needed and thank God for her sisterhood. I wasn't losing the gift of this opportunity.

I jumped in the van, silently thanking whoever left the keys in the ignition, and took off out of the lot. It seemed to take forever for the metal gate to slide open, but when it did, I was gone.

I didn't have to be back at the bakery, as my brother and sister were handling stuff, and it closed very soon. Luckily, that would be the place Ax would look.

Who the hell was I kidding? He wasn't coming to look for me.

He got what he wanted, and I was the idiot who

gave it to him. The stupid pill I took this morning sure did a bang-up job.

The outside of the house was dark, and a chill went down my spine as I looked around my surroundings. The letter creeped through my thoughts, and I had to push it out

It wasn't happening. Couldn't.

Since my car was at the bakery I opened the garage door and slid the van inside. I'd have to remember to call Marley, and he'd get my car here. I waited for the door to completely close, and I was locked in my garage, taking a huge breath once it was down.

The barking started as I closed the door to the van. She was waiting for me. Like she always was.

Opening the door, a little ball of white and black fur came bouncing to me, the bit of light from inside shining bright. I swore she was part rabbit because the pup really did hop like one.

Scooping her up, I cooed, "How's Mommy's baby? Did you have a good day?" Little Gizmo started licking my face and squirming in excitement.

"That good, huh?"

We sat on the couch, and Gizmo automatically flipped on her back for me to scratch her belly. "Oh, this again. Wish someone would scratch my belly," I grumbled to myself.

I'd just made one of the biggest mistakes a woman could make. Fucking an ex who broke their heart. Always said I'd never do such a thing. I was smarter than that.

No way would he worm his way anywhere close to my panties.

Then one kiss, and I was a puddle of mush and the worm got in.

It had been a while since I'd been with anyone, but that was no excuse.

He kissed me, and I was lost to it. The feel of him. The taste of him. Just ... him. My whole body came alive just reliving the night in my mind.

It was hard in that moment to remember the hurt he'd caused. The devastation he portrayed. No, all I thought about was getting off, and that was even worse.

I'd loved that man with everything I had, and I hated to think it, but when he kissed me, when he was inside me ... it felt like home. Like I'd just now came back to Sumner, and that was dangerous.

He couldn't have that kind of pull on me again. I couldn't allow him to envelop me in his life only to tear it away. I wouldn't risk my heart being pulled out from my chest.

No. I wouldn't.

Gizmo jumped, and I heard it too. The sound of a motorcycle.

You have got to be kidding me. He didn't even try to go to the bakery; he came directly here. A place he'd never been before.

A place he had no stamp on. No memories.

If he came in here, there would be memories, and that would kill my sanctuary. It was the one place in

Sumner where I could be without anything reminding me of Ax Monroe.

And here he was, wanting in my space.

Did he even know I had a dog? Maybe her bark would be enough to keep him away. Gizmo was only fifteen pounds. Let's just say her bark was bigger than her bite.

The light of day was dissipating as I carried Gizmo and peeked out of the window. The man in question parked in my driveway like he'd done it a million times. He took off his helmet and shook his hair, then put his baseball cap on backward. Why did he still have to wear it like that to this day? In high school, the same thing. Made the girls swoon and still did... Dammit.

Maybe I should grab his hat and cut it up, then he wouldn't look so damn hot.

Who was I kidding? With or without the hat, he would still be hot. I'd seen him without it several times and had first-hand knowledge.

He swung his leg off his bike and made a beeline for the front door. He looked my way, and I snapped the blind closed, but the smirk I caught on his lip told me he saw me. Well hell, that worked well.

Gizmo was going nuts now, barking and jumping at the door as if she could open it herself. "Shh ... it's okay. Calm down," I whispered stupidly. Ax already knew I was here for God's sakes.

Gizmo was a bit territorial of this home. She allowed family and Mrs. Denolli from next door, who took her out during the day, to come inside. Mailman? Nope, hated for her to be on the porch. Package delivery? Nope, barked to high hell. Girl Scouts? Nope, but I didn't know if that was because she knew my cookies were better or if it was them.

Family was good too, but that was her limit.

Maybe she would scare Ax. Terrify him into running for his bike and driving away. I found myself laughing with my hand over my mouth when a banging came to the door.

It wasn't my doorbell. It wasn't a knock. No, this was a balled-up fist threatening to break the door down and shaking the damn house banging.

Seriously, Ax?

Gizmo kept barking, jumping, turning around in circles and attacking the door too. Normally I'd tell her to settle down, but in this instance, she could bark to her hearts content until Ax left. Because he was leaving.

"Indie, open the damn door," he yelled from the other side.

I placed my palm on the wood, knowing he was right on the other side. I could feel the hurt he inflicted and how wounded my heart was by this man still to this day. "Just go, Ax. You can hear my dog; she'll bite ya."

He started chuckling. "That thing wouldn't scare an ant, let alone bite it. Now let me in."

Scare an ant? How the hell did he know how big my dog was? It could be a ferocious Rottweiler for all he knew.

"She's tougher than you may think." I shook my

head. "There's nothing to talk about, Ax. Let's just forget what happened, move on from this, and let it go," I tried.

"If you don't let me in, I'm gettin' my tools and pickin' the locks."

Shit.

I knew he could do that. He tried to teach me once upon a time, but I wasn't very good at it. Give me a cake, I'm golden. But picking locks wasn't in my wheelhouse.

I laid my forehead against the door.

My will was too strong to give in. He'd have to get his picks and do the work if he wanted in. Screw him. Who did this man think he was?

"I'm not lettin' you in. You want to talk. We can talk through the door," I told him, standing up straight and throwing back my shoulders.

"We're not fuckin' talkin' through the damn door, Indie. Open up."

The poundings started once again.

"Then I'm going to take a shower. You can go back to the clubhouse."

Ax growled on the other side, making a smile tip my lips.

"I'm not goin' anywhere," he retorted.

"And I'm not letting you in," I clipped back.

"Fucking hell."

I heard his boots stomp down the stairs, and I then peeked through the slats to see him going back to his bike. He opened a compartment and came out with the pick kit in his hand.

He would get in, but he'd have to work for it. I wasn't the same wallflower he knew years ago. Time made me stronger. No matter how weak in the knees he tended to make me.

"Shh... Gizmo, enough." Yeah, she didn't listen to me at all. Instead, she kept barking, wanting to see who dared to enter her space.

Taking a step back, I went and sat on the couch. Even when he picked the lock, he'd still have one obstacle. That being the chain I had on all my doors.

Sounds from the door told me he was already at work. There was a deadbolt and the lock for the handle. He popped the handle way too easily and getting a stronger lock for that was definitely on the to-do list.

"Come here, girl."

Gizmo looked at me then started barking harder, obviously knowing someone was trying to get in. Smart dog.

The handle on the door turned and then a faint "Fuck," came through the door, making me smile.

"You know, you could just give up," I called.

"I'm gonna spank your ass for this."

A flush crept my cheeks, and bold as brass I responded, "Love to see you try that one."

"Oh, Indie. You have no idea the challenge you just threw down," he said, going at the dead bolt.

A thrill shot up my spine, then I chastised myself for it. The deadbolt turned way too quickly too. Investing in a security system needed to be high on my priority list. When the door opened just a couple of inches and then stopped, his body hit the door as if he thought he was going to make it through.

I burst out laughing. Yes, full-out belly laugh.

"Good luck getting through that one," I said with a smile in my tone. Might have needed a thicker lock, but I bought the most expensive chain the internet had to offer. Take that, Axton Monroe!

Gizmo took that opportunity to jump through the little crack, and I jumped to my feet, all joking aside. Traitorous bitch went right to him. Now what?

"Gizmo!" I yelled, moving to the door and unlatching it.

Ax held Gizmo in his arms who looked happy as can be.

"Traitor," I muttered to the dog. "What happened to girl code? I feed you, for Pete's sake!"

He stood there like a dark angel ready to attack. Whether it was heaven or hell, no way I could know.

Gizmo went quiet, looking between the two of us.

"Give me my dog," I ordered to his smile.

"Nope."

Anger bubbled. "What do you want?" I asked in a clipped tone.

Him being here... I just didn't know how I felt about it. Not to mention him not letting Gizmo down. She seemed to like exactly where she was.

"Pretty sure I'll have some killer bruises tomorrow," he said on a smirk.

"Good. Now you can give me Gizmo and go."

Ax didn't wait for an invitation to enter. He just walked right into the house, grabbed the door, shut it and locked it, then put Gizmo down. Gizmo looked up at the man begging with her eyes to be picked back up. He even had the effect on dogs; what the hell was up with that?

"Well, come on in," I said in the most sarcastic tone I could muster. I scooped up my dog who began to wiggle, wanting down. See, she was a traitor.

"Let the pup down," he told me.

My hand went to my hip. "Ax Monroe. Do not come into my house and tell me what to do with my dog."

He lifted his hands in surrender. "Just thought it'd be better than dropping it."

I hated it when he was right. Setting Gizmo down, she went right back to Ax who bent over and picked her up. She immediately started licking his face.

"Traitor." I mumbled again under my breath to Ax's chuckle. "Talk. What do you want?"

He stepped closer to me and looked deep into my eyes. "Everything."

My entire world ground to a halt. He wanted everything. What the hell did that mean?

Funny thing about heartache ... I remembered when he took everything from me.

Squaring my shoulders, Ax needed to know I wasn't some naïve young girl anymore. I was a strong, capable woman.

"You want everything, Ax. Well, you had all I could ever give, and you destroyed it. Sorry, bud, but the well has run dry, and I'm all empty with no fucks left to give."

CHAPTER FIFTEEN

HER BREATH STOPPED, BUT I DIDN'T PUSH IT. I KNEW Indie. Knew how much she could take at one time, and for what I had planned it would take a little finesse. "Thought you said you needed to get to the bakery?"

Her eyes flared. "Let me guess ... you know we close early on Saturday."

"Of course. And you're off on Sundays. It's on your door." He smirked. "Baby, been comin' to your shop damn near every day since you opened; I know the fuckin' schedule. I also know Meadow has a thing with cleaning, and she's quite particular about it. She prefers to close the shop so she stays on top of the sanitation."

The light dawned on her as she shook her head. If she could, I had no doubt she'd want to strangle me.

Too bad that just made her hotter, and I'd love to see her try.

"Tell me I'm wrong," I challenged.

Was I a fucking douchebag for what I did to her? How I hurt her? Absolutely, but not for one second had she ever left my mind. I remembered everything about her and her family because as much as her siblings could drive her crazy, one thing about the Fallon family, loyalty was everything.

The pup was cute and all, but licking my face was getting old, so I set her down and took in the space.

Shock? I wasn't sure that was the right word for it, but something close to it.

Now I knew that Indie's mom was a hippie back in the day, and her GramO, who was fucking awesome too. But I had no idea that Indie liked that feel for her space as well.

It wasn't full-blown hippie. More of that boho thing that Austyn talked about wanting to change her living room into, and we gave Ryker shit because of all the bright colors and plants that Austyn would kill in the first week.

Stepping further inside the entrance, the colors hit me at once, and I questioned myself about giving Ryker shit.

The living room had a subtle orange on the walls, but the couch, pillows, and carpet were all bold in your face colors of blues, purples, greens, bright oranges and every other color under the sun. And plants. The woman had them in so many different sized pots on the floor, on tables, and some hanging from the ceiling in these net things, making me wonder how the hell she got them up there.

The coffee table looked as though it was made from recycled wooden pallets that had been sanded and stained. The floor had a rug with every color in the rainbow woven together in shapes of diamonds, squares, and rectangles.

The couch was a bright bluish-green color that she had to have custom made because I'd never seen the color before. Tossed on it were so many pillows, she had to throw some on the ground to even sit on it.

Taking a few more steps, in and off to the right was a dining area. It was slender as opposed to the living room, like it had something behind it. The walls had lower cabinets and shelves filled to the brim with books and other stuff. I made a note to check that out later when I could actually stop and look at the pictures.

The large long table was wooden as well and looked as though it had the shit beat out of it. More plants in the middle of it with chairs and pillows pushed into the sides.

"Sure. Why don't you make yourself at home and go through my house looking at all my personal stuff? I mean, I did invite you into my space." Sarcasm dripped from her tone.

"I'm gonna fuck you on this butcher block table," I announced, moving through the dining room, and my finger skated on the table as I went into the kitchen. Yeah. This was what took up a ton of space.

It had a wall of windows that showed off the back-woods in Sumner.

Orange. She had fucking orange cabinets and a refrigerator. Never fucking seen that before. Didn't know they even made that shit. The walls were a bold green, and even with all the different colored bowls, it all felt like it went together.

"Yeah ... that's not happening. Fucked me once; it was fun. Have to say grown man Ax knows what he's doing. But you won't fuck me twice," Indie said from beside me. I knew the last part was laced in memories of the past and not just about the sex we had. "Can we get on with the talking portion of this conversation? I'm ready for you to leave."

The dog started barking, then ran over to the door and rang some bells. Indie followed and knelt to pick her up. "Does Gizmo need to go potty?" she cooed in a voice I'd heard moms talk to their children in, and I raised my brow at her, not ever hearing her like this.

"Shut up. No one asked you." She turned on her heel, slid the back door of the kitchen open, and let the dog out. She didn't shut the door and stood there keeping an eye on Gizmo. She was trying to distance herself from me. Too bad that shit wasn't happening.

"Gizmo, Huh? Thought you'd choose something like Marley or Hendrix."

She rolled her eyes to the ceiling and crossed her arms over her chest, pushing up those beautiful tits. "Why on earth would I name my dog after my brothers?"

"They both bark and shit a lot. They both think they have a bite."

A smile tipped the corner of her mouth. I fucking loved that. Teasing. Joking around. It felt like we'd never stopped seeing one another, yet everything had changed. So much had changed with the both of us. But my feelings for her never had. If anything after today, I felt her through every cell of my body.

"Talk, Ax. Time's a tickin'. I really need some sleep. I've been working on Mazie's cake around the clock, and I'm wiped. I don't have the energy to fight with you. Just say it already."

"First, you need food." Moving to the orange fridge, it was one of those old-fashioned looking ones with the handle horizontal, I opened it. It was stacked and had a built-in freezer at the top but didn't have a separate opening from the cover.

"What are you doing?" she asked from further away, so I knew the dog hadn't come in yet because she was still at the door.

Inside I found some ground beef, a bottle of red wine, and a small container of crushed garlic. I pulled it out and set it on the counter. Then I started opening and closing the cabinet drawers, trying to find what I needed or a close second.

"Gizmo. Come on, girl. I need to go murder someone going through my stuff," she yelled out the door as I heard barking coming closer.

I chuckled. Finding pasta, a can of tomato sauce, and an array of spices, I went on the hunt for pans. Every time I opened another cabinet, I smiled. Everything: plates, cups, and bowls were in bright mix-matched colors that went together so perfectly you'd never know they weren't an actual set. At least to me. I was used to paper plates and red Solo cups.

Finding the two pans I needed, one purple and the other teal, I got to work.

"What are you doing?" The voice came from right behind me over my shoulder.

"Cookin' you dinner."

She shook her head. "No. You're not. I'm not hungry."

I leveled her a look. "You've busted your ass all day, and probably this week, helpin' out my club. So I'm cookin' you dinner. Sit down, pet your dog, and chill the fuck out."

She wanted to respond, and before her brain could catch up with her actions, her stomach growled, giving her completely away.

I pointed the newly found aqua spatula at her. "See, that's what I mean. Sit. Relax."

"How do you know how to cook? If you're makin' pasta, I don't have any marinara sauce." She sounded further away. I looked up to find her sitting at the small island off to the side of the kitchen area. It had four chairs that all butted up to it. They gave a view of the kitchen and of the tall windows. It was a really peaceful scene.

"I'll make the sauce. Don't have much fresh but I'll make do." There was only dried basil and oregano, but it'd be okay.

"Who taught you to cook?"

Normally this small talk bullshit would be a real turnoff. Hit it, get it. Done.

This was totally different, though. This was Indie. I wanted her to know me. Not Ax the biker. But Ax the man, who I was now. Dad always said the man and the biker were one in the same, but even with him I saw a difference between the two. When he was with Mom, it was like his world lit up. When he was a biker, he was badass. There was a thin line between the two. But it was there. That small softness he allowed in for her.

I'd never let anyone that close.

I began breaking up the meat I just dropped in the pan, hearing it sizzle. "My mom. She said that every man should know how to make at least seven meals."

"Seven? Why seven?"

I continued breaking up the meat and giving it a stir. I moved to the drawers, searching for a can opener. "One full week. Just because a woman marries you, doesn't mean she's gonna cook for you. She always said we needed to be prepared for that shit."

Indie chuckled, and I turned to look. Her laugh was beautiful. Her little Gizmo sat in her lap, loving getting rubs. *I hear ya, buddy. I'd like a few rubs from her myself.*

"She also said that a woman didn't want to cook all the damn time and her boys wouldn't be the men who demanded food on the table at a specific time. So, she taught us if we were hungry, we cooked."

"I would've thought fast food would be your meal every night," she stated.

I lifted my shirt and showed her my abs. "You think I could keep this shit up by eating McDonald's every fuckin day?"

She slowly trailed her eyes over my abs, then shook her head and asked, "And she taught you how to make marinara sauce?" completely blowing off the abs. Indie didn't need to worry about it. She'd have her hands all over me soon enough.

I nodded, letting her off the hook as I found the can opener and opened the tomatoes. "I'd like to have some Italian sausage in here with the beef and fresh spices, but we work with what we got."

"I feel weird with you cooking for me," she admitted. "In fact, I would feel much better if you would just walk on out that door climb on that steel horse, and cowboy your way right on down the road."

I didn't even try to stop the laugh that escaped. "Get used to it. One, I'm not going anywhere. We can both be stubborn, Indie, but you should know I won't back down. And two, I am cooking for you. I'm here, you're hungry, and tired, so I'm cooking to make sure you aren't still hungry when I put you to bed. My mom didn't just teach me seven recipes like she did Raid. I have a whole arsenal of recipes to show you." I looked around, then held the top of the can and turned to her. "Garbage?"

"Under the second cabinet. It pulls out."

Ahhh, she was finally relaxing a bit. Finding the

spot, I opened it and grabbed what I needed to throw away.

"Can I help at least?" she asked, and I shook my head, seeing the bottle of wine I'd pulled out of the fridge. Going back to the top cabinet, I found glasses in it. She didn't have a glass with a stem on it, so I grabbed one without and poured some of the wine in the glass.

Walking over to her, I set the wine in front of her as her eyes traveled up my body. "Um. Thanks?" Her breathing hitched, and I fucking loved it.

I kissed the top of her forehead. "Anything."

Without giving her a second, I moved over to the beef, stirring it around adding some of the seasonings. Putting the other pot on the stove, she had this spicket that came out from the wall for water. I turned it on and filled up the pot, turning it on high to boil.

"Why do you come into the bakery every morning?" she asked, surprising me, but I continued stirring then adding in the tomatoes.

"You've got good coffee, but great fuckin' lemon bars."

I heard her chuckle. "That is true, but why, Ax? I want to know why for years you've come into my place, my space? I've left you alone, not bringing up our past. Why can't you do the same for me?"

Turning, I made eye contact with her. "Needed to see you every day. Wanted to see you every day."

"That makes no sense, Ax. What we had in high school was burned to the ground."

We needed to talk about this, but I wanted to be sitting with her, focusing completely on me while we discussed our past. This didn't seem as personal. I wanted to be able to touch her.

"We'll talk about this. Promise you that. Let me finish dinner so we can sit together and talk. Me having my back to you half the time while talking isn't how I want to do this."

She cleared her throat. "I kinda like your back to me. Makes it easier."

I smiled down at the sauce. "Yeah, but this shit isn't easy. We'll get there."

"Seriously, Ax. Whatever."

She was totally giving me attitude just because she didn't know what else to do. It had been her fall-back even when we were together before, but this time it had a bit more spice to it. It was fuckin' sexy as hell.

"When did you decide to open the bakery and make cakes?" I asked, putting the pasta in the boiling water then giving it a stir.

"Really, Ax. Do you even want to know?"

Setting the spoon down, I leaned my hip on the counter and crossed my arms over my chest, staring her down. "Yes. I wanna know fuckin' everything. From the moment you left to this moment now. If I didn't, I wouldn't have asked."

She lifted her glass and took a sip of her wine. Thinking. Contemplating. Hell, if I knew. "Just turn around, and I'll talk."

"Easier?"

"Yeah."

"Only this time, Indie." I turned to finish up the sauce and tasted it. Adding a few more spices, she finally began to talk, giving me a huff along the way.

Fuck, she was cute. If this made her talk, I'd do it.

"As if I want to tell you anything," she growled, but then started. "After graduation, I needed to get as far away from Sumner as I could. Needed a new start. New life."

Fuck, I'd done that to her. Fucking hated that.

"Ended up in Seattle, Washington if you can believe that."

No, I actually couldn't. That was on the other side of the country, and she liked the sunshine. Heard up there it rains a lot.

"It was always cloudy there, or at least it felt like it because when the sun shined it was like a vibrance came to the city. Truthfully, I loved it there. Even went to the University of Washington and got my degree."

"Always knew you were smart. What did ya get for your degree?" I asked, giving the pasta another stir.

"Art and a minor in Business. I'd thought about taking online master classes before opening Fallon's Bakery. Now I'm glad I didn't. Even with grants and scholarships, college is not cheap."

"Damn. That's awesome, babe. Proud of ya."

The only thing I could hear was her dog's collar jiggling and Indie's deep intake of breath.

"Um ... thanks?" She posed it as a question instead of a statement.

I grabbed the colander out of the cabinet and put it in the sink. Went over to the pasta and picked up the pot, dumping it in to drain. Letting it rest there, I stirred the sauce once more then took a taste. Not half bad with what I had.

Filling the large spoon with a little of the sauce, I took it over to Indie and held my hand under it to prevent any spills. I held it up to her lips and offered, "Tell me what ya think."

Her brow quirked, and I could tell her inner panther wanted to scratch me. Surprisingly though, she opened her lips as I gave a blow to the sauce so it wouldn't burn her.

Placing the spoon between her lips, her eyes stayed connected to mine as she took in the deliciousness.

When they widened, I pulled away.

"Oh my God. You made that from the scraps I have in my kitchen? I'd love to see what you could do when you had access to a store and everything you'd want."

My heart thumped in my chest, and when her hand went to her mouth, I knew she'd finally caught what she had said. The little vixen wanted me to cook for her again.

That shit wouldn't be a problem.

Indie shook her head, probably trying to clear out the indication she just allowed to slip. "I'm starving. Can we eat?"

My brow quirked. "Thought you weren't hungry."

A smile graced her lips. "Shut up and give me

food, or better yet, I'll get it myself. Matter of fact, thank you for your consideration and kindness in preparing me a meal. Now kindly go home."

She moved to get off the chair, but I put my arm in front of her. "Sit. I'll bring it to you. And, baby, you should know I get off on the attitude, so push all you want—the pull won't be denied."

"You don't have to wait on me, Ax. I can do things for myself," she snipped back.

I got so close to her, she had to tip her head to see me. "Queens need to be takin' care of, Indie. So you sit."

Her mouth moved, but nothing came out of it. Speechless. I could do with that. Slowly swiping my nose against her cheek, I turned away and went to the food.

"Does this mean I get a tiara?" she asked as I mixed the pasta and meat sauce in a bowl.

"Ab-so-fucking-lutely. I'll put my mom on it. She knows where to get that shit."

"Ax!" she yelled my name in a scold. "Do not ask your mother to get me a tiara. That was just a joke. I don't need a damn crown, but I will take the title of Queen at least for tonight if it means you will do what I want."

She'd be my queen every fucking day of our lives from this moment on. She just didn't know it yet. Mom might have taught me how to cook, but Dad taught me how you treat the woman you love. Yeah, I fucking loved her. Never stopped.

It was time for me to put up or let it go. I was no fool. Letting Indie go again wasn't an option.

Pulling out two plates, I dished out the food and walked over to Indie who had put little Gizmo down and was curled up at her feet.

"You wear the queen shit with honor. Not many get that title in life."

She rolled her eyes then inhaled deep. "This smells amazing. Thank you, Ax."

Cupping the side of her face, I brushed my thumb over her bottom lip. "Anything for you, Indie. Anything."

I didn't wait for her response. Instead, I turned around and got the utensils, napkins, and a glass of wine for me. Now wine wasn't in my top ten of what I liked to drink, but I couldn't find beer or any other liquor in the house. This would just have to do.

I sat next to Indie, giving her what she needed. She didn't waste a moment digging right into the food. The first moan had my cock hardening, and I swore she was doing it on purpose because at the fifth one, I was ready to throw her on this counter and fuck her brains out.

"What about you?" she asked after swallowing.

"Me?"

Damn, this shit wasn't half bad. Indie was right. I could make it better with fresh ingredients. That would be for another time.

"Yeah, you, Ax. What have you been doing over the years?"

Most of what I'd done she couldn't know. At least

for now. Therefore, I went the easier route. "Club business mostly. Then, of course, work."

"Work? Do you work at the garage?"

Many of the Ravage men worked at Banner Automotive, but since we'd expanded our income streams, we all had to branch out and take more on.

"Nah, I work at X. Live there too."

Indie's back went rigid, which was a good sign. If she didn't like me working at X, it meant there wouldn't be as much resistance as I initially thought. But knowing Indie, anything was possible.

She wiped her mouth with her napkin. "You work and live at a strip club?"

"Yep. Work as a bouncer or, at least, I oversee the ones there. Mine and Raid's place is on the top level of the building."

Turning to her, she was twirling up some of the pasta, but she had a distant look on her face.

"I'd give anything to know what's running around in your head right now."

This was a moment I thought about many times. Indie and me, sharing space, a meal after a good fuck. Only, I never imagined she would shut me out, build the walls.

Younger Ax wouldn't have the patience or tenacity to endure. I did this shit, though, so I would see it through. No wall, no defiance, nothing would hold me back from continuing to fight to have her as mine again.

CHAPTER SIXTEEN
Indie

AX MONROE WAS COOKING AT MY STOVE, CREATING something that had my mouth watering. He could cook?

I had no damn clue. From the smell alone, it had to taste good. From the stuff I had in the fridge and cabinets, I didn't think it could make this space so aromatic.

Not to mention, with his back turned to me, his ass was on full display in his jeans. Somewhere along the line he'd taken off his cut. Why did he have to be so attractive?

Answer. *What was the question again?*

This man did not need to know what I was thinking at all because deep inside me anger bubbled like in a cauldron threatening to spill over.

He worked around strippers all day. Fucking lived there and had easy access to fuck whoever he wanted,

172 | RYAN MICHELE

whenever he wanted. Like that was something new with all the "Mommas" around the club, but it still cut.

And that shit cut deeper than I would like to admit.

It shouldn't matter. I shouldn't have these feelings. So why were they so damn strong, pulling me this way and that? Part of me wanted to cry, while the other part wanted to cut his dick off. And both of them were wrong.

Ax wasn't mine. He gave that up years ago. He gave me up.

I had zero right to feel anything about this situation whatsoever. I didn't want to feel. I didn't want to think.

But damn, I did, and I wanted it to stop.

Seeing my plate was empty, I started to escape and got up saying, "I'll clean..."

My arm was grabbed, and I was back in my seat. Somehow he turned it to fully face him, and my plate clattered on the counter. I really hoped it didn't break. My other teal one did and this was my last of the color, and it happened to be my favorite.

Great time to think about plates, Indie. If I could roll my eyes at myself I would. What was that tombstone going to say again...

"Ax, I..."

"Stop." His tone was so intense yet calm that it had me pausing to take him in. His eyes were lit, and it intrigued me more than it should. "One step at a time, Indie. Breathe."

Shit. I wasn't breathing? Only then did I take in a breath, and it felt like my head started to think a bit.

"Do you want to help me clean up?" I asked, avoiding this entire situation. I didn't want to talk about it. Think about it. Deal with it. And here it was, right in front of my face. I also didn't want his help cleaning, but at least if we stayed busy my mind wouldn't wander.

Ax shook his head, his locks following his movements. While I loved when he had his hat on backward, I also loved his hair just like this; wild and free, nothing holding it back.

My fingers itched to touch it, so I clenched them into fists to keep them still. No way was I touching him.

He leaned over and pulled me closer to him. Even with me standing and him in his seat, he was still taller than me. We were perfect height like this, and his damn lips were so close.

My pulse picked up as he ran his nose along my cheek. Why did this man have to do this? Why. It was my damn trigger with him, and he knew it. The brush of the nose did it every damn time.

Heat flooded me, and I clenched my hands tighter, feeling my nails biting into the skin.

"There's a lot we need to catch up on." He started, but it was hard for me to concentrate with him running his hands up and down my arms and his face so close to mine. Distracting. That was what this man was doing. "Know we went our own directions, but it's time we found our way back."

Something about what he said snapped me to the present, and I pulled back, breaking free, even taking a step so he had to reach out his arms to touch me. *Our way back?* Was he out of his ever-loving mind?

He had to be. There was no back. There was no fixing what he broke. There was none of this shit whatsoever.

"There is no going back, Ax. Too little too late. It's over. We both have moved on with our lives. That was our story, but the book has been finished; the cover slammed shut. You made choices that deeply hurt me, and nothing you say is going to fix it. It's like a piece of glass once it shatters; the pieces can't be put back together again because there will always be shards that never fit back in place."

He shook his head and pulled me into him again. "Would you stop doing that?" I growled low, trying to pull back to which he just stared at me. "Anything is fixable. Glass can shatter and it may take a fuck of a lot of glue, but I've got a ton of it and will fix this."

Ax stared at me in a way that no man had ever done. As if I were the most precious thing on earth and he'd do anything to protect me. I closed my eyes to cut off the sight. I couldn't take it. I couldn't take him. I knew he wouldn't protect me. He didn't before.

He released my arm and cupped my face, and his thumb traced my bottom lip.

God, why did this man have to be this man? He could be anyone else except Ax, and I'd fall hook, line, and sinker. First the nose brush, then the thumb.

Now I was holding on by the tips of my finger-nails, and I refused to let go and give in. I couldn't. I couldn't.

"Open your eyes, Indie."

I didn't want to. Didn't want to see what was reflected in them, but I did anyway and met his eyes, sucking in that anger.

"Know I fucked us up. Young, dumb, but I don't live my life with regrets except the pain I caused you."

My mind drifted, and I was unable to stop the past coming forth.

"Whore!" Was called out as I moved through the hall-way, each step coming like lead weights. The name calling doesn't shake me; I couldn't give two fucks what anyone thought of me, but the cat-calling, the whistling. All of the unwanted attention was too much. What happened to live and let live and all that shit? It was relentless.

"Is there a sign-up sheet for you? I want in!" another boy yelled out. I kept my head down and moved quickly, wanting desperately to get away.

Away from here.

Only no place felt far enough in this very moment.

"Yeah. From what I saw you're loose enough to take three or four of us at once." This came from a different voice, but I didn't stop to look.

"We can all take turns." Laughter burst out as I ran out the doors of the school and to my car.

Tears flowed down my face.

The damage was too much. I'd never come back from this.

Ax. He did this. He couldn't fix this. Heartbreak and hatred had become one in the same. I had more questions than answers but no desire to even see the man to ask a single one.

I was a ghost. Non-existent. I went from having friends, to not in the blink of an eye. I went from being with the most popular boys in the school, to being a whore who fucked anything and everything.

And nothing from Ax—or Raid, for that matter, which was something that just hit me in that moment. It wasn't just Ax. There were two of them who had betrayed me. No, I shouldn't feel safe with either of them.

Shit. That made it worse.

"Yeah. You did more than fuck us up, Ax. You humiliated me which led to my torment and didn't say a fucking word to anyone who called me a whore, knowing that wasn't me. That I had zero to do with your little tape. You were a coward, and I lost respect for you."

His eyes closed slowly, and I wished I could hear what was going on in his head. His eyes slowly opened. "I know. I'm so fuckin' sorry. That isn't even a strong enough word for it. I should've handled every step of it so differently. I didn't. Forever my greatest mistake is shutting you out."

I pulled out of his grasp and moved to the other side of the island, putting some space between us. Being that close to him wasn't helping the anger and frustration. It kept growing with each word that was spoken.

Hated to admit it, but he was right. We needed this. Needed to get everything that happened out and close this chapter of our lives. I always wondered why he chose to let me swing. Why he allowed the entire school to believe I was a whore. Why he never said a single word to solve it. That hole never healed. Maybe doing this would make that part of me not hurt as much. Maybe it could heal and finally give me peace.

My gaze met his.

"Do you even understand how teenage girls' minds work? We're preprogrammed to think everything that happens to us or around us is our fault. We should've, would've, could've changed the situation. Do you know how many times I laid in my bed not understanding how you could tell me you love me one day and then throw me to the wolves and out like trash the next?"

The pain of that teenage girl filled my heart, and for the first time in a really long time, I allowed it to open and bared my soul.

"Crying," I spoke without hesitation, "I cried until there were no more tears, and then somehow I cried some more. That was all I did for what felt like forever. Picked apart every little thing about myself wondering what I could have done differently. Whatever a teen mind could throw at me, I thought it and felt it. The biggest was I wasn't experienced enough sexually. With what I was accused of, that one hurt. You were my only. How could I get anyone to believe me over you? Like, you wanted your freedom to go off and screw everything that walked, fine. I get it. I wasn't enough—that was the bottom line. I got your message loud and clear when everyone told me how you were fucking anything that was warm. I was just the little virgin girl who gave you everything. Heart. Soul. You were the boy who took it all and left me nothing but shamed and destroyed."

"Indie, you're beautiful. It had nothing to do with you."

My head shook. "You're so full of shit! It had everything to do with me. You let the entire school think I was in a threesome with you and Mr. Baker!" I yelled at the top of my lungs, making Gizmo bark. The rage inside of me just poured out. It was a switch I had no control over. "You didn't deny it. You egged it on. Pushed it to the point I was so humiliated I didn't attend graduation, just left Sumner! If you wanted more, all you had to do was tell me. Tell me that what we were doing wasn't enough for you. Why add to my heartache with the embarrassment, humiliation, and defeat? Why, Ax, just why?"

"Please." He started. "Just listen."

I let out a haughty laugh. "Don't feed me some line, Ax. You could've stopped that shit at any time. Told the school it wasn't me. But no, that video went to fucking everyone in the school. The girl had her back to the camera the entire time, so there was no way of proving that it wasn't me. And you, or Raid, or whoever in the hell were having a hell of a time. If you wanted to have sex with her and the teacher, fine, but to cheat on me and let everyone know about it and think it was me ... you're a special brand of cruel. You're a fucking asshole, Ax!"

"Raid was being blackmailed by Mr. Baker."

This gave me pause, but I was still burning red. I remembered all the times I would tell myself it wasn't him. I watched the video over and over, wondering if I was that bad in bed or if my mind was simply wishing it wasn't Ax in the video but his twin brother, Raid. I convinced myself I was being naïve and desperate to say it was Raid. I made peace with his betrayal of me because Ax never once denied being in the video. If he wasn't the dude on the screen, then surely he would tell the world and save me the heartbreak.

He didn't because *it was him*? My head pounded, and my palms were sweating as all the unresolved emotions built inside me, adding to the tornado already swirling around me.

"Mr. Baker had some pull with the club that we didn't know about. It was just enough power, we came to find out, to cause issues with the club. Since Raid had already started a flyby with that fucker, it put Raid in a fucked up situation when he tried to pull out of it. We were young and fucking stupid."

"This makes no sense. All you had to say was a teacher had sex with a student and get Mr. Baker canned," I retorted. "It would've been over! He would've been gone, and my life wouldn't have been ruined!"

His head shook. "Not how things work unfortunately."

"I'm losing you here. Why the hell was I brought into this! If this was between Raid and Baker? It had nothing to do with me!" At this point I was yelling because this bitch was pissed the fuck off.

"No, not at first. When Raid tried to pull out of fucking him, Baker decided to get collateral on Raid to keep his mouth shut. Baker set up the camera and found the girl who had similar hair as yours. He taped Raid fucking the both of them and told Raid that if he didn't continue their fuck-a-paids, he'd say it was me and you on the tape fucking Baker. It was the only reason that Raid took his shit for so long. He was trying to protect us from this recording getting out."

I huffed hard, not hiding the bite in my tone. "Since we all know the tape went out to everyone, why the hell didn't you say something then? Why did you go along with it? Why didn't you say it wasn't me because you sure as shit knew it wasn't me or you for that matter. Yet you allowed me to think it was you!" Fire burned my veins. I'd wanted the truth, but fuck it wasn't easy to hear any of this.

"Had to at the time. I couldn't let my brother hang in the wind for that shit. Yes, he fucked Baker. Yes, it was on tape. But Baker was playing hardball. The best thing for us to do at that time was call Baker's bluff to get Raid from under his control. See if Baker would follow through on saying it was us or Raid. As fucked up as it was, it took away his power in the play."

Could one's head actually explode? Because right now it felt like a strong possibility. "Why? Why destroy me? Ignore me. Turn your back and walk away without a word!"

"It was how we had to play it for a few weeks until we came up with a game plan. Had to get the club involved and get out from under Baker's thumb. Fuckin' so sorry you got dragged into this. I tried to get you out as soon as I could. You heard that, right?"

My lip tipped in a snarl as if this helped at all. "Oh yeah, I heard. Months later when I was hundreds of miles away from my family and school was out, so your clarification fell on deaf ears. No one really wanted to believe the truth, even when you told it. The farce y'all created and went along with for months was the better story. Great timing, by the way, after I was already gone. Too little too fucking late."

"Having everyone turn on you wasn't what I'd thought would happen, but once it did, I couldn't stop it. I had to protect Raid and the club."

"So you left me swinging. Great. Good to know." I grabbed the half empty bottle of wine on the countertop and took a healthy gulp. Fuck it. Setting it down, I reached for the cabinet under the island and pulled out Jack Daniels and a bottle of Jim Beam.

Not getting a glass, I unscrewed the top of the bottle of Jack and took a heavy swig. It burned all the way down but didn't erase the pain that was threatening to take me under.

He stepped closer and I moved back, bottle in hand. "No. You stay right there, or this conversation is over now and you're leaving my home."

He halted at my tone. "Indie, I was stupid. So

fuckin' stupid. I thought I was protecting you too. With Baker's eyes off of you..."

I interrupted him. If I had the power to burn him to a crisp with my eyes, he'd be ash. "Protect me? Are you kidding me right now? You have to be joking. You were not protecting me," I spit out. "You heard all the things people said to me. The names I was called. The taunts and threats made against me. How they were going to catch me after school and..." I couldn't finish the words. I didn't want to give a voice to it.

He looked me deep in the eyes. "But no one touched you. Or your stuff. Never a thing on your car or locker. It was words, but no one laid a hand on *you*."

My head shook. "Is that what you thought? I was stopped in the locker room...."

"And did he touch you?"

Thinking back, I relived the fear I felt being alone and trapped by Derk in the locker room. I hated to admit it, but he was right. Something spooked Derk, and he disappeared after only stepping a few feet in front of me. "No. How?"

"Liam. He knew what was going on and hid in the shadows, keeping his eye on you once we saw what was happening."

"Why? Why let the school think it was me if you were going to have someone watching out for me? If you loved me, why would you allow that? That isn't love, Ax."

His head hung, and I could actually feel his regret, which I didn't know was possible. "I know.

Now. I'd thought we'd get it settled and I'd be able to tell you everything. It took longer than I thought, and then you were gone. You hated me, and I deserved it. More than deserved it. Fuckin' killed me watchin' that shit. At the time I couldn't find another way out."

"Do you know that to this day people come into the bakery and call me a whore under their breath. They think I don't hear them because I fully ignore it, but I do hear them, and each time it takes me back to that time. What you did has scarred me Ax. No matter how much I tried to heal it, stitch it or staple it, my heart bleeds to this day. All you had to do was say a single word, and it would've stopped. You didn't. So no, Ax. You didn't protect me. Even with someone 'watching' me. You did nothing. Just sat back and watched me fall."

He opened his mouth to talk, but I shook my head, and he stopped.

"I loved you. Loved you with everything inside of me. Would've done anything for you. Anything. You could've asked me to meet you somewhere, tell me we could never talk about it and not to ask questions. And you know what. I would've come. Never asked a question and would've been right by your side. That was how much I loved you. How much you meant to me. And you decimated it. Everything we'd built over our time together burned to ash and blew away in the wind."

I felt the tears well in my eyes, and I didn't stop them. There was no reason to. He had to know how much this was killing me. Clutching the bottle, I took another drink. It didn't matter. No matter what I did, nothing would numb it. It was too raw now, talking about it and feeling it once again.

I could've swore I heard Ax gasp, but I didn't stop.

"Even as young as we were. I knew you were my one. Knew down to my soul you were my forever. Sounds stupid to say that about someone in high school, but for me it was true." My gaze met his. "You were my future. Every time we talked about getting married and me riding on the back of your bike until we couldn't ride anymore, I could see it ... feel it. The family we'd create, the life we would build together. All of it. And in one day you shattered it, Ax. When that video came out and you said nothing—you broke me. You broke us."

"Baby." My head shook.

"Don't. Listen, Ax. While as twisted as this story is, I know you'd do anything for Raid and your club. Always knew that. Never disputed it. BUT... I thought I was in that group as well. That I ranked up there with them. Turned out, I wasn't and that was worse than the name calling and torment."

"I'm so sorry, Indie. I never wanted it to get this far. Never. I misjudged Baker. Never did I think he would release it, but we pushed, and he pushed back. Once we played our play, our hands were tied."

I nodded. "I believe you. I truly do, Ax. But that choice came with the cost of me." I exhaled deeply. "Thank you for telling me. For trying to close that wound. Now the past is closed, and we can move on." Damn, I hoped I wasn't lying to myself here.

He came closer before I could say anything and grabbed the bottle out of my hands and put it on the counter. His arms then wrapped around me. How the hell he moved so quickly I still didn't understand.

"I fucked up. Wish I could go back in time, knowing now what I knew then. But I can't. I can spend every single day of my life making it right. I will show you how much I love you. How much I know I fucked up. How much I'll fuckin' grovel until the day I leave this earth."

My heart broke. So many times I wanted to hear he wanted me. That none of this shit happened. But it was too late. "It's too late, Ax. I've already mourned our relationship. Already put it past me."

"Now who's lying." His brow quirked. "You just told me how the wounds I left bled to this day. How the love you had for me was forever. That means I have a shot. Small as fuck, but it's a chance, and I'll fuckin' take it because having you in my arms, in my life, isn't an option anymore. I've fucked up, but you're the only woman I've ever loved."

When his lips came on mine, they sucked the air from my lungs. With all the emotions running high, I gave in. Yes, I was weak. But the girl who once loved this boy with every breath I took selfishly wanted one more taste.

CHAPTER SEVENTEEN

Az

I'D FINALLY HAD THE CHANCE TO TALK TO HER.

Holding onto that shit for so long felt like a weight had been lifted off my shoulders. Or maybe that was just because she finally understood. She was currently in my arms, kissing me like a starved woman.

Didn't she realize how starved I was for her? Anything for her. I would never make the same mistake twice.

We were such morons, Raid and I. We were so close to getting our cuts and thought we could handle Baker and not get the club involved.

Too cocky. Too self-assured. And it bit us in the ass. Bit me in the ass.

If we would've gone to the club first, none of this shit would've blew up. It was a hard lesson both Raid and I learned. The club was family. The club would stand by us. Always knew it growing up, but we were kings in the school and didn't think it would go as far as it did. Thought Baker would back down. He didn't.

Everything got fucked.

My father was pissed as hell, and it was why my mom had a really hard time with Indie and my breakup. She blamed me as she should have.

We had more to talk about. There would always be more to talk about, but it could wait.

Now I needed to feel her. Know she was with me once again. Taste her and etch her so hard on my heart and soul she'd never disappear.

This was it. I knew it. She was it.

Grabbing her by the ass, she wrapped her arms and legs around my body, and I carried her though the house. Gizmo was barking, but I didn't give a fuck.

I needed her more than I needed air in this moment.

Nothing could erase the past. I could only hope that our future wouldn't be tainted with my bad decisions.

Kissing her slow and deep, I laid her on the bed, following behind and landing on top of her. Skating my hands down her side, I went under her shirt and felt warm, soft skin. A groan left her lips, making mine vibrate.

My cock was hard as granite, but I didn't give a fuck. Worshiping her was the only priority. She needed to feel what I did. Needed to understand where this was going. That she was mine and I was hers.

And fuck me—I was coming to the realization that she'd always been mine.

Leaving her lips, I kissed down her neck and up to her ear. Her nails dug into my back. I wanted her touch. Lifting up, I pulled off my shirt, placed my hands under hers, and pulled it off, then I reached around and undid her bra before tossing it to the floor.

My lips trailed down her body between her breasts. Her fingers laced through my hair and pulled as she squirmed underneath me.

Leisurely, I kissed her breast rolling my tongue around her nipple. I stopped to nip and tug, listening to the labored breathing from her beautiful lips.

"Ax," she gasped as I bit down just a touch harder on her nipple. "Oh my God."

"Not God. Me. Only me."

Following down her body, I licked and sucked down to her bellybutton. She pulled my hair rough, turning me the fuck on. This woman undid me.

Stripping off her pants and underwear in a flash, I nestled right between her thighs.

Pussy had always just been pussy.

Indie... She was never just pussy. She was everything. She was the only pussy I wanted for the rest of my life.

The taste of her washed over me as I sucked, licked, and smelled her beautiful, aroused scent.

She tried pulling me closer, then pushing me

away only to bring me back once more. Indie didn't know what she wanted except chasing the orgasm she undoubtedly would have.

Unrecognizable noises came from her lips as I teased and flicked her little nub, adding two fingers into her tight channel and stroking deep.

Her back arched off the bed as a scream tore from her, and her pussy tightened around my fingers so hard, I couldn't move them momentarily. Damn when she came, she came hard.

When she released my fingers I stripped myself of my clothes and slid inside her on a groan. Fuck, she felt like home.

Our eyes met as I remained deep inside her. I didn't move a single inch, wanting her to feel me. All of me. Body. Heart. Soul.

"Ax," she gasped, her hand coming to my cheek. I leaned into her touch but didn't move my body, just kept her filled with me. Kept us connected. Bonded. Tethered together.

"Yeah, baby."

"Please," she whispered, her eyes scorching me. She was on fire, just as I was, her hands going to my ass and squeezing hard.

"Feel me," I returned and painstakingly slowly moved inside her.

"I feel you," she returned back.

"No, Indie." I stared into her eyes, wanting to dig into her soul. "Really feel me. Feel what's happening here. Feel me. This right here, this is everything right after so much has been so wrong between us. You and me."

A tear rolled down her cheek, and I hoped like fuck she was able to feel our connection. I leaned down and kissed her breathless, my hips thrusting in and out of her no longer gentle. No longer slow.

Over and over, I kept moving inside of her so fast the bed kept crashing to the wall. I didn't give a fuck. I needed her. Wanted her.

Lifting up and peering down at her, her hooded eyes told me once again she was close.

And since I was ready for her, I was ready to blow myself. As soon as she let go, I followed, spilling deep inside her. My body twitched with each jet of my come as I filled her to the hilt.

I lifted her leg and rolled us to our sides, staying inside her.

Kissing her softly I said, "Sleep."

"Ax, I can't sleep with you inside me. Let alone want to. I need to clean up, and you need to go."

My head shook. "No. Not tonight. I need inside you, having you surrounding me. I need you."

Her eyes flared. "You're not sleeping here. This was a goodbye fuck. It was not a get back together fuck."

It was as if she were trying to erase what I just said, but I wasn't letting her off. "I need you, Indie. Just as you need me. Tonight. Please give me this."

Several moments passed before she let out a heaving breath and settled down.

"Everything has been wrong in my world since

you left it. Call me selfish, but I have this moment, and I can't release you. Not again," I whispered to her as she drifted off.

Never again would I let this go. Connected as one, bound together from the beginning, she had always been mine.

CHAPTER EIGHTEEN
Indie

"HOLY FUCKING SHITBALLS!" I HEARD SCREAMED IN THE distance. It took me a bit, but my mind finally cleared from the sleep haze. Looking over, my sister Meadow and mother Delilah stood at the door of my bedroom.

"What's wrong?" I asked, blinking my eyes from the offending light.

"Oh, I don't know ... you have Ax fucking Monroe in your bed with his naked ass on display," Meadow said, irritated.

"And what a beautiful ass it is," said my mother in her calm voice. She was all about love and happiness. No doubt she'd be in bed with this man if she had the opportunity.

"Thanks," Ax grumbled but didn't bother to cover up.

Sitting up, I pulled the covers over my naked body. "Can you get out? I'll be out in a minute."

"Oh, you have some serious explaining to do," my sister said on her heel, turning and leaving the room. Mom just stood there staring at Ax.

"Seriously, Mom. Stop staring at him and close the door behind you—please."

She smiled wide then followed my sister.

Reaching over, I slapped Ax on the ass hard. "Get up and get dressed."

I released the blanket, got out of bed, and made my way into the adjoining bathroom. Turning on the shower, I brushed my teeth while waiting for it to heat up.

This was not good.

Of all the people for my sister to catch me with, Ax Monroe would only be below Charles Manson. That was how much my sister didn't like Ax. She was there for me through all the pain of that damn tape and Ax's betrayal. Listened to me cry. Felt my anger and even took me to Hendrix's place and had me chop wood with an ax. Each hit I pretended it was the man in question's head.

It might have been a bit extreme, but it helped me more than I ever thought.

My entire family knew how Ax crushed me. Even saw the tape to my utter dismay. They had disdain for him along with me through the years. All except Mom and GramO, who after the truth came out did a one-eighty on Ax. Which pissed me off.

And here I was in bed with the man who caused me so much heartache.

Hell, we ended up screwing like rabbits instead of me kicking the man out of my house. My sanity was taking a serious hit.

Over and over I scrubbed my teeth, taking all the frustration out on the poor things. But at least they'd be clean. I was mad at myself. I was mad at him. I was mad at life. I didn't want to be mad anymore, and I wanted to be able to let it go.

And then what the hell was last night? I just threw myself at the man and let him fuck me. Him wanting me to feel him. For the love of God, I did. I felt how sorry he was, and it scared the living shit out of me. He didn't protect me. How could I just let that go? Just forget it ever happened? He made it all sound so easy, but when push came to shove, would he have my back?

Spitting out the paste, I felt the water in the shower, adjusted it and got in under the spray, putting my head fully in it. Hoping to wash away something, hell if I knew. But it felt good.

The curtain from the shower opened, and a large body came in with me, his heat at my back. God, he was so warm, and in combination with the water it felt magnificent.

Why? Why did this feel so good yet hurt so damn much?

Lifting my head out of the water, arms encircled me and pulled me in closer. I could feel his hardness against my back, and my core throbbed. Tears welled in my eyes.

I wanted him. And I didn't want to want him.

That was it—he was going to kill me through sex. Yep. Screw the heartbreak and all the feelings there; it was the sex that was going to be the end of me.

His lips came down to my shoulder as he began to give small kisses up and down my neck, my head lulling to the side to give him better access. The kisses added the tongue, and I reached back and clutched onto his hard thighs for support.

Ax definitely grew over the years. No longer was the little boy I fell for; now, he was all man. Every inch man.

His lips came to my ear. "We've gotta be quiet or your family will hear." The words were so rough and jagged, my need for him increased, and my head fell back fully to his chest.

"We can't," came out in a barely there whisper, mostly in a false response because I wanted it. Wanted him.

Ax wasn't like his high school self when it came to sex. No, now he was demanding, intense, sure of himself, and unbelievably good at finding just the perfect spot for me.

"Hands on the wall," he ordered, and my clit throbbed. My traitorous body followed his instructions.

His hands gripped my hips and pushed them up, and without any other touching, he slammed into me. My entire body moved up, and I stood on my tiptoes and tried not to fall on my ass with all the water around me.

The feeling of him inside of me was different, but also the same. I'd always felt comfortable with Ax. He was gentle with me always. Now, he was not. His thrusts were powerful, confident, and meticulous.

He'd grown in his exploration times. As soon as that thought hit, I shut it down. Thinking about other women or men he'd been with only made the ugly, jealously monster rise in me. There was no time for that.

Moans escaped my lips, and his lips immediately came to my ear. "You want them to hear you, don't you? Want them to know how good it feels to be in my arms with my cock ramming into your hot body over and over again. You want everyone to know you're mine."

This again was new. The dirty talk. Never knew how much I loved it until now. It turned me on even more than his cock. Or, at least, a close second.

"Shut up and fuck me," I told him, not meaning any of it.

He thrust in hard. So much so, I felt him so deep inside me there was an instant of pain that quickly turned into pleasure.

"Your pussy is so fuckin' tight around me, squeezing and wanting my come." He nipped my ear with his teeth and used one of his hands to reach around me and begin to rub my clit. Holy fucking shit.

That did it. I bit hard into my bottom lip, trying desperately not to scream like I wanted to as my body began to shake and tremble. He didn't relent; instead, he continued pounding in me over and over again, riding me through each wave of pleasure.

He began speaking softly in my ear once again, which only set me off again. "Yeah. I want that lip bruised and bloody so you remember this all fuckin' day. Want between your thighs to ache for my cock and your pussy to feel so empty without me."

Either the orgasm never stopped, or I'd had another because my insides were quivering and my legs threatened to give out on me.

I had no clue where I was. Mars? Africa? The sun? Hell if I knew. Ax took me on a ride where I went out of my mind.

He turned me and lifted me, and my arms wrapped around his neck as he thrust back inside me. The tile was slick and hard against my back, but I didn't care. He'd have his bruises if he wanted them.

"Fuck, Ax. Oh my God," I moaned, stuffing my face into his neck.

In this position he hit the hot button inside me, and I came once again; Ax followed behind me.

The shower was so hot I could barely breathe and felt as though I was gasping for breath.

He pulled my hair gently and lifted my face to his. "You okay, baby?"

I nodded stupidly.

"Need you to breathe so I can clean you up. Your family is gonna wonder what's taking so long."

"You don't give a shit if they wonder anything," I countered and felt his chuckle as he sat me down on my legs, holding me until I got my barrings.

"Nope." He swept the hair away from my face in that way I loved. "Don't give a fuck who hears us."

A smile came across my lips. "Will you let me shower now?"

"Fuck no." He then proceeded to lather up soap and began washing my body as though we had all the time in the world. And I let him. Even let him wash my hair. Each second of it, all I could do was be in the moment with him. Feel him. Take him in.

He was damn good with keeping himself wrapped around me so I couldn't think. Couldn't breathe. Couldn't do anything but be in this moment with him.

I had this feeling that in the end he was going to crush me more than he had before. If he did, there'd be nothing there but dust.

"I'm going to strangle you," my sister announced as I came out of my bedroom, leaving Ax in there to finish doing whatever in the hell he needed to do. Hopefully he was getting his shit together to leave so I could think. I really needed to think.

"Take a number. I'm number one," I clipped back, then went to my mother and gave her a hug.

"Is that Indie?" I heard from the kitchen and felt my stomach drop to my feet.

"GramO is here?" I asked, eyes wide, looking at both my sister and mother in utter shock.

"Yep. She's got a lot to say too. Probably heard you

in the shower as well," my sister said, turning and moving through the living room, dining room, and into the kitchen.

Great. So they heard me having sex. With the man who destroyed me once upon a time. Lovely. Not that sex had ever been a taboo thing in our home. I just didn't want my GramO hearing me scream out Ax's name, especially since I hadn't said the man's name in years.

"Come on." Meadow yelled as I made my way to the kitchen. Yeah. This was going be a fun way to start a Sunday.

GramO was cleaning up the counter and putting dishes in the dishwasher.

"Don't do that," I said as she turned to me and raised her brow. She didn't leave any room for discussion, but I went over to help her, going to the stove and picking up one of the pots.

"Hear you have a friend here," she said, running the water and starting to wash the dishes. We'd gone round and round about the dishwasher. GramO had a thing with washing the dishes then putting them in the dishwasher. Like what's the point?

But I gave up that argument. It wasn't worth the breath. She'd win anyway. She always won.

"Just say it," I told her, waiting to hear her scathe me and tell me what a mistake I was making. That she heard me and knew what was going on. Something.

"About time," she said just as the man in question

came into the room, both stunning me momentarily. What the hell did she mean about time? She knew how badly this man had hurt me.

"Hello, ladies," he announced with his dark hair wet from our shower. My treacherous body tingled at the thought and stilled my ability to ask GramO what she meant.

Meadow put her hand on her hip.

Mom smiled widely.

I didn't know what to think. GramO said about time... What the hell did that mean? I wanted to ask her, but not with him in the room.

"Hello!" Luna, my other sister, called from the living room, closing the door behind her. Gizmo was going crazy with all the company. Me, I wanted to go back in my room and lock myself in it.

"You've got to be kidding me. What is this? Visit Indie day?"

Meadow smiled at me. "Yep. Had to come see what my baby sister was up to."

All I could think was I was so glad she didn't bring the kids.

"We're in the kitchen!" I called out as Ax moved right to Mom, bent down and kissed her on the cheek. Then he went to Meadow who stopped when he did the same thing to her. Then he made a trip to GramO.

I was so focused on GramO and Ax that I missed my sister coming into the room.

Ax towered over GramO and had to bend down

deep to kiss her cheek. "Hello, ma'am," he said on a smile, still bent down and looking in her smiling—yes, smiling—eyes.

Was I in the twilight zone here? Had to be. GramO had seen the devastation that Ax left me in. She knew the tears I cried to her. And now she was welcoming him like he never left a day and was a regular staple in my life. What did she know that I didn't? I wanted to know. Then again, I didn't.

Shit. How'd my life turn into this emotional rollercoaster when all I wanted to do was to make damn cakes!

"What the hell did I just walk into?" Luna said, catching my attention. As always, she was dressed to the nines with a pencil skirt and blazer. It was the weekend, and she still looked like she was going into the office. Professional was the only mode she had. Fun ... not so much.

"The fun that has become my life. What are you doing here?" I asked her, fully turning from Ax and GramO as they started talking in hushed tones. It took everything I had not to storm over there and hear exactly what they were saying to each other.

What was she telling him?

What was he telling her?

I wanted to know so badly, but alas I had to deal with my family.

"And hello to you too," Luna said, making her way to me, and part of me felt bad for snapping at her.

"Hi. Now why are you here? Why are you all

here?" I asked, turning to GramO because she started giggling. Yes. Giggling. I was in a different world. Laughing I'd heard my whole life. Giggling like a schoolgirl, not so much.

My mother hip checked me, nodding over to GramO and Ax. "That one already has Olive around his finger."

I rolled my neck, then looked up at the ceiling seeing plants hanging. I really needed to water all of them. Hello ... random.

"Shut it," I said to her, then to the room I asked, "Is anyone gonna tell me what's goin' on? Did I miss something or forget we were having a party?"

Luna lived hours away in Atlanta and didn't come to Sumner often. Something had to be up.

"I came to make breakfast," GramO said, pointing to the grocery bags I hadn't noticed on the counter. This was a great thing considering she was an excellent cook. The sausage, biscuits and gravy needed medals.

"Okay. So that one has a pass," I announced to GramO's chuckle. And I thought I heard Ax's in there too. "Now you three?"

"I had a little bird chirp in my ear yesterday," Meadow said.

"Bird? Did you kill it?" Yes, I was a sarcastic bitch. Fully admit it.

"You want me to kill your niece?"

For the love of God. "What does Farah know?"

"Mazie called her."

I was going to strangle my niece.

"Rah told me. I told them, and we're here to find out why you were running out of a building at the clubhouse with Ax on your heels and Princess stepping in to let you leave."

"You need a life," I grumbled.

"Oh I have one, but yours was a bit juicy this morning."

I looked over at Ax who had a wide grin on his face. "Shut up," I growled at him, making him smile wider.

I wasn't going to get far with this crowd.

"I knew I should've dropped her cake," I told the room, and everyone burst out laughing. Mazie. I didn't even put two and two together on that one.

Rah, as we called her, went to the same school as Mazie. But I didn't think they were close enough to call each other and gossip. Never crossed my mind. Rah never talked about Mazie, and I knew she wasn't on the volleyball team with her because I'd been to the games.

What a small town this place was.

"The cake was pretty cool too," Meadow stated.

"It was. I have a picture on my phone." Saying that brought up the thoughts of those two men coming toward me, and I felt myself shiver. A strong body was at my back arms, going around me tight. I looked up to see Ax, knowing he protected me last night, but how long would that last? When would the time limit be up?

"They won't touch you."

"How did you know what I was thinking?" I asked.

"It's my superpower," he said on a grin.

My eyes rolled as I turned back to my family who were all staring at me.

"So, this is a real thing then?"

"No," I answered just as Ax replied, "Yes."

"Well, this is gonna be fun," Mom said, moving to the counter to help GramO with the groceries.

"You good?" Ax asked into my hair then kissed the top of my head.

"Yeah. I'm good."

When he released me, a coldness filled me that I tried to shake off. Seeing him going over and helping Mom and GramO ... that warmed me right back up.

"Tell me what the hell he's talking about? Who hurt you?" Luna said, slamming her purse, or should I say bag, down on the countertop.

"Yeah. Spill," Meadow said.

"Can I at least have coffee first?"

"No," they both returned in unison.

"I'll get it," Ax said, going to the coffeemaker and getting it started. Who was this man? Cooking? Coffee? Kissing my family? Giving me confessions and the best orgasms of my life. I was a bit dumb-founded.

"Uh ... thanks," I responded, seeing his smirk from his side profile. He was eating this shit up.

"Anything. Told you that."

A gleam came to both my sisters' eyes, and I

narrowed mine. "Not a word," I whispered under my breath.

They both chuckled then sobered, wanting an answer to their question.

They heard what had happened with the tape and Ax's recant of it. Mom and GramO were way too forgiving if you asked me.

So, I sat down at the island and told them the tale from the night before, having to add in the part about Ax carrying me out of the clubhouse since Mazie thought it would be great to tell my niece about it.

"There's more to the story," Luna said.

Ax slid a cup of coffee in front of me, and it looked perfect. "How did you know how I take my coffee?"

"I'm observant. What would you ladies like?" he asked Meadow and Luna, who both appeared in shock the man was asking their preferences. After a few beats, they gave theirs as Ax leaned down in my ear. "You gonna tell them how I fucked you against the wall until you screamed? Sure Olive would love to hear all about it."

A growl came up deep in my throat. "No. Now go," I ordered, only to hear the man chuckling again. "I'm so happy I amuse you."

He pulled away. "More than you know."

Meadow leaned in. "Did he really do that?"

"I'm not talking about it. Stuff happened. I came home, he showed up and we ... well ... talked."

Meadow burst out laughing just as Ax dropped off the other two coffees.

"Talked? Guess we did that too," Ax said, leaving us once again.

There weren't many secrets I kept from my family. We were pretty open when it came to life. Even talking to GramO about things. But here in front of him ... that wasn't going to happen.

It felt strange and uncomfortable. I never wanted to feel uncomfortable in my home.

"Yes. Talked. And he made me dinner."

"You didn't make this mess?" my mother said, washing some of the dishes. "I mean, it smells amazing and would've loved to try it if it had been put away and hadn't sat out all night..."

"I'll make it for ya sometime," Ax offered.

I turned to Ax. "Don't you have somewhere to be or something to do? You can see my house is full, and we have a family meeting that I seemed to have missed the memo about, so yeah, you can go."

He held his arms out wide. "What, and miss a morning with five beautiful women? Not gonna happen. Besides, I need GramO to teach me how to make her sausage gravy."

"Oh boy. That's a family secret," GramO responded, shaking her head.

Ax smiled at her. "Don't worry. I'll be family soon enough."

Holy shit. Butterflies danced in my chest.

"That's not happening." I retorted as Ax looked to me and winked.

"Yeah, it is." He was seriously going to kill me this time.

His confidence was an allure that pulled me in. Instantly, I threw my walls up and blocked off my heart. And added my soul in there too. He was dangerous, and I knew with everything inside of me that he was going to hurt me.

How? I didn't know.

But it was coming.

CHAPTER NINETEEN

THE DISHWASHER WAS RUNNING, SO I WASHED THE REST of the breakfast dishes by hand. GramO did teach me how to make her sausage gravy, and when we all sat down at the table in the dining room, everything felt right.

If only my brother and folks were here, the morning would have been perfect. That would happen at another time.

My cell rang, and I had to look for it. Drying off my hands, I moved to my cut that was laying on the side of the kitchen counter with my hat, and pulled out my phone, seeing my father's name.

"Hey, ol' man."

"Asshole. Told you to cut that shit. Need you at the Pick. Old Red just touched down in his private jet and wants to meet. Get here now." The Pick was right on the border of Sumner. Having Old Red meet us there was giving a very clear statement that he was not welcome to enter the city limits. How he would respond to that, no one would know.

Fuck. What a way to screw up a perfectly good morning. I needed weapons. Not just the ones I kept on me or my bike.

"Give me ten, and I'll be there."

"Later," my father said, cutting off the call.

Indie came into the kitchen, carrying glasses and set them on the counter next to the sink. "I can get these. You don't have to keep doing all the cooking and cleaning, ya know."

"Know that. But like doin' it. Told you, you are the queen. My queen. Get used to this shit." I leaned over to kiss her lips gently. "But I have to meet my dad at the clubhouse. Can I see you later?"

Why on earth was I asking if I could see her later? Because I would be seeing her later. That I had no doubt, no matter her response.

"No," She returned.

"At the bakery then?" I leaned down to her ear. "Always wondered what it'd be like to fuck in that walk-in freezer of yours. We'll have to try that out."

She shivered. "Ax..." Indie started, but I deepened a kiss to her lips, making her go silent.

Damn, she tasted good. "Gotta go," I said, pulling away. If I wasn't mistaken, there was a bit of sadness to it, but she wiped it as soon as it came.

She couldn't hide much from me. Never could.

"Bye," she responded quietly, and I pecked her lips.

"And, baby, I will see you later," I explained, then moved away putting on my cut and heading to the other women in the house.

After all the goodbyes and boots on, I was off to the clubhouse.

Yeah. There was no denying I loved Indigo Jamison Fallon. Just hoped it didn't take her too long to get with the plan. If it did, I wasn't afraid to push. Yeah, I'd fucked up. I'd atone to that for the rest of my life. But she was mine.

The entire ride to the Pick, which was about twenty minutes, all I thought about was the taste of Indie. How she moaned. How she moved on me. Replayed every single moment I'd had with her yesterday and last night.

My cock was so fucking hard by the time I got to the meeting place, I wished she were here to relieve it considering the shit was going to hit the fan in a matter of time.

Bikes were lined up, and I noted Raid already here. Seemed I was the last to show. So be it.

Swinging off my bike, putting my helmet on the handlebars, and putting my hat on backward, I moved to the door and opened it wide. The darkness had me pulling off my glasses.

"About fuckin' time. Where were you? Had to cover your ass at X." Raid came up, his strides quick.

"With Indie."

His brow lifted. "Is that right?"

"Yeah. Now what the fuck's goin' on here?" I asked him.

"You wanna start this with Indie again because she's not gonna let this shit go."

A red haze fell over my eyes. Brother or not, I was pissed. "She's fuckin' mine. End of story. Don't give me any shit about it. I took that shit for you. Don't fuckin' forget that."

"I know, Ax. Somethin' I'll never be able to repay. Anything you need, I'm there."

"Know that."

My head shook. "I feel like we're having a warm and fuzzy moment, so can we cut the shit and deal with this mess?"

His hand came to my shoulder, giving me a squeeze.

There was clatter in the room as we entered. After saying my greetings, Cruz spoke. "Listen."

We all shut up, giving him our attention.

"Old Red is on the way. We are getting ourselves out of the shit Nick put us under. Be vigilant. Nox, Deke, Ryker and Green outside, keepin' an eye. Micah in the back room watchin' monitors. Buzz, Breaker, Ax and Raid, you're with the rest of us while we talk to Old Red."

Having my uncle be the cause of this just pissed me off more. I fucking hated that man. He would be dead sooner rather than later.

"He'll be covered. We'll be covered. Don't want a fuckin' blowout, but who the fuck knows at this point. It's why I didn't do this at the clubhouse or X." He looked at his phone. "Five minutes and I doubt he'll be a second late."

We all broke off.

The Pick wasn't anything special. Cruz bought it for this exact purpose. To have meetings away from our loved ones and away from our club. It was smart. After all the shit that had gone on over the years, it was an actual necessity.

The building was nothing special. The outside looked like a log cabin, and the inside was sheetrocked. Everything was painted gray, walls and floor. Two tables sat in the middle of the room, and Cruz sat in the middle, GT and Cooper on either side of him. My father and Uncle stood behind them, and Raid and I moved next to them while the other Ravage men took a seat in the open space.

"He's here," Micah called from the other room.

"This is gonna be fun," I grumbled to my father who elbowed me in the side.

The door opened, and in walked one who could only be called Old Red. Shorter in stature with long red hair and red beard. He had a beanie on his head and wore jeans and a flannel shirt. Anyone who saw the man on the street wouldn't know he was a billionaire who practically ran Las Vegas.

"Cruz," Old Red said just as four more of his men followed him in.

Cruz stood as Old Red walked up to him. "Old Red." Cruz held out his hand. Old Red looked at it and gave a smirk, taking it and shaking it.

"Glad to see ya have backup." Old Red chuckled, sitting in the seat across from Cruz. "Go," he said with a flick of his hand, and the men who came with him found spots in the building to either sit or stand.

"Let's get down to it," Cruz told him, not giving in to the small talk. It was what made him our President. He had a way of cutting the bullshit.

"Right. Which one of you is related to good ol' Nick?" Old Red asked.

"He's our brother," my father said, pointing to him and his brother.

"Who else?" he asked.

"What do you mean?" Cruz asked him.

"Nicko had a lot to say. Guess his nephews are in here too."

"That's me," I answered to Raid's, "Me."

"Two doubles or is my vision finally givin' out on me?" He chuckled. What he found funny, I had no fucking clue.

"Let's get on with it," Cruz said, eyeing the man.

"Wait. Where's the young one?"

Booker. Fuck.

Booker didn't take but a second before he was standing, saying, "That's me."

"Any why aren't you standin' with the family."

"Cause I told him to sit his ass down," Cruz said, and Booker instantly sat again.

"I respect that," Old Red said clicking his tongue. "Okay, here's the problem. Nick owes me a lot of cake. Said you were part of his crew and had the cash. He says he's in the family. Then you call me and say he isn't with you. Do you see my dilemma?"

"Your dilemma is with Nick. Not fuckin' us. He's

never been a part of this fuckin' club and never will
be. His family's written him off. Don't know what you
expect from us," Cruz responded.

"See, that's where you're wrong." Old Red started,
but Cruz cut him off.

"I ain't wrong about shit. That motherfucker is on
our radar, and just for using our name he will have
his head ripped from his body."

Old Red's brow tipped.

"So if you want your money, you'd better get it
from him before he stops breathin'."

Old Red threw his head back laughing.

This fuckin' man was nuts and spitting in the eye
of the tiger.

"Funny. But that changes nothin'."

"The motherfucker told you lies. That doesn't put
us up for his cash owed," my Uncle Breaker said.

"Havin' all these men here, you obviously know I
have reach far and wide." Old Red started. "Means I
have a reputation. I don't ruin that shit for anyone.
Nick owes money. He said he had you as backers. I
can see he's a lying piece of shit, but that doesn't
resolve my problem."

"You just said it, ol' man. *Your* problem. Not
Ravages." GT said, lacing his hands and putting them
behind his head as he leaned back.

"Ahh... But it is our problem. I tell ya what. I have
a deal for ya. Will cut your entire club from anything
Nick owes me."

"Why the fuck should we do that?" my dad
barked. "It's his fuckin' problem. Not ours."

Old Red shook his head. "Know you're top dog around here. Got that shit. I'm top dog everywhere. You do this for me, you're out. You don't. You'll have problems."

This pissed me off royally. No one came into Ravage and said this kind of shit. The problem with sticking a bullet in his head would mean more eyes on our club, and that wasn't an option.

Couldn't help but wonder what Cruz was going to do.

"We want this shit done with." Cruz told him. "What is it?"

Old Red smiled wide. "Knew you'd see it my way."

I could hear Cruz growl from here, no doubt pissed as fuck to be put in a corner. No one fuckin' put him in a corner. No one. It had to be taking everything he had inside of him from jumping up and killing the man.

"Don't push it," Cruz said low.

"Got some packages that need delivered. Four crates. I have an address for you to drop them off."

"What's in them?" Cruz asked.

Old Red tsked and shook his head. "That's for me to know and you to not. It's best that way."

Cruz looked at GT, who was pissed as fuck but lifted his chin. Then he turned to Cooper who had a snarl on his face but lifted his chin as well.

"Deliver this and done. We don't want to see your face in Georgia again. Or you won't be walkin' out of here unscathed."

Old Red stood up. "Yeah. I know. Surprised you

haven't shot me already from your track record. But many people know I'm here, and you don't need trouble at your door. You do this, and Ravage's debt is clear. Nothin' else owed to me." He looked to my father and Uncle. "You'd better say your goodbyes to Nicky boy. He's fuckin' dead."

"Where's the shit?" Cruz asked, standing up from the table.

"In the back of the SUV. We brought it with us."

Cruz crossed his arms over his chest. "You had this shit planned."

Old Red smiled once again. "You know it." He snapped his fingers, and one of his men came up with a piece of paper and handing it to Cruz. "Location. Tonight."

"Fucker," Cruz said. "Get the fuck out and don't come back."

"Pleasure doin' business with ya," Old Red said.

"Dryerson. Get the boys outside and get the shit in here. Micah," Cruz yelled loud, and Micah came out. "You head to the clubhouse and get the Tahoe back here. Now."

"You got it."

Both Dryerson and Micah left the building as Cruz turned to us Monroes. "That motherfucker will die, but we get him first. We'll deliver him bloody and broken to Old Red. You get him here. I don't give a fuck how you do it, but you do it now."

Cruz pissed was never fun. Him pissed at us, really fucking sucked. Only made me want to find Nick even more.

"We're on it."

"Ax and Raid, you do this delivery with Deke, Ryker, Micah and Dryerson. Got it?"

"Yes."

Cruz opened the paper, then handed it to me. I read it and showed it to Raid.

Fucking hell.

CHAPTER TWENTY

Ax

"BOSS, THIS SHIT IS MOVIN'," DEKE SAID, SITTING ONE of the crates down inside the Pick.

"What do you mean movin'?" Cruz asked, taking a step forward.

Ryker brought another one in. "Yeah and fuckin hissin'. What the hell are we movin'?"

The crates were made of wood and had no slats in them. Just solid. But sure as shit it sounded like something moving ... or slithering.

"It sounds like a fuckin' snake." This came from Green who brought another in followed by Dryerson. Four crates.

Four crates filled with what?

Cooper shook his head. "No fuckin' way. We don't play with fuckin' reptiles. Old Red's lost his mind."

Cruz turned to Dryerson and Nox. "Open one."

Dryerson and Nox looked at each other, then

shrugged. Tug handed them a flathead screwdriver and a hammer. It didn't take much to work the lid loose.

"I'll fuckin' shoot it," Ryker said, pulling out his gun.

I was on board with him. It wasn't that I had a problem with snakes. I had a problem with delivering a package with snakes in it. That was fucked up.

Nox pulled the top off, and two snakes jumped out of the box. Not fully but enough to have Nox dropping the lid and stepping back from them.

"You have got to be shittin' me." Cooper steamed, anger pouring from his presence as his father stepped with him.

Nox moved over to the wall and grabbed a walking stick. Why it was there I had no fuckin' clue, but it was there. "Are these fuckers poisonous?" he asked, trying to get them back in the container with the stick.

"Fuck if I know. I'm no snake expert," I answered, pulling out my gun. "What the fuck is going on here? Is Old Red fuckin' with us?"

"Don't think so," Deke said. "Look at their stomachs." One jumped out of the box and landed on the floor. Nox put the stick on the reptile's head not allowing it to move a muscle as Raid put the lid back on the crate, not wanting any more to come out. Fuck that.

"What the fuck?" I asked, moving closer and kneeling. "They have something inside of them." Taking my finger, I pushed on one of the nine large round masses inside the snake. "And it's fuckin' solid."

"Are you tellin' me that whatever we're takin' to someone we don't know is lodged inside of snakes?" Micah asked, and I shook my head.

"Bet it's coke or heroine," Deke said, coming up to the snake and pushing on it. "They put it in bags and make the snake swallow it. They don't give a fuck if the snake dies, just that the product gets to where it needs to be."

"You're shittin' me," GT said, coming to stand next to his son.

"Nope. One snake here probably has ten grand in it. Depending on how many snakes are in these crates, we're payin' for Nick's shit. Old Red just doin' it a different way."

"Fuck me. Simple delivery my ass. Old Red is one smart son-of-a-bitch," Cruz said, hands on his hips and looking down at the reptile. "He knew the entire time he'd get his fuckin' money. Nick. I want to fuckin' skin him alive. Slowly and painfully."

Anger bubbled inside me as I clenched my fists, turning to my brother. "Dead."

It was all I had to say for Raid to know. He would find Nick. We would find him first and then bring him to the club. That motherfucker would pay for this.

"Understand Old Red is just doin' business," Uncle Breaker muttered to everyone. "But this shit, we aren't some errand crew for an old fucker with too much money. Yeah, Nick is getting delivered in pieces to Old Red."

"Club's got too many irons in the fire right now to have issues with a bookie from Vegas," GT stated what we all knew. "While I would love to teach Old Red that no one has the upper hand on Ravage, this seemed like a short-term sacrifice for the long-term gain. We had a reputation for transports, so to an outsider we took a job from Old Red. From a club to Red standpoint, we did our part, and he'd keep his word and goes away. I saw this shit as a win-win in the long run, even if my pride wanted to fuck up Old Red's world by killing his shipment and delivering Nick instead."

"We're all Ravage, so what do you think, brother?" Cruz asked us all.

Anger bubbled inside me. Frustration flowed through my very veins. No one got one over on Ravage. Old Red didn't either, but the mere idea of letting him think he had the upper hand for even a moment pissed me off. Nick could die ten times, and it still wouldn't satisfy the need for vengeance inside me.

Short-term sacrifice for the long-term gain.

That I could do. Nick would pay either way, and that was the true victory here for all parties involved.

CHAPTER TWENTY-ONE
Indie

HANDS MOVED OVER MY FLESH, WARMING ME AND MY core. A moan escaped my lips. Rough fingers glided under my panties, finding my clit immediately and made small circles.

Wetness pooled, and my hips began to move, chasing the orgasm that was building inside of me.

Lips caressed my neck, trailing up and down.

My eyes spluttered open.

It wasn't a dream. My body was in full arousal, and just by the smell I knew who was behind me. I didn't know which was running higher. Passion or anger.

"What are you doing here?" I groaned, searching for the orgasm he kept teasing me with and hating myself for it.

"Needed you," he responded, and my body shivered. Why did he have to say things that got to me? Why? Dammit.

"Would you just give it to me already?" I grumbled as he lifted my leg, and he was inside me. No preamble. No waiting. Just him and me connected in a punishing thrust that quickly put me over the edge.

Ax stilled behind me, surprising me. From what he'd shown me so far, he had the stamina of a horse.

"Go to sleep," he whispered.

"You're inside of me. I need to clean up considering you didn't use a condom again. You really need to start using protection, Ax, or I'm not going to fuck you anymore." What the hell did I just say? Again?

He chuckled. "Yeah, you will. Now sleep."

One would've thought I'd never get to sleep, but I did.

I'D WOKE up this morning alone in a cold bed.

Would it be moronic to say that I hated the coldness he left behind?

And I knew I wasn't crazy and it wasn't a dream. I felt him between my legs and the mess he'd left me to clean up this morning. It was like he wanted me covered in his come all damn day. Hell, maybe he did.

Now who was the stupid one? And I didn't have the excuse of being a naive teenager. Nope I had years to learn. Yet, here I was. His come leaking out of me.

Where he went? I had no damn clue. How he got in my house? I had no damn clue. How he locked up behind him? I had no damn clue. What the hell we were doing? Once again, I had no damn clue.

After cleaning up and getting ready for the day, I made my way out to my car. Locked the doors and then had the garage roll up. Pulling out, I looked all around, searching, not knowing exactly what I was looking for but scanning all the same.

I hadn't told anyone about the note. Part of me thought it was a dream and it never happened. At least, that was what I wanted it to be.

My hands trembled as I watched the garage shut completely, then I drove to the bakery.

Pulling up, the darkness was still only illuminated by the moon and street lights. It was part of being a baker. Since most people came to the shop first thing in the morning, that meant I had to work early.

I turned off the car and put the keys to the bakery in my hand, ready to go. I absolutely hated having this fear. I'd thought it was over with, and here it was creeping back into my life.

Opening the door, I moved inside and flipped on the lights, locking all the bolts on the door. Seeing there was no one in the bakery, I breathed out a sigh of relief.

It was time to get busy.

Kneed. Roll. Press. Over and over again I repeated the process, putting together some loaves of bread. They always went quickly, and I liked having them in the windows first thing.

Frustration hit me, and I took it out on the dough. Had to admit it was good therapy.

If nothing else, it would be well prepared for baking.

As the early morning began, Kali and Conner came in to work the front. Marley didn't say a word to me when he got in, no doubt pissed at me about the Ax situation because I knew my sisters didn't keep their mouths shut. They had no capacity for it.

After getting the initial baking done for the day, I moved over to the lists of cakes that needed to be worked on.

From there I got lost in figuring out how I was going to keep antlers on a three-foot deer without them falling off and not having any stabilizers besides the dowel rods.

This creation was for a hunter's birthday and the woman, I assumed his wife or girlfriend, gave the actual picture of the deer this man shot to recreate.

There would be some serious airbrushing just to get the colors right.

"Hey."

The word made me jump, and a small pot of brown dye fell over on the countertop. I'd been trying the technique to get the right colors. The cake part wasn't a problem. It was perfecting all the key elements in the cake design.

Especially the little whiskers that had dew on them. That was going to be made with candy. No way to make cake look like glass.

Turning, Blaine smiled down at me. "Sorry, didn't mean to scare ya."

I grabbed the pot and luckily it only had a small bit inside and was easy to clean up.

"Sorry. I get in the zone and well, you know."

"Yeah. I know. What's this one going to be? Looks like wood," Blaine said as I turned back to the cake. He was right; the small piece I was working on was really coming along to look like a tree, and then I could transfer it in the same way for the deer.

"Deer with a mount." I grabbed the picture I'd received and showed it to him. "Even got a pic."

"Wow. That's crazy talented you can do this stuff. Can't wait to see it when it's done." Blaine smiled. This time, though, there were no butterflies. No excitement. No intrigue.

It scared me that I had no idea what to do with that. I really didn't want to think it was because of Ax. If that were true, I'd really be screwed.

"Thanks. This one will be done hopefully by Friday since the party is Saturday. Lucky for me, though, they are coming to get it, and I don't have to lug the thing myself."

"Speaking of lugging. How did the car cake go?"

Flashes of Ax touching me, kissing me, feeling me made my body tingle. That cake would be forever known as the Ax cake. No other way to put it. And the confusion that was my life at the moment didn't help things at all.

"Great. She loved it and, better yet, it got there in one piece. That's what I was scared of, but we made it free and clear." Well, the cake did. Me, not so much.

"I love that you love what you do." There was this

twinkle in his eye, and this strange feeling came over me. Was he going to kiss me? Right here in front of everyone. Better yet, did I want him to kiss me?

No. I didn't think I did.

Not after the way Ax had kissed me the other night.

Just then I was grabbed from the side and hot lips were on me, devouring me, consuming me.

Ax. I knew by the smell of sandalwood and leather.

Easily I fell into the kiss just as the world around me disappeared, and the only ones around were Ax and me. His arms wrapped around me, and I followed, wrapping mine around his neck. My fingertips went to what I could reach of his hair under his hat.

"What the fuck?" Someone cut through the fog as I pulled back from Ax, noting the very angry man standing beside us. Shit.

"Um ... Ax, this is Blaine. Blaine, this is Ax," I introduced, feeling utterly stupid.

Ax put his arm around my shoulders, pulling me further into him. As we both looked at Blaine, he had fire in his eyes.

"Who the fuck are you?" Ax asked, and I felt his mood change as his body stiffened, and he clutched me even tighter.

Fuck. Was this going to be a big dick contest? I so didn't want to deal with that shit. Ax and I were ... hell, I didn't know what we were. Dammit.

"Blaine. Her man."

Ax's eyes shot to mine, now he's pissed as hell at me. *Lord, save me from alpha men.*

"That's fuckin' hilarious considerin' my cock was inside her only hours ago."

Blaine's accusing gaze came my way, and I held my hands out. "Look. Blaine, you and I only went on a few dates. Friends, remember? Yes, we were seeing each other, kind of, but we were not exclusive, and we discussed being friends. Ax, I have no clue what the hell is going on with us, so just let me breathe."

Ax leaned down to my ear. "You'd better get this fucker out of here and away from you, or I'm gonna have to kill him."

My body stilled. "No, you won't."

"Fuckin' try me, babe. I'd do it with my bare hands for him just touching you. If he fucked you, I'd torture him before I killed him."

"You're nuts."

"Never said I wasn't. Told you the other night you're mine. No one fucks with what's mine."

I pulled away from him to get some distance.

"One, I do not have to explain myself to anyone. Two, this is my place of business, and I will not have some cock fight in it. Three, get whatever you came for and move your asses right out the door," I demanded.

The energy I was expending on this pissing game was what I needed to be working on my damn cake.

"You're fuckin' cute," Ax said to me. Then to Blaine he said, "Get the fuck outta here. Don't come back. She's my girl and if you come near her, I'll cut off your dick and shove it down your throat until you choke to death.

"Ax!" I chastised. "Stop that!"

"Nope," he answered without a shred of doubt. This man was going to be a handful. Did I really want to deal with that shit?

Fuck... I did.

"Please go, Blaine. Thank you for stopping in."

"Seriously, Indie? I didn't think you were some biker whore."

That was when a fucked up situation became completely out of control.

Ax didn't even wait a second before he was on Blaine. Fists were thrown with a cringeworthy crunch as Blaine fell to the floor of my bakery with a thud. Ax didn't give him a second to breathe. Instead, he was on top of him. Somehow Blaine got a few punches across Ax's face before he scrambled off the ground and got to his feet.

"You piece of shit."

Ax stood, blood coming from his mouth and a wide smile. His eyes were completely dark, and menace ripped over him.

Shit. Ax was going to kill him. Straight up murder him.

They locked together, each throwing punches. When they crashed into the first table, I gasped. The second, I got angry. The third, where I'd been working, well, I was fucking livid.

Going over to the mop sink, I pulled the hose and

turned the cold water on full blast. I didn't know if the hose would reach, but I was willing to try it.

The hose almost made it, and I pulled it as tight as I could, pulling the trigger and spraying both the men who were destroying my kitchen.

They coughed and fluttered, backing away from each other. I turned it on to both of their faces just because I was pissed. I'd never waterboarded someone but fuck me—this felt good.

After a few minutes, I released the nozzle.

"Both of you get the fuck out of my bakery now!" I screamed, knowing the entire place would hear me, but I didn't care. Not only did they mess up the cake I was working on, but they also trashed two others I'd hadn't frosted yet. No amount of frosting would fix this mess.

"Babe. I'm..." I held up my hand with the nozzle in warning.

"I will spray you until you leave, Ax. Don't test me. You've ruined this entire space." My focus went to Blaine. "You too. I'll do what I want to do with my life, and both of you can fuck right the hell off. Now get out!"

My breathing was coming in ragged breaths.

"What the fuck happened here?" Marley asked.

"Yeah ... what the hell?" Meadow followed behind him.

"Great, you two can help me get these assholes out of my bakery. I don't give a shit if you have to call the cops or hell, the President of Ravage to get Ax out right now. I'm so pissed I can't even think. And, Blaine, I don't know who'd you call, but he goes too!"

All that work just down the toilet because these two hotheads couldn't have a civilized conversation for two minutes.

"Babe. Sorry. I'll help..." Ax started, and I could feel his sincerity, but I wasn't in the mood for it.

"No, you won't. You'll leave along with Blaine. Now!" I ordered, then started spraying them with water again. Screw them.

Come into my place and ruin my things.

No. Just no. Not happening.

"I'll be back," Ax said, grabbing Blaine's arm who tried wrenching it away, but Ax had a pretty strong grip on him and it didn't release. Ax pretty much frog marched Blaine out of the bakery.

All my customers stared at me in shock. I'd bet anything I was a hell of a sight.

"Sorry, everyone. Don't let these two jerks ruin your morning. Enjoy it. Free lemon bars for everyone," I stammered out with a small smile.

My sister chuckled behind me as I turned to her. "Don't know what you're laughin' about. You're helpin' clean this mess up."

Fuck my life.

CHAPTER TWENTY-TWO

Ax

My grip tightened on this asshole as I walked him through the bakery and out the door, all eyes focused on us, but I didn't give a fuck.

We were both completely drenched from that fucking hose. Indie sure knew how to break up a fight. I hadn't had water sprayed on me like that since Raid and I were little boys and Mom was pissed at us.

I threw 'Blaine' on to the sidewalk. He tried to steady himself but was unable to and fell on his ass. He reached his hand out behind him, and the crunching sound of a bone breaking made me smile. His screams did even more. Fuck yeah. Hurt, mother-fucker. Hurt.

I bent over and got in his face. "You come near Indie or this bakery again, you will not walk away from it. Do you hear me?"

"Fuck you."

"No, fuck you. Don't you ever call Indie a whore. You obviously have no idea what a whore is, and who she fucks is none of your business. She's mine. Has always been mine. Will be mine until we're both dead."

"You think you're so tough with the leather biker shit. She deserves so much better than you," he charged back.

"You think I don't know that shit? Doesn't matter. Only she matters. And make no mistake, I'll be your worst fuckin' nightmare. Try me."

Blaine scrambled to his feet. "Fuck you."

"Really, that what you have to say? Just go…"

It took Blaine a few seconds, but he was off and going. I pulled out my cell, then pushed a few numbers and connected.

"Brother. Need a favor. Can you and Booker come help me at Indie's bakery?"

"What the fuck did you do?" Raid asked me, a smile to his words.

"Beat the shit out of some fucker Indie was supposedly seeing. Tore up her kitchen and need some help cleanin' it up before she literally cuts my balls off."

"Already fuckin' whipped," Raid teased.

I didn't even fight the proud smile on my face. "Damn straight. That woman is mine. Do any fuckin' thing for her. You gonna come?"

He chuckled. "Give me ten. I'll get ahold of a few others."

"Thanks, brother," I responded, disconnecting the

call. I pulled out a smoke and lit it, inhaling deep. Over the years I tried to fully quit, but sometimes I just needed it.

Back against the wall of the bakery, I waited for my reinforcements. What I wasn't prepared for was five bikes pulling into the lot.

Raid, Booker, Deke, Green and Ryker all shut down their bikes, got off, and came my way.

"Thanks, brother," I responded to Raid, grabbing his hand and shaking it, then nodded to the others.

"You think we wanna miss this shit?" Ryker said. "We wanna see how Indie blows."

"Fucker. Come on."

I led the group of my brothers and Booker into the bakery. All eyes were on us, but mine were only for the three cleaning up the mess I'd created.

Moving behind the counter, I didn't listen to the teens telling me we shouldn't go back there with shudders in their voices; probably afraid we'd rip their heads off. Which at this point, I would.

"Thought I told you to leave, and here you bring all the dwarfs in like I'm fucking Snow White. Great!" Indie was so damn sarcastic. She might have thought it was a turn off, but she was completely wrong. "Clue in, fellas, this isn't a Disney movie. We got this all under control. So pack up all that male testosterone dying to save the day, and go do what it is that you do in your free time."

I wrapped her in my arms and kissed her deeply. She hit me on the chest and bit my lip, and I hoped like hell she drew blood.

Pulling away just an inch, I said, "You have no idea how hard I am right now."

"God. Would you just shut up already?" Before I could say anything, a handful of cake came to the side of my face. "Taste it. Maybe it'll shut you up."

Raid and the rest of the brothers started laughing uncontrollably, and I followed suit, pulling Indie to me and rubbing my face all over her. Her screams were adorable as the cake covered her with each movement.

"I'd love to stand here all fuckin' day and watch you two make out with cake, but I've got shit to do," Booker said full of snark.

"And you, my friend, are asshole smurf," Indie claimed.

"I thought we were dwarfs, not smurfs?" Ryker chimed in.

Indie grabbed a bowl filled with blue icing. "Assholes I could make it a reality assholes."

"This is a circus, and we're the ones providing a show for the entire town of Sumner," her sister groaned.

I didn't give a fuck, but with Indie's sigh, we got to work cleaning up the kitchen.

With all of us, it didn't take long at all. We even booted Indie, her sister, and brother out of the way. Her brother wasn't too pleased. Probably heard about our Sunday morning escapades.

He'd have to get used to it.

I wasn't goin' anywhere.

"Damn. You owe us beer and pizza for this shit,"

Green said, sweeping up the floors after all the tables were set right and we were almost done.

"Quit your bitchin'. I think we need to get some more prospects to do this shit."

The last two we had flaked out, and Cruz put a hold on giving anyone else leather for a while. Understandable. We had a few hang arounds who would probably make it to the prospect stage, but nothing was set in concrete yet.

Except maybe the two who didn't fit in. Concrete held nicely on them.

"Agreed," Raid said, putting all the cleaning things away in the back closet.

"We're out," they announced as I made my way to Indie who I found in the far kitchen where she was stirring something in a very large bowl.

"Hey, Indie."

Her eyes flew up at mine, and the fire wasn't there as hot as it had been. "Hey."

She moved with the bowl and dumped its contents in the huge mixer. "Whatcha makin'?"

Her eyes cut to mine. "Cake since you Neanderthals destroyed what I had prepared to frost."

A chuckle escaped me. "All cleaned up and ready for ya."

"Thanks," she grumbled as if she didn't want to thank me for anything, but also appreciated the help.

"I did it. I'll clean it. Gotta know now; you have Ravage at your back. We take care of our own," I told her frankly.

She stared at me, her hand halting. "I don't have

Ravage at my back, Ax. Just because we had a little heart to heart and fucked a couple of times, doesn't mean I'm with you. You need to get that through your head. All is not forgiven. I don't trust you. You have to know that."

Part of that was complete and total bullshit. She knew what we'd shared. There was no going back only forward and proving every fucking second that I would protect her with my life.

"You keep tellin' yourself that, but, babe, mark my words—there isn't a place in this world you can hide from me. What we've shared, that shit is solid. As hard as a concrete structure for us to build a life on."

Indie looked down at her batter then turned on the huge mixing machine. It was loud and she was probably trying to drown me out, but too bad. I made my move to her and wrapped my arms around her stomach.

She stiffened, then relaxed into me. "You've lost your mind, Ax."

"For you. Always had my mind scrambled when it came to you. It's how I know."

Her voice was so soft it was a whisper. "Honestly, Ax. How on earth am I supposed to just forget you left me out to dry? How am I supposed to not feel that hurt you caused me every time I look at you? Please tell me because I don't see how this 'future' you have for us would work."

I hit the button on the mixer, switching it off, and turned her around to face me. Cupping the side of her face, she leaned into the touch and I swiped my thumb over her bottom lip. Her eyes closed briefly on a gentle sigh, then opened.

"All the cards out on the table here, Indie. No one but the club, ol' ladies, and now you know that Baker was blackmailing Raid. That part is between us. I'm putting my trust and faith in you. I know you can't do it right at this moment, but I'll make you see how happy we can be."

"Since all the cards are out, what about women? If I already don't trust you, how the hell would I be able to trust you working at a strip club?"

"Full disclosure. I've had a lot of women since you. Easy lays to get off on. Never. Not once in my life has anyone ever compared to you. That was how I knew that if you ever gave me the slightest shot again, I wouldn't fuck it up. I'd grab onto it with both hands and never fuckin' let go."

"How do I trust this?" Wetness pooled in her eyes, and I leaned in to kiss each one, hoping to wipe the pain away from them. Fucking hated she felt she couldn't trust me. Trust was earned, and I had a lot to make up for. I knew I'd hurt her. Fixing it wouldn't be easy, but I was in it for the long haul.

"Because I'll prove to you every fuckin' day that I'm your man. No one else's. You own me, and if it takes the rest of our lives for you to believe me, I'll damn well do it."

The tears began to roll down her cheeks. "You scare me."

My heart cracked. Fucking hated she felt that way, but she had to know. "You scare me too. Having my heart in your hands to crush to dust is a heavy weight. I'm trusting you to keep me safe."

"God, Ax. You can stop now."

My brow quirked. "What?"

"All this mushy shit; I have to make cake. Tears don't go with frosting."

A smile graced my face. "Never. Shit will get heavy, but as long as we talk about it, we'll be just fine."

"Okay, so let's talk about the fact you not only work at a strip club but live there as well. How the hell am I supposed to feel about that one?"

I leaned down and kissed her lips briefly. "Soon enough I'll be movin' in with you." Her body stiffened. "And not one lady in that place holds a candle to you. Once you see that, I believe that you'll know."

"You are not moving in with me, Ax," she growled low, making me chuckle. "I'm serious." She started, and I held my finger to her lip.

"For now I'll move my shit into your spare room until I get it sorted. That's one thing off your list of not trusting me. I won't be living at a strip club anymore."

"You've lost your damn mind. We are not living together."

"Babe. You fell asleep with my cock inside of you. People can't get closer than that. We're gonna do this and ride it out. You'll see." I'd make her see that we fit together.

"This is moving too fast," India said quickly. "I just... I don't..."

Brushing the pad of my thumb over her lips again, I had to bend down and take them briefly. Pulling back, I looked deep into her eyes. "When I left the other day and GramO was still there, what did she have to say?"

Her eyes grew wide, and I knew I hit something there. That old woman had a wisdom that Indie respected. She gave me a piece of her mind before I left that day. She liked us together as long as I didn't fuck it up again. Because if I did, she'd hang me by my balls. She knew the story the rest of the world knew. Sex tape went out there. I never disputed who was in the tape until it was all over. By then, it was too late.

If I fucked this up, I'd want her to hang me by my balls. Fuck, even rip them off, and that was saying a lot coming from a man. I loved this woman and would do anything for her.

Indie gave me a little push. "Shut up and move. I have cakes to bake."

My head shook, and I gripped her tighter and held her to me. I licked the side of her face, chewed, and swallowed. "Fuckin' great cake, Indie."

She pushed at me. "Stop licking me!"

"But you taste so fucking good." As I licked the cake off of her, she tried to fight me off but burst out in a fit of giggles as I erased the cake from her face.

"Ax! Seriously! I'm clean!"

My lips attached to hers, and she stopped pulling away from me, kissing me back. I lifted her and placed her on the stainless-steel table and then maneuvered between her legs. Deepening the kiss, Indie didn't fight me. She took me for everything I had, giving back what I gave.

Yes. I loved her. With every fiber of my soul, I loved her.

The door to the kitchen swung open and a, "Stop that! People eat stuff off those tables. Out!" Indie's sister Meadow cried as we pulled away. "Anyway, we have a volleyball game to get to."

"Shit," Indie said, somehow getting out of my grasp and hopping down from the table. "Let me get this in the oven and tell Conner to get it out, and I'll deal with it in the morning.

"Volleyball?" I asked, wondering what the hell they were talking about. Indie never played volleyball in school.

"Yeah, my oldest, Trinny, plays," Meadow filled in. "She has a game tonight against her rivals, so we're all going to cheer them on."

"You have fun with that shit." I moved to Indie, pulled her into my arms, and kissed her hard. "See ya later."

Then I turned to leave, knowing I wouldn't be without Indie for long. Now she was under my skin, and I had zero reason to pull her out.

CHAPTER TWENTY-THREE
Indie

"YOU SERIOUSLY CANNOT FUCK HIM ON THE COUNTER IN the kitchen. That's so gross," Meadow told me as I put the cakes in the oven and turned on the timers. She was right, but so wrong. I would've let Ax screw me six ways until Sunday on every surface of this place if he wanted to.

Not that I'd let him in on that little tidbit of information, but it was very true. I was completely and totally screwed when it came to Ax Monroe. As much as I hated to admit it, he was partially right.

I'd missed him. My soul missed him.

But how did someone get over such a betrayal? I couldn't just say *oh you were young ... it's okay.* That wasn't going to happen. It wasn't okay. It wasn't right.

It took me years to even try to get trust back within myself. Yes. I had my family but trusting a man had not come easily because of Ax's actions.

If I closed my eyes, I could see myself in that same place as a teenager, crying and full of so much pain she didn't know how to process it. Each moment like a ticking timebomb just waiting to explode at just the slightest touch.

Those years building myself back up, putting faith in myself, and finding my strength were the hardest of my life. I had to put walls up where there hadn't been before, seal them with concrete, and reinforce them with steel.

But I'd done it. On my own and came out on the other end a woman who knew what she wanted in life. Knew what her priorities were. Knew her mind and inner strength. Knew the world around her could be cruel and how to survive it.

Sure, Ax stepped in from the bikers who wanted to attack me at the club, cooked dinner for me, and cleaned up my bakery when he made it a mess. All nice things, and with any other person, I might've given him more credit for it.

But it would take so much more before I could trust him.

I was still working on forgiveness because GramO always said that forgiveness was for you, not for the other party. Years later I was still working on that, which was so much easier said than done.

Ax now with his proclamations of being together and letting the past go. Did he really think it would be that easy? For him, he had no ramifications. In school, he was still the popular kid. He was still a biker. His brother was still his best friend.

The only one who got hurt from this was me. The innocent girl who fell in love with a boy with a reputation, and I should've known I would not be the girl he changed for.

But had he really changed? I just didn't know anymore, and everything was blurring.

"Just stop. Let me get myself together," I snapped at my sister harsher than intended.

"Yeah, considering there's cake in your hair and probably up your shirt."

"Dammit," I growled, going to Conner and handing him the timer. "This goes off, take the cakes out. Marley will be here to close down the place. Got it?" He nodded, not saying a word. Did I look as crazed as I felt?

Nevertheless, I didn't have time and turned back to my sister. "I'll meet you there. I'm gonna go home and change first."

"You've got an hour and a half. I came in early because I eat the shit here. No way do I want sex juice on it."

"Now who's being gross, woman?"

She chuckled. "Sad but true ... but it is kinda hot. I'll meet ya there."

We both took off out the door, but I paused momentarily at her words. From my sister ... the one who hated the man just as much as I did.

Once again, I hated to admit it but sex here, with him would be hotter than hell. Shit, I had it bad for the man who broke me all those years ago. How was that possible?

Those walls I'd built up were beginning to fall faster than I could put them back up. This did not bode well for me.

I stopped at home and took a quick shower because the cake in my hair was not coming out any other way. Damn man.

I'd made it to the gymnasium with ten minutes to spare. Never thought I'd be in my own high school on the regular, but with Trinny playing volleyball from sixth grade on, I was here more than I really wanted to be. High school looked exactly the same. With two nieces, Trinny and Farrah, I knew the kids acted the same as well. The clicks, cool kids, jocks ... all the drama. They both loved to tell their aunty all the shit they wouldn't dare tell their mother.

I hoped that when I had kids, mine would tell me all the shit that Trinny and Rah told me. Not that I'd like it, but I'd love to be a mom who could be there for her kids to talk to no matter what the situation was.

I don't know... Maybe when a sex tape of 'you', your boyfriend, and a teacher leaked out. Yeah, that one was not fun to tell my mother.

How she'd already forgiven him, judging from her reactions, I wished I could follow her path. *Please let me follow the path.*

Meadow waved goofily at me, standing up in the bleachers as did Mom. GramO smiled upon my approach. Devon, my brother-in-law and Meadow's husband, came down the few stairs from where they were sitting and took my hand to climb up the bleachers.

"You know you don't have to do that," I replied on a smile, absolutely loving that my sister had this in her life. She deserved to be pampered. This man opened the doors for her all the time. Like all the time. I'd be surprised if he didn't do it when she went to the bathroom just so she didn't have to touch the handle.

"Help a beautiful woman? Hell, I want to!" he teased with a wink, giving my hand a squeeze and releasing it as I sat next to GramO, who was on the end of the bleachers. She always loved sitting on the aisle. Said it was the best seat in the house, when there was a fire or you had to pee.

She was wise, but nuts sometimes too.

"Hey, GramO. How ya doin'?" I greeted, leaning in and nudging her shoulder.

Her hand came to mine, and I took in each line, wrinkle, bruise and freckle. Each mark was a stage in her life that made her the woman she was today. It was also a reminder of how many years she'd been on this earth. It sucked that the ones you loved got older. If I had a genie, I'd wish for time to reverse itself. It was something I hated thinking about and was why I cherished each moment I spent with her.

No one ever gave you a manual saying when your time would be up. I prayed that wouldn't be in the cards for a really long time.

"I'm good, child. I should ask you how you're

doing." She squeezed my hand even harder, bringing my eyes to hers as she wiggled her eyebrows.

The deep breath I sucked in didn't stop the laugh that bubbled out. "GramO. Stop that. We're just writing the last chapter of our story. We needed to do it and get it all out there so we can move on."

"Oh, my dear, your story may've had some serious bumps in the road, but it is nowhere near the end. If anything, it's beginning again. Like what you had before was the prologue, and now you get to the meat and bones. He messed up. Huge. He knows it. You can see it in his eyes. You can feel it when he looks at you, especially when you're not paying attention."

This made me curious, but she kept going so I couldn't ask.

"Like you were precious, and if he so much as blinked, he feared you'd disappear. One thing I know. Don't have a twin but know down to my bones that I'd do anything for my family. He might've gone about it the wrong way, but he's older now. Wiser. He realized that losing her was the consequence to his choices. And let me tell you, Indie, he won't make that mistake again." She gave my hand another squeeze.

I leaned into her ear. "How do I trust him, GramO? He didn't stop the kids at school from taunting me or spreading rumors. He never said a word. Not about the tape. Not about me not being in it. How do I let that go?"

"Everything in life is a risk. Some come out good. Some come out bad. But I know my Indigo

Jamison, you are strong, quick-witted, super smart and won't take any of Ax's crap. You're not the same woman as you were before. You've grown and learned a strength I always knew was there, but you had to develop. You've changed and experienced life outside of the city of Sumner. Realized that it didn't matter what the people of this town thought because you knew who you were inside. You knew there was a bigger world out there. Whatever obstacles come up in your life, you know you can weather the storm. You've got my grit and determination."

I felt the tears starting to well up but pushed them back as best as I could. Here we were, in a gym of all places, having this conversation. This needed to be an "in the living room with a bottle of whisky talk."

"You love him. Have always loved that man, and he knows what he almost lost forever. The crowned jewel you are... He won't make that mistake again, dear. I swear it." GramO shrugged, and my heart swelled. "And I told him if he hurt you again in any way, I'd cut off his balls."

I burst out laughing so loud everyone around us started staring, but I didn't care. "I love you. You know that?" I told her, wrapping my arms around her and hugging her tight.

"I know. And I you."

Others obviously, seeing the heart to heart GramO and I were having, began to interrupt and say hi. Yes, there were those who remembered the past, but ninety-nine percent of the time, it was just me—Indie, the woman who bakes like a dream.

Thinking back, really there were only a few who still said things under their breath, and it was mostly old bitties.

Maybe more had let it go than I'd realized. Because each time I thought about it, it was so raw and fresh.

When the whistle went off, the stands erupted, including my family, taking me out of all the thoughts swirling in my brain. Where was the off switch when you needed it? Guess volleyball would be the way out this time.

Sumner was a small town which meant the teams were small, but the Raiders were really good, and Trinny, my niece, led the pack. Loved that for her. I was never good at sports, never really interested in them either. Sure, I went to the games, but being athletic, not so much.

"Go, Trinny!" I yelled, jumping up and clapping like a mad woman. Trinny looked up and rolled her eyes at me, but I saw that smirk. She loved her auntie Indie no matter how much I embarrassed her.

Once the game got underway, my head swiveled back and forth between the ends of the court, getting up and cheering each time our team, the Raiders, got a point. Which was good because the game kept my mind off of what GramO told me and everything else my heart was feeling.

Right before the end of the first match, with only two points to go to win, a quiet hush went over the court like some mystical power entered the space. The players' focus went off the game and moved to the entrance of the gym, standing stock still with gaping mouths.

When I followed their gaze, my mouth followed the others and dropped open wide. "Oh my God," I breathed as Ax Monroe dressed in jeans, black T-shirt, boots, backward black hat entered the gym.

It wasn't just him though... No, Raid was at his side.

Hot. Smoking drop-dead hotness was entering a teenage hormonal zone. The women in this place were going to cream their panties.

Judging from the parents in the audience, they were in the same boat. One even fanned herself with the team roster like she was going to die of heat stroke.

Lord, save me from hot men.

The only thing that could be heard was heavy breathing and surprised gasps. Not even the roll or bounce of the ball.

Why on earth were they here? Didn't they realize they were causing a complete scene just for showing up and being, well ... them? Everyone knew the Ravage MC, but I knew for a fact that they'd never shown up to a volleyball game since Trinny played. That would not be something easily forgotten.

"Did you know they were coming?" Meadow leaned over and asked quietly because if she didn't the entire place would hear her. It was that quiet.

"No." I stood, and Ax's gaze came directly to me. I

started to make my way down the bleachers to him, thinking maybe he just wanted to tell me something he forgot and would leave quickly, but he shook his head and I stilled.

Please tell me they aren't planning on staying here. There would be no way these girls could concentrate with all this testosterone oozing out of them. Hell, the parents were going to need to go bang in the bathroom at this rate. They oozed so much sex.

The entire gymnasium watched each step they made, their gazes swinging to me as they looked to see who Ax had his eyes on. The group took the steps of the bleachers two at a time, and I could hear the girls across the gym sigh heavily.

Yeah, some things never changed. It was that way in high school as well, and while they were hot then, now it wasn't right to have that much sex appeal.

"What are you doing here?" I whispered to Ax, who grabbed me around the waist, pulled me to him, and kissed me hard. His lips were so perfect, and I got lost in them. All the emotions felt like they were being sucked out of me, and he was taking on that burden for me.

Then I could feel it. The eyes that were boring into us. We were not somewhere that this would be appropriate. Shit. I pulled away and gave my head a little shake. "Again. What are you doing here?"

"We came to watch the game," Raid said, leaning over and kissing my cheek like he'd done in the club-house. I still wasn't sure how I felt about him and the situation. He looked to the row behind my family, where other parents sat. "Would you mind movin' down please."

"Please?" I asked Raid with a quirk of a brow, being a smartass. Sometimes the sass just came out. Sue me.

"I do have manners. When I want to use them." His smile widened, and I shook my head with one tipping my lips.

As Raid sat down, I introduced Raid to my family although they knew who he was. It felt like the right thing to do, in the middle of a gym with everyone not even pretending to not gawk.

I sat in the same spot as before, and Ax sat right behind me. He pulled me back to rest between his legs. When I made a move to stop him, his grip tightened in warning, and I cut my eyes up at him.

"What?" I asked him.

"Just relax, Indie." His tone was so kind and gentle that the fire dissipated, and I relented.

Unfortunately, sitting like this was comfortable, so I ended up not arguing.

Even after their entrance and seating, the game was still stalled like the people were waiting for some cosmic sign to start again.

"You caused people to go stupid," I chastised Ax.

He chuckled and then whistled so loud my ear rang. "Is there a game goin' on or what?" he asked loudly, and I could see Trinny's face was beat red. Yeah. The Ax effect was in high gear.

Soon after his words, people came out of their

trances, and the game got underway. The Raiders missed the point, and mentally I blamed it on Ax.

"You're gonna start a riot in the gym," I grumbled to him as he leaned down to me.

"Anything for you."

I looked up. "Would you stop with that?"

He smiled. "Never."

Returning my focus to the game, I felt him behind me the entire time. But it didn't stop me from cheering on my niece, even jumping to my feet when they won the first set and during the second when she served and got the team seven points.

What I didn't expect was Ax and Raid to cheer right along with me.

Yeah. Shit. I was officially in trouble.

CHAPTER TWENTY-FOUR

Ax

PEOPLE COVERED THE BLEACHERS AND KEPT GETTING IN front of GramO as the game got over. What the fuck was wrong with these people? Respect was lost to some. Everyone wanting to be the first here or the first to leave. Slow the fuck down already.

I whistled loud, and everyone around us stilled. Moving quickly, I got in front of GramO. "Ms. Olive, may I?" I held out my hand, and she took it, smiling.

We went down the stairs slowly, those around us still stopped. If I had to be a bastard to let the woman get out safely, I would be. That being said, I flat out was a bastard so I didn't give a fuck. GramO was the matriarch in Indie's family, and she deserved the respect of that. People who didn't have respect for someone just because they weren't wearing a cut pissed me off.

They were the reason the world was turning to

shit in so many places. Here in Sumner, I'd do anything in my power to stop the leaching. Respect and loyalty came in all different ways.

On the last step, GramO looked up at me as if to tell me something, and I leaned down. She came up to my mid/lower chest. She was a little thing, but I had a feeling she packed a hard punch. I wasn't wrong. "Thank you, son. Now you get my grand-daughter and you grovel until your knees bleed, then heal them up and grovel more. My Indigo deserves the world, and if you're not one hundred percent in, you turn away from her now. If you're in, be all in. Don't hold back because if you do, you'll lose her and this time it'll be forever."

Yeah, her punch definitely hit hard, right to the soul.

"I'm all-in, Ms. Olive. Swear it. Indie is my queen and she always will be respected and treated as such. You have my word."

She smiled and put her hand on my cheek. "Now get that brother of yours over here to help me out to the car."

"You really need help?" I asked, raising my brow.

She smiled wide. "Little ol' me? Of course. And he's a looker. I'm old, not dead."

I burst into laughter and waved my brother down who came immediately. "Can you walk Ms. Olive out?"

He grinned and held out his arm to her. "This beautiful woman? Absolutely. Nothin' I'd love more."

GramO smiled as Raid led her out of the crowded gym.

A feminine hand came to my shoulder, and the scent of sweet vanilla came to my nostrils.

Indie.

"Thanks for being so nice to her," she said as I spun her around so we were face to face and wrapped my arms around her tight, pulling her to me.

"Hey!" she protested, but I didn't give her a moment to say anything else as my lips were on hers. What was only hours I'd waited to feel her again felt like years.

Only thing I wanted in this world was my cut, family, and Indie.

She put her hands on my chest and began to push back but didn't stop kissing me. She was at war with herself, and she had every right to be.

Her head was telling her I was a worthless piece of shit and never to trust me again. While her heart was telling her she loved me and she could trust me until my dying breath.

At least that meant I was cracking through a bit, and I was going to take it and run with it. Any opening she gave me I'd prove I was the man she needed.

Pulling away, I rested my forehead on hers, our breaths intermingling between us.

"You have to stop doing that," she said panting.

"Never, Indie. Never will I stop taking what's mine."

Her head shook, causing my forehead to move with it. "I'm not yours, Ax."

"Right. I'll remember you when you're riding my cock and screaming my name."

She huffed. "Just because you're spectacular in bed doesn't mean we're together or taking this any further."

I pulled back to look in her eyes, a small smirk playing on my lips. "Spectacular, huh?"

"Of course, that would be the one thing out of everything I said you'd pick out. You're such a man."

A chuckle escaped. "Damn right, Indie. Man. Not a punk kid who fucked up the best thing that ever happened to him. That shit ain't happenin' again."

"Awe, how cute." A woman's voice came from beside us. Lexi Jones. Was a bitch in high school and never lost her bitchy attitude, which she proved from her next comment. "Back to your threeways I see. Guess some never grow out of their depravity."

Indie turned, her arms crossed over her chest. "Why are you such a bitch? Jealous? Wish it was you? Whatever it is, I don't care. Leave me alone."

"I'd never," she gasped, putting her hand to her chest. "Me, jealous? Of what? You have nothing for me to be jealous of."

"Considering you just said the word jealous twice in your rant, I'd say that was a sign."

I moved to step in, but when Indie's head whipped to me, eyes blazing, I took it as a sign she had this and I needed to stand back. Not an easy thing to do, but I did. For her.

Lexi leaned in close. "Take your sign and shove it up your ass."

Indie chuckled. "So that's what you're into, yet I'm the one depraved. Makes sense and all."

"What's goin' on here?" Delilah came up to us and asked.

Lexi's head swung to her, and a smug grin came to her lips. "Did you see the tape?" Lexi shook her head. "Don't worry. You'll be able to see it soon. I guess it was reuploaded to all social media sites earlier today. Soon everyone will remember what your daughter truly is."

Indie gasped beside me, and that was the time I stepped my ass in and pulled Indie behind me.

"That shit had better be pulled and wiped in the next fifteen minutes. If it's not, you'll have Ravage at your fuckin' door."

"You can't do anything to me. My husband is the mayor, or don't you remember?"

"Bitch, he was appointed because we allowed it. We own his dick more than you do. So you are very wrong. I can make your life a living fucking hell."

Lexi swallowed hard. Her husband obviously kept her out of the loop which was good for him, but now it was bad that she knew. Not my fucking problem. "I'm..." She started then turned tail and ran out of the gym like the coward she was.

Turning back to Indie, the panicked look on her face told me everything I needed to know. She was scared to death this video would make its rounds again.

Grabbing my phone, I pushed Raid's number who picked up on the third ring. "Where the fuck are you? We have to get to X," he greeted.

"Video is makin' its rounds. Cut the neck off. Get Micah on that shit and get it wiped for good."

"You're fuckin' shittin' me."

"Nope. Put the Mayor and his wife on notice. Wife was the one who uploaded."

"On it." He disconnected.

"I'm not doing this again, Ax. I can't."

"And you fuckin' wont. That I can guarantee. That fuckin' cunt thinks she can bring all that shit back up again; she's sorely mistaken. Not only that, this entire town knows it wasn't you. Made fuckin' sure of it."

Pain split through her gaze. "I have nieces now, Ax. They go to this school. They do not need to even think that I was part of an affair with a teacher."

I pulled her close. "Hate to tell ya this, babe, but they probably already know. But they also know it's not you; just some random bitch."

A tear fell from her eye, and I wrapped her up tightly in my arms.

"Swear to you, Indie. I'll take care of this shit. You have nothing to worry or even think about. It'll be destroyed today."

The thing was back in the day once everything came out, Dad and Raid went through everything they could to wipe that video from existence. Where this bitch supposedly got a copy I didn't fucking know, but I would find out.

My guess would be her fuckin' husband kept a

copy of it for collateral, thinking it would be something he could hang over our heads. Or Lexi could be just a big enough bitch that she copied it without us knowing.

This time, it would be destroyed. Every megabyte of that shit would be erased. We had my father, Micah, Deke and Austyn who could do anything with technology. Those fuckers would find it if it were there.

"We just talked about all of this. Why now? Why…" She paused, pulled back, and looked into my eyes. "A few days ago she came into the bakery. I made her coffee and then she coughed under her breath, calling me a whore. I told her that the gas station had great coffee and she'd be better off going there. She was not happy."

"That'd do it, but, Indie, I'll handle it. Let me have it on my shoulders to deal with."

"Like you did last time? We both know how well that went." She huffed, and I felt the tightness in my chest.

"So fuckin' sorry about that. I will not make the same mistake twice. Please try to trust me."

She swiped under her eyes just as it fell from her lid. "This is big, Ax. Make it or break it. And if it breaks, there's no goin' back."

Indie threw that down like the ultimate challenge.

And I would not fail her. Not a single bit.

Exiting the gym, Raid stood outside.

"How in the fuck did that tape get out?" Raid started just as I made it to my bike. "Indie just took off out of here like a bat out of hell. I'm guessin' she's pissed as fuck."

"And you'd be right. Lexi Jones. That fuckin' cunt. She always was one, so why I thought she would've grown up, I'll never know. Need to take a ride."

"Brother. I've got Micah, Deke, and Dad on that shit. We have to get to X. Princess called and said there are six bachelor parties and she only had two down. We need to cover."

I grabbed my helmet from the handlebars. "Fine. But in the morning we're payin' Lexi and her husband a visit."

"Sounds good to me. They'll find the shit."

"Right."

CHAPTER TWENTY-FIVE
Indie

THAT STUPID LITTLE COME-GUZZLING ROAD-WHORE cunt-sucking twat-waffle uploaded that damn video. To threaten me with it? I'd never really envisioned killing anyone, well accept Ax back in the day, not that I'd carry it out, but with Lexi, I felt the red rage filling inside me.

If it came down to it, would I really be able to kill someone? I hoped like hell I'd never have to find out.

Trusting Ax ... that was an interesting thought. As much as I thought there was nothing between us, there was. I just didn't know how to get passed our past.

Gripping the steering wheel, I started my car up and waited my turn to pull out of the lot. I noticed Raid by his bike, but he wasn't paying attention to me. His back was turned, and he was on his phone.

That strange unease hit me and prickled up my spine, making the hairs on the back of my neck rise.

The parking lot had so many cars moving in and out I couldn't see anything out of the ordinary. Scanning, nothing looked amiss. Just parents, family, and kids getting into cars.

Except, I couldn't dodge the feeling of eyes on me, so as soon as there was an open shot, I took it and headed home.

The feelings I had were completely gone by the time I pulled up to my house, opened the garage door, and pulled my baby inside.

Gizmo was there to greet me, and after a few loves, she needed the restroom. "Hang on there, little one."

The lights in my house were set on an automatic timer. I didn't like Gizmo being in the dark, nor did I like going into a dark house.

Flipping the outside lights on, I unlocked the slider and let Gizmo loose, then stepped out into the night air. It happened to be a beautiful night. Quiet with the stars in the sky shining bright. One in particular brighter than the others.

Memories flashed me back to the past.

"This is beautiful," I told Ax as we lay on the blanket under the stars. We were all alone on top of one of the hills right outside of Sumner. I'd only been here with Ax, and this was our second time.

"You're beautiful," Ax replied, pulling me closer into his body. God, I loved him. Loved him with everything inside of me.

My mother warned me never to get to attached to a boy in high school, but I couldn't help it. Ax had me wrapped in his snare, and there was nowhere else I'd rather be. He was it for me. I wanted him for the rest of my life.

"Look." *Ax pointed to the sky where a shooting star flashed across the darkness.* "Make a wish."

That night I'd wished to be with Ax forever, and it didn't turn out as I'd planned. Instead, it left me torn wide open. Now he was back in my life. What that meant, I was still up in the air about. And now this tape coming back to life... How did my life turn so hard on its axis all of a sudden?

Gizmo started yapping or barking' one could call it either. Maybe a yapbark?

I shook my head at my crazy thoughts. "Come on, Gizmo! Time to eat."

She bound in like I knew she would. Girl loved to eat. I locked the door and gave her the food, then proceeded to make something for myself. Popcorn at the game did not cut it, but the look on the girl's face who Ax bought it from was priceless.

Sitting down to eat, the doorbell went off. Ax didn't ring bells. He just picked locks and came right in, so it couldn't be him.

Gizmo started barking as I put down my fork and went to the door. I peeked outside the window though the blinds. The front lights were on, but no one was there.

No one in front of the door waiting to come in.

No one walking on my driveway or the street.

"You heard that? Right, Giz?" Surely, I wasn't hearing shit now. I had enough on my plate as it was dealing with Ax, the tape, and life. Lord knew I didn't need anything else.

Gizmo yapbarked, her head moving up. "I guess that's a yes or, at least, that's what I'm taking it for."

I wasn't stupid. There was no way in hell I was opening that door, especially when I saw nothing. I'd seen a few horror films, and I wasn't going to be the stupid bitch who let the crazy ax murderer in to slaughter me up. If there were something there, I'd want to see it in the light of day. Not the dark of night.

I rested my back to the door. Why on earth was that the first thought I had? An ax murderer? Seriously? It'd been forever since I'd watched Emily D. Baker and listened to the trials and her commentary. Was I warped from watching true crime sometimes.?

Ax was crossing all of my wires as of late.

More than likely it was kids doing the door dash. I wouldn't be surprised if I stepped on a bag of dogshit on my front stoop in the morning. Too bad for them I used the garage. Ax could have the pleasure of stepping in it if he attempted to come into my house tonight.

While part of me wanted to stay awake and see if Ax would show up, it was past ten, and I had to be up in a few hours for work. A yawn escaped.

Ax would either have to use his magic to get in, or he'd have to come another time. I really wasn't sure I wanted him to come at all. That was a lie. I'd felt safer with him here. How fucked up was that? The one person who'd destroyed me as a teen was the one man I felt the safest with.

Changing my clothes, I dropped Gizmo on the bed and climbed in behind her.

I put on the Hunger Games and quickly fell fast asleep.

CHAPTER TWENTY-SIX

?

OH MY INDIE ... CUDDLED UP IN THE BED ALONE WITH her dog.

She thought having that other man in her bed would detour me.

No. Nothing would detour me for what I wanted. For what I needed.

She was mine.

Watching her chest rise and fall steadily, I pulled out my cock and began stroking myself. With each breath, I pulled and tugged harder and harder until my come exploded into the grass.

Indie...

She would be mine.

I would take her from here, and she'd forget all about everyone but me.

We were destined to live our lives together.

And we would. I'd make damn sure of it.

CHAPTER TWENTY-SEVEN

Ax

It was a very long night at X. Many people thrown out after fights broke out.

All of it just made me later and later. Then adding in coming here, I wasn't able to slide into bed with Indie before she went to work. That pissed me off.

Good thing I had a couple to take it out on.

Both Raid and I watched the three children get on the school bus, and no one else had left the home yet.

Not bothering knocking, I twisted the door handle. The dumbasses had nothing locked and the door swung open as we charged in.

"Honey, I'm home," I yelled as we walked inside, noting everything was perfectly clean and orderly. Not a beer can or speck of dust anywhere. My parents' home was always clean, but it was lived in. This was not. It was on the flipside of fun.

"What the..." John Corbon came through the home and stopped in his tracks when he saw us moving toward him. "Why are you in my house?"

"Where's your bitch of a wife?" I asked.

John pointed his thumb behind him, not saying a word about the name. "In the kitchen."

"Let's go," Raid ordered as we moved into the kitchen.

"What's goin' on?" Lexi asked, smiling, which fell at the sight of us. Then her gaze flipped to her husband. "I didn't mean to..."

"What did you do?" John asked his wife, turning to her and staring her down. She shook her head, her face scrunching up.

I moved to the butcher block and pulled out a knife and started cleaning under my fingernails. Intimidation. The bitch was so scared of us. Let her sweat. If I had to use the knife, at least it was handy.

"I... I..."

"Fuck me," I growled moving closer to the woman. "Do you have a copy of the sex tape video of Baker and the threesome?"

It was John's turn to freeze, then he exploded. "You have what?!" He yelled at his wife. "For fucks' sake. Please tell me you don't have that shit."

"I..."

"Do you have any other words but stuttered 'I's'?" Raid clipped out, the night wearing on him as well.

"Answer, Lex. What the fuck is goin' on?" John clipped, moving closer to her as I took a step back again.

Lexi put her hands up and took a step back, then another. The counter finally stopped her, but John got close in her space. "Answer me."

"I told Indie that I uploaded the sex video to social media."

"What!" He exploded. "Have you lost your fucking mind!"

"I was mad." Lexi started quietly.

"Mad." John chuckled darkly. "You were fuckin' mad and decided to get involved in shit that could kill you. Shit that was supposed to be dead and buried years ago! Really fucking smart." John had gone to school with us, therefore he knew about the tape, but like most people in Sumner it wasn't even a thought anymore.

"It just came out when I saw them." She started.

"You're absolutely ridiculous! That shit just doesn't word vomit out of your mouth! Do you have a copy of that shit?" John cut her off. Lexi nodded. "Fuck me." He turned around and scrubbed his hand over his face. "Where?" he barked.

"On my computer, the cloud, and on the flash drive in the safe."

John whipped back around to her. "You're insane. Legally insane and need to be in a ward. Three copies? Three. Not just one, but three. Anymore? Because I swear to Christ if you have more and don't tell me in this moment, your life will be hell until you take your last fucking breath on this earth."

While I was impressed with John's reaction, he was taking all the fun, and I hated that shit. But he asked what I needed to know. It also appeared that miss perfect Lexi didn't live a happy life and knowing her husband would make it hell helped.

"On the drive cloud no one knows I have. But that's all. I don't have anything else."

"You have a fucking drive I don't know about?" Each word had John getting angrier and angrier. "Did you upload it?" John asked.

Lexi shook her head. "No. I stopped myself before I did it."

"Maybe you do have a few braincells left in that arrogant head of yours," John grumbled. "Take what you need. There are tablets, laptops, external computer hard drives and a tower to the desktop. I'll get the key to the safe," John said, not even waiting a second to move out of the room. Had to say this impressed me too.

Raid grabbed his phone and dialed out. "Come in. Get the shit." Deke and Micah were outside in the Tahoe waiting for our call. If these people had this video anywhere, these two could find it.

"I didn't mean to cause trouble," Lexi cried as I moved to leave the room and follow John.

Turning to her, I stared her down. "You ever talk about or post that video in any way, you'll be dead, and they won't find your body. You stay away from Indie and the bakery. You stay away from the volley-ball games or any game that Indie is at. If you walk into a store and she's there, you walk out. You don't come near the Ravage MC or anyone associated with us. You do, I'll turn your ass over to Princess and my mom, and I'll stand back and watch. Then I'll put a bullet in your head."

Her eyes widened as fear gripped her. She had no idea who she was fucking with, which was stupid on her behalf.

"Not fuckin' around with you, woman. Swear on my life. You do, say, think anything, and I will destroy you."

Moving to the upstairs, I heard John moving around to the left and went in that direction through the door. He was tossing shit around his office, ripping out the cords to the electronics and tossing them to the ground.

He looked up briefly then back down before grabbing the tower of the desktop and putting it on top of the desk. "I cannot fucking believe her. She's been in this town all her life. She fucking knows better than to mess with the MC ... yet here she goes, bringing up this shit. And she has copies! She has a serious death wish." His head shook.

John pulled a set of keys out of the top drawer of his desk and moved to the wall. "Fucking moron."

"Sounds like you love her," I replied sarcastically.

He huffed. "When she pulls stupid shit like this, it's fucking hard."

"This isn't the first time?"

"She thinks she's high on the fucking hog and nothing can touch her because I'm mayor, and she has that shroud of protection. Flaunts it, and look here—it came back to bite her in the ass. So fucking stupid."

"Get a hold on her. I'll put a bullet between her eyes and not think twice about it."

He nodded, then put a code into the safe, inserted a key and opened the door wide, not really having any "normal" reaction to me killing his wife. If someone told me they were going to kill Indie, they'd have a bullet in their head immediately. "Lexi! Get your ass up here!" he yelled, and two seconds later both her and Raid came into the room.

"Get the drive now."

She hustled to her husband and pulled out two flash drives, handing them to John. He looked down at his hand. "Two fucking copies. So now we're up to five. I swear, woman. You'd better tell me where every one of these are."

"That's all in the safe."

"Get your laptop, computer, phone and tablet."

Her eyes widened. "My phone."

John snapped. "Yeah, your fucking phone! They need to wipe all the shit to their satisfaction. We might get it back. We might not. Fuck if I know. We'll get new shit if we have to."

Had to admit, I respected this man. He knew what we would be doing with all this information. Most of the time we'd have to beat the shit out of people before they talked. This was a serious change of pace.

"We need usernames and passwords," Micah said, coming into the room. "It'll make it easier. But know

I'll be able to hack it without those. Just saves us time."

"I'll write mine down," John said, then looked at his wife. "You too."

Tears rolled down the woman's face. Personally, I didn't give a shit. She made her bed.

What I did give a shit about was not being able to punch someone and get my frustrations out since John was being very open about it. Had to give credit where credit was due.

It just proved how much pull the Ravage MC had in Sumner, Georgia. Even the mayor knew the consequences.

"We'll see about returning your shit. But don't hold your breath," Deke came in, saying with a shrug. "Usually don't do that shit."

"Usually," I replied. "It'll be up to Cruz."

John nodded and tossed his phone to the top of the desk as well. "That's a city-issued phone." He reached into his back pocket and pulled out a second phone, then tossed it next to the other. "That's my personal." He then leaned down and wrote some things down.

Deke held out his hand and took the paper.

"Keep your bitch in line," Deke growled, grabbed the shit he could carry, and left the house.

"Write down all the clouds you have as well," Micah threw in, looking at Lexi. "And don't fuckin' tell me you don't have them because I'll track them through your IP address. I don't give a fuck if you have a VPN because I'll still find it."

Lexi went white as a sheet then hurried to the desk like her ass was on fire, and grabbed a pen and paper, writing it down.

After all this was done and all of Lexi and her children's electronics were taken, I held my hand out to John. It was unexpected to him by the shocked look on his face that he covered quickly, but he held his out as well, and I shook it. "Thanks for makin' this shit easier than spillin' blood."

"Sorry about it. Had no fucking clue she had it. I'll find out what else she has on this other drive. If it's anything to do with the club, which it better not be, you'll be the first to know."

"No offense, but we'll find it sooner than she'll tell ya," Raid said.

"We'll be in touch."

Leaving the house and moving to our bikes, Raid stopped me. "You think he's hidin' anything?"

"About us. No. About other shit, sure. Who doesn't have secrets? But he's a man who knows the position he's in and our position. He also knows he'll be dead alongside his wife. He's not a stupid man."

"Right. Headin' to the clubhouse. You?"

"Bakery."

Raid held out his fist, and I bumped it with mine.

Driving off, I headed to the bakery.

Parking in the lot, I entered the bakery, and the sweet smell of vanilla hit me and I inhaled deep. Indie wasn't at the front counter, and I shifted my gaze to the cake area, and there she was with her back to me.

Meadow was at the counter as I made my way to it, to go around and get to Indie. She held her hand up. "Hang on there, big guy," she said, and I stopped and looked at the woman. "No cake flying and no hanky panky."

A chuckle left me. "I assure you, I do not do hanky panky. Fuck your sister senseless—of course."

She smiled and playfully slapped my arm. "Stop that! There are kids here."

"If you have sensitive ears here, then maybe you shouldn't be bringing up hanky panky."

Meadow looked up at the ceiling. "I cannot believe I'm having this conversation with you." Her head moved back down. "Seriously, though... Don't hurt her. You will have a family of Fallons that will dismember you and feed you to the pigs."

Another chuckle left me. "To the pigs, huh?" My brow raised questioningly. It was a very astute statement considering pigs ate everything and left no evidence behind.

"I watch true crime like my sister. We know how to hide a body."

"Your sister watches true crime?"

"Since you don't know that yet, I'm sure I have nothing to worry about."

I placed my hand on her shoulder, and she stilled. "Love your sister. I fuck up, I want you to feed me to the pigs. We're on the same page."

"As long as you know where we stand." She then stepped out of the way. "I look forward to my trip to the pigs!"

A huge smile lit my face as I made my way to Indie. She was molding cake, and I couldn't exactly tell what she was trying to make.

"A whale?" I asked, and Indie jumped, the knife in her hand flying up, but I caught it quickly.

"Why in the hell are you scaring the shit out of me?" she retorted, standing from the stool and putting a hand on her hip. I set the knife down on the stainless-steel table.

While her stance was cute, I really needed my arms around her. She was stiff for a few seconds, then the breath went out of her, and she followed suit.

"Sorry, Indie. Didn't mean to scare ya," I whispered in her hair.

She really deflated then. Only then did I feel the tension fall from me. I needed this woman like a drug. Like air. She was everything.

"Are you okay?" she asked, pulling back just a bit, but we were still very close.

"Why do you ask that?"

"Just seemed to have tension in your body until you wrapped your arms around me."

Loved how she knew me. "Long night. Talked to Lexi and her husband." It was her turn to tighten. "No, Indie. It's okay. We have all their electronic shit and all copies of what Lexi had. She was bluffing about putting it on social media. She's just a bitch, and her husband was not happy with her."

"Oh..."

I leaned down and brushed my lips against hers. "Told you I'll do anything to protect you."

Her eyes glistened. She closed them and burrowed into my chest. Fuck, this was the best feeling in the world.

I loved this woman.

CHAPTER TWENTY-EIGHT
Indie

"WHAT? WHERE?" I ASKED AX AS HE HELD MY HAND and pulled me to his bike.

"Don't ask so many questions, Indie. You'll ruin the fun."

I rolled my eyes. "I'm always going to ask questions, Ax. That's me."

He grabbed the extra helmet from his bike and put it on my head, strapping it down. "You do know I can put on my own helmet right?"

"But this is more fun."

His smile was broad, and I felt myself falling into it. I'd missed that smile. The one where I knew he was thinking something and desperately wanted to know what it was. Yes, that was his killer smile.

"Fun for who? You?"

"Promise it'll be fun for the both of us." He leaned

down and kissed me stupid, then hopped on his bike, and I got on the back.

Without a second thought, I wrapped my arms around his waist and snuggled my front to his back. When the bike started, I could feel the beast under me.

Ax was seventeen when he got his motorcycle license, and I was the first one on the back of his bike. He'd take me for long drives on the winding roads with nothing but the breeze and sun surrounding us. I loved those days.

We just rode to wherever we ended up, and then we'd come back home. Personally, I always loved the trip there best just because of the excitement of the unknown, something new. But riding back wasn't bad in the least.

I braided my hair, and it hung long down my back. The leather coat and jeans would protect me from the wind. It was nothing fancy, but when a man says "get dressed to ride a bike, and let's go" you do what you can.

How he knew I was home was a mystery. I'd only walked in the door fifteen minutes ago. But there he was, ready for a ride.

I sucked in a deep breath smelling dirt and grass as Ax took off like a shot.

We rode for a while, my body completely giving over to the freedom that came when I rode with Ax.

In the zone so much that it wasn't until the lights caught my attention that I knew where we were.

He killed the bike and I got off, having to shake

my legs just a bit. It had been a long time since I'd been on a bike that long.

Ax got off, unsnapping my helmet and putting it in the little case of the side of his bike.

"A carnival?" I asked, hearing all the sounds instantly once the bike shut off. Music and laughter billowed out as the lights flashed in every color of the rainbow.

People were everywhere, and the bell on one of the games rang in the distance.

It was time for me to smile and look up at Ax. "I haven't been here since the last time you brought me."

Ax ginned, leaned down, and kissed me on the temple. "Come on." He took my hand, and we walked through the grass hand and hand to the entrance.

A childlike giddiness filled me. When I was a child, my mother would bring the five of us here on the ride bracelet day when we could ride and ride and ride until we puked.

It was a huge challenge on who could last the longest. The spinning tilt-a-whirl did me in every damn time.

When I relayed this story to Ax, he brought me to the carnival. While our challenge wasn't going until we puked, it was seriously fun.

"I am so winning!" I told Ax as we made our way to the entrance, and I reached for the cash in my pocket to pay.

"Don't even think about it," he growled at me, making me stop and look up.

"What?"

"Don't wanna know the men in your life, but if one of them made you pay for shit ever, they'll be on my kill list."

I shook my head and elbowed him. "It's 2022, Ax. Women pay for stuff now."

He stopped and pulled me up against him. "Gotta know this about me, babe, and you gotta let me do it. It's important to me. It's how I was raised. You've seen it with my folks. Already told you, you are my queen. You've gotta give me the space to take care of you. That includes payin' for shit. Includes cleanin' the kitchen. Holdin' your hand and keepin' you close. It's not that I don't think you can do it on your own. I know that. You've been doin' that, and I'm not gonna take over your life. It's important to me to do what I need to do for you, whatever that may be. Here right now, that's payin' for everything and havin' a fuckin' great time."

Was I breathing?

No. There was no way because my chest was so tight it felt as if my heart had completely stopped.

Heat flooded my skin and the soft breeze of the night gave me goosebumps.

My hand even trembled holding the cash that I slowly put back in my pocket, and I kept it there, unable to move it again.

He stared deep into my eyes, and I could feel his heart pulling to mine.

"I don't know what to say." My trembling voice came out on a whisper.

"Nothin' to say. Just let me take care of you."

"Then I get to take care of you," I fired back without thinking. Without going to that time in my life when he'd hurt me. Just being in this moment with him. The boy I'd fallen in love with all those years ago.

He smiled wide. "I'd fuckin' love that."

His lips took mine, and only then did I take my hand out of my pocket and wrap them around his neck placing my hand at the bottom of his ballcap to feel his hair.

Home. That was what Ax Monroe felt to me. Home.

Shit, I was in trouble.

He pulled away and tugged my hand. "I'm winnin' this time."

A smile grew on my face.

"Hell no. It's my turn."

He took care of all the costs, and I didn't say a word. Hell, he wanted to spend his money on me ... fine.

"What do ya wanna go on first?" he asked pulling me to the tilt-a-whirl, and I stopped in my tracks. He jerked with my movement.

"Ohhh no you don't." I planted my feet.

"Come on. I know how much you love it," he teased.

"You want me to puke?"

He laughed full out. "Not particularly." He leaned in close to my ear. "Considering my mouth will be on every part of you, vomit isn't my thing."

My body shivered at the thought of his lips on my body, but I snapped back. "Okay! Tilt-a-whirl it is!"

This made him laugh harder, and he pulled me in tight, giving me a hard kiss.

"Smartass. Roller coaster it is."

A sense of adrenaline flowed through me as the anticipation of the rush hit me. The thrill of the ups and downs and twists and turns. "You're on."

I released his hand and took off running. Unfortunately, time had not made Ax slower as he wrapped his arm around my stomach and threw me up over his shoulder. I cried out, laughing, "Put me down."

My hair flew around, my braid hitting me in the face as he smacked my ass hard. "Nope. That's it. I'm carryin' you."

"Oh no you're not, Ax Monroe. I have two legs, and I can walk!"

He positioned me in the same way he carried me at the clubhouse over his shoulder. His ass was right there and I started hitting it as Ax walking toward the ride.

"You big oof. Put me down!"

"Nope, you'll take off on me. I should've brought some damn rope to tie you to me. I'll remember for next time."

"The hell you will."

"Excuse me."

Ax stopped suddenly, and I jostled at the quick movement. Lifting my head and peering over Ax's side, a short, older man stood there with a cane in his hand and had it pointed up at Ax as if it were a gun.

Well, he did, so I guess it worked.

"Miss, are you in trouble?"

Awe. It was nice to know that there were people out there who would actually take the time to make sure everything was okay. That I wasn't being taken against my will.

"She's fine," Ax said and started to move, but the little guy was quick and moved his cane so it was right at Ax.

I figured this wasn't going to end well. Ax didn't take well to being told what to do or how to do it.

"Sir, I'm fine. He's just being an overgrown caveman who thinks I don't have legs and can't walk."

A hard slap came to my ass, and I returned the favor and surprised Ax as he hitched me just a bit. It made me smile knowing that I got him. It was the small things.

"You're not just tryin' to tell me what I want to hear, are ya?" the older man asked, and Ax chuckled.

"If anyone told Indie what to say, she'd claw their eyes out," Ax replied, and I grinned wide at the older man.

"Right, and I know where his balls are located. So if I really wanted him to put me down, one kick to those and he'd drop me. Hard, but it'll work."

"Young love." An older woman with styled grayish hair came up to the older man and put her hand on his cane, pushing it down. "Now, Harold. You know better than to involve yourself in love."

"She was screamin' for him to put her down. Just wanted to make sure that she was okay."

The woman smiled at Harold, then leaned over to kiss him on the cheek. "You're a good man. Let's let these two go have their fun."

These two were absolutely adorable, and part of me wanted to put them in my pocket and take them home.

"Thank you, Harold. I really appreciate you stopping to check on me. You never know, this big oof could've been kidnapping me, but alas, he is not."

Both Harold and his woman grinned at the two of us.

"Can we go now?" Ax asked, and I smacked his ass.

"Be nice! I like them."

"You just met them," Ax said as the blood started rushing to my head.

"You need to put me down; I'm getting light headed."

Without another second, he set me down and held me tight. "Are you okay? Your face is red."

"You were holding me upside down; what did ya think would happen?"

"Not that we'd get stopped by this guy." Ax nodded to the couple.

"Ignore him. He loses his manners when it comes to others around me. Or so I'm learning."

"How long have you been together?" the woman asked.

"Milly. Didn't you just say not to get involved in it?" Harold told his woman.

"Shut it." Milly looked to me. "How long?"

I was curious, so I asked her. "How long do you think?"

"Years. Maybe sevenish," Milly said, and my head tilted. That was about the time we would've been together had he not fucked it up.

"Really?"

"Yeah," Milly said. "You've been together for a long time, but something pulled you apart."

My body stiffened. "What?"

She only smiled. "Just be happy. Love is pure, but it's complicated. Love can hold you high in good times and get you through the tough times. Love can also hurt. It can break and bend. There will be fights and miscommunications. But it's the strongest bond you'll have. One you can trust and count on. It goes both ways, so hold on to it tightly."

"We're not together," I told Milly, and Ax growled.

"Are too," he retorted.

Milly smiled wide. "You are and have been in each other's hearts."

"Now enough of your mumbo jumbo," Harold said.

"Even after fifty-three years, you still think it's mumbo jumbo? I swear sometimes I want to take your cane and hit you with it."

Harold very wisely moved his cane to the other hand out of Milly's grasp. "Woman. I know you know what you're talkin' about. I'm sayin' let these youngins' get on with their night instead of standin' here talkin' to us."

Milly side-eyed him, and I just knew he was going to get it when we walked away.

"Thank you for your kindness," I told them.

"Nice to meet ya," Ax said, and Harold's brow lifted, but he kept his mouth shut.

"Bye," Milly said as Harold nodded.

"Bye."

We walked away, and I didn't know what to think.

Ax held my hand as we headed to the roller coaster. "Was that weird or just me?" I asked him.

He chuckled. "You don't remember who that is?"

I looked up, my brow lifted. "Milly?"

He smiled. "Remember the side show that was here when we were probably in grade school?"

"Yeah..., but I've never been to it."

"Milly was the fortune teller for years."

"No way! You're lying," I said, shocked.

He stopped and wrapped me in his arms. "No, actually I'm not. Guess she's really good at telling people's future."

My head tilted. "Good? She said we've been together for years. We're not even together now, Ax. She's very wrong."

"Stop sayin' that shit. We are together. And babe. Think about it. You've never been away from me. I tattooed you on my arm to carry you everywhere after you left."

"What? The one on your arm? That makes no sense. A heart, an eye, and claw marks. I don't get it."

"Look closer. The eye is yours. I gave my artist a picture of you, and he recreated it. 'I' for Indie. The bleeding heart because my heart has been bleeding since I made you leave my life. The claw marks are because you're a panther when you want to be, and you sliced me because I deserved it."

"You thought of all of that with the tattoo?"

"Yeah. I needed you with me. I'm the one who fucked up and couldn't let you go."

Lord save me. Yeah, I was in trouble. Shaking my head, I asked him, "So what Milly said about being together seven years. That you had the tattoo. I'll go with that."

Ax ran his nose over my cheek. "You go with whatever you want. Know you've been with me. Know that I never thought you'd give me a sliver of a chance, and I'm not lettin' go of you. Now, enough of the heavy. Let's have fun."

Yes. We really needed to move on. "Please. And I'll be the winner."

I smiled wide, held his hand, and we started walking.

His warmth had that hard shell I'd put around my heart cracking and breaking.

He didn't know, but I stole one of his shirts and had worn it to bed over the years. I still had it.

I'd never let him go over the years either.

CHAPTER TWENTY-NINE

Ax

HER LAUGHTER WAS EVERYTHING. EVEN WHEN SHE smashed her bumper car into mine and caused mine to stall, which was hilarious to her.

I gave as good as I got, but she had a thing about running from me and then sneaking up on me. It seemed to be a pattern with us.

One that was breaking. No more being away from each other. This was it. Her and me.

"Bring it in!" Came over the loud speaker just as I plowed into Indie.

She gasped. "You AxHole!"

I burst out laughing and headed into the lane and parked.

Moving quickly, I gave Indie my hand, which she took, and helped her out of the car. Wrapping my arm around her shoulders, I pulled her to me tightly as we walked away from the ride. 'AxHole? What the fuck, Indie?"

"Yep. That's what I call you when you piss me off which is like all the time."

"You should get that tattooed on your ass. My Axhole. That way I can claim it."

She stopped in the middle of the walkway, and I pulled her to the side quickly before a bunch of teenagers ran into her.

"No way in hell I'm getting that tattooed on me. Never. NEVER!"

I kissed her hard and pressed her back to the metal trailer we'd just come out of, my hand going to her back and under her shirt. Pulling away, I whispered. "Right here is where I'd put it." I brushed her skin, and she shivered. "Then I'd have you wear your shirt up so every motherfucker who saw it would know that you're mine."

Indie rolled her eyes. "New topic! Here, fishy fishy!"

She pulled out of my arms and began to walk away. I grabbed her hand and held it the entire way to the fish bowl game.

We'd already done the rides minus the tilt-a-whirl.

Now it was time for me to win.

"Come and try your luck!" the man inside the tent said as we made our way to the side of the square table. "You wanna win this beautiful lady a beautiful beta fish?" he asked.

"Hell no. I'm gonna win him one."

"Right. Keep tellin' yourself that," I said back, handing the man the cash. We'd play until we won. It was our challenge. When we were together, she told me about her siblings challenge at these things. Since I didn't want her to puke, I upped the ante.

People thought throwing a ping pong ball in a small hole to get a fish was easy. Fuck no it wasn't. Even with perfect aim, if it hit the water just right, it would bounce out. It'd probably cost me a hundred bucks for a small fish, but I didn't give a fuck then and sure as shit didn't give a fuck now.

"Smile," Indie said, holding her phone in front of us with the fish in the background. I smiled as she snapped the picture.

"You need to send me that."

"Hell no. This is my bragging picture for when you're carrying the fish that I won out the door!" She laughed as the carnival man with the tag saying Gibler set up the balls for us.

"One at a time. Alternate," I ordered.

She picked up a ball and then waved it at me. "Yeah, yeah... I know the rules. Get ready to go down."

"You do remember that I won this last time."

Her head snapped to mine. "That was a default! You paid that guy off!"

I chuckled. "Prove it."

"I was standing right there! You cheated and just paid for the fish. That's not winning. If I can remember right, I've won once, and once was a default because you paid them and you have zero. The big goose egg, baby. I've got this."

"It's one-one. This is the tie breaker, and I'm winnin' you that fuckin' fish!"

"Nope. Not happenin'. I'm first," Indie called.

"What? No. Flip a coin. Make that shit fair."

She cocked her hip. "What happened to ladies first?"

I looked around dramatically. "Where's a lady?"

She clocked me in the stomach, making me cringe. Didn't see it coming, so I didn't tighten the abs. Needed to remember that shit. "AxHole!"

Indie pulled out a quarter and tossed it in the air. "Tails," she called out, and the damn thing landed tail's side up.

She jumped up and down. "Hell yes!" Her tits shook, and my tongue wanted nothing more than to lick and suck until she came in my arms.

Fuck, now my cock was hard. "Would you go already?"

Indie looked down at my cock, which only made it harder, and smiled. "Tease."

"You have no idea," she taunted, then turned to the game.

Indie was absolutely hilarious bending down, lining up balls, then switching her aim to go high, then low. Her face was serious as hell.

It was my turn to pull out my cell and snap a quick picture of her.

She was so focused she didn't say a word about it.

She let go of the ball, and that fucker bounced out of the damn tent.

"Oh, baby. You lose your touch?"

"I'm warmin' up. Let's see you!"

My turn, I totally bombed. The ball went flying, but Gibler caught it, and Indie laughed.

"I can see you're rusty too."

"Shut it and throw," I teased.

Balls flew everywhere. In the square. Out of the square. Anywhere but in the fucking glass bowl. Time ticked by, throw after throw. Each of us giving the other shit the entire time. Every time I missed, it made Indie laugh, and I found missing wasn't such a terrible thing.

"Shit!" Indie cried out once the ball flew out of the bowl after going in. "Did you see that! It went in and bounced out!"

"Your cash is out," Gibler said.

"How much have you paid already?"

"A hundred and twenty dollars," I told her.

Her mouth dropped open. "No way."

"Not gonna lie to ya, Indie."

She swallowed and looked at the pricing. "So each round of five balls was five bucks each. That's ten bucks a go. We did twelve rounds?"

"Apparently."

She sighed huge. "We're done."

"Why do you say that?"

"Ax. We're not putting another hundred bucks down on a fish. I can go to Walmart and pick up one for five bucks."

"Let me do it one more time."

She shrugged. "Wasting your money."

I smiled and handed Gibler a five dollar bill, and he set up the balls.

I tossed the first, and it landed in the bowl.

"No way!" Indie cried out as I threw the second ball, and it landed in the bowl.

"You're cheating," she accused me with her hands on her hips.

"Nope." I threw the third and missed. "See."

The next I missed.

I held up the little ball. "I've already won you two of these guys. How about three?"

"Ax, how are we gonna get these home on the bike."

I shrugged. "We'll figure it out."

One last toss had the ball landing in the bowl.

Indie stood there slack jawed. "How in the hell did you do that?"

"Three fish for the biker man," Gibler yelled out loudly, trying to get the attention of all of those around us. More business and all. He got busy putting the fish into bags then tied the bags off.

"Ax. I don't think Gizmo will like these. And they can't be in the same tank or they'll kill each other. What am I going to do with three of them?"

I smiled as Gibler handed me the fish. They had such big air bubbles in them, they looked like balloons.

My gaze swept over the crowd, noting a mom with

her three children. I nodded their way. "What'd ya think? Presents?"

She grabbed onto my arm, smiled, and kissed me on the cheek. "Perfect."

It was the first time that she really initiated the kiss, and it was just a peck. But fuck, it meant a lot. It meant I wasn't in this alone. That she was right there with me.

Walking over to the kids, Indie spoke. "Excuse me. We just won these fish and don't have a home for them. Would you be interested in taking them off our hands by chance?"

The two little girls and one boy's faces lit up with excitement.

"Mom, we tried forever to get one of those!" the little boy yelled out.

"He's right. I spent fifty bucks so all three of them could try. It didn't end up working out. Are you sure?"

"Absolutely."

I reached out my hand, and each child came up and grabbed one.

"What do you say!" the mom scolded.

"Thank you."

"Thank you."

"Thank you," were all said at the same time.

"You're very welcome."

"I appreciate this. They were so upset when they didn't get one. This made their day."

"Glad to help," Indie said as I lifted my chin, and we turned to walk away.

Indie wrapped herself around my arm, holding

me tight. Her head even brushed my shoulder a few times. Fucking loved that shit.

"I say we both won on that one. We'll have to have a rematch," Indie told me as we made our way around the park.

It felt fucking awesome she was talking about a second time. She was there with me. Fuck yes.

We made our way over to the fun houses. There were three of them, each with a different theme. "Let's do that one." I pointed to the optical illusion house.

"Oh, I like that one. I wonder if they've changed it," she said, excited as we made our way over.

I reached in and handed the man our tickets then a fifty. "Twenty minutes. No one in."

The man took the money and as we went it, he put the chain up with the closed sign.

"Why'd you do that?" Indie asked.

"Because I can't go another fuckin' second without bein' inside of you."

Indie took off running, but that was the thing with optical illusions. You could never tell what way was up or down. I caught her by the black and white spinning wheels that covered an entire wall. If you looked at them too long you'd get dizzy as fuck.

"Hands on the wall, Indie," I ordered her as I pinched her nipple through her shirt, and she let out a low groan. She followed my direction.

My lips attacked her neck, kissing, sucking, biting, and licking. Every fucking inch of her skin there.

Her body moved in time with mine. Her ass

grinded hard against my cock. Hand at her belly, I moved it down to unbutton her jeans and skated it under her panties. The silk of them felt soft on my skin.

Going through her curls, I wasted no time finding her clit and rubbing.

I didn't know if the guy up front would follow my instruction or not, and no one saw Indie like this but me.

Her hand left the wall and clutched to my hand, and I stopped. "What's wrong?"

"I can't. Not in public. There could be cameras."

It hit me then. She was right. We'd been down this road before.

She shook her head. "Can't do it again, Ax. Just can't."

I pulled my hand out and rebuttoned her jeans, turning her to face me. She wouldn't make eye contact with me, so I lifted her chin with my fingers. "You ever feel uncomfortable or don't like somethin', you tell me. Always. I'm sorry, babe. Didn't think about that. Just wanted you so bad that my cock wouldn't stop pointin' your way."

She chuckled at that, breaking up the tension that had grown in the space between us. I kissed her gently. "Let's go on the Ferris wheel."

She bit her bottom lip and nodded.

Fuck, my cock was hard as hell now, but I'd do anything to make Indie feel safe with me. She needed that, and I wanted to give her that any way I could.

Holding her close to me, we got out of the

funhouse and made our way to the Ferris wheel without much being said. My huge mistake put a damper on the night, and I could feel the tension come back to Indie.

Fuck.

I hadn't thought about it. Never crossed my mind.

But it crossed hers, and worse—it made her try to close herself off to me.

That was not what this night had in store for us.

We arrived at the ride, and I handed the man our tickets and he put us in some rickety tin cart with a latch on it that would not save us if it tipped over. As high as this fucking thing went, you'd think there'd be something more secure.

"Behind you," he said, pointing to the harnesses, and I nodded, getting Indie's and giving it to her. It wrapped around under her arms and stayed attached to the metal.

I did mine up. All of this in silence.

Putting my arm out, I wrapped it around her and pulled her into me. She didn't resist coming naturally and resting her head on my shoulder.

"I'm sorry I freaked out on you." She apologized, shocking the fuck out of me.

"No, Indie. I'm sorry. I wasn't thinkin'. You were totally right."

"Thank you for stopping," she said quietly.

I cupped the side of her face so her eyes would meet mine as the ride started going up and up. "Always. You don't like something, Indie, you tell me. No hesitation. You're safe with me. Fuckin' swear it."

Brushing my lips ever so slightly against hers, I whispered, "Love you, Indie. With everything inside of me. I love you. Never said those words to anyone but you. It was true then. It's been true the entire time we were apart. It's true today. You hold my heart in the palm of your hands, Indie. And you have my dark and battered soul. You're the only one I've ever wanted. Ever needed. Please see it."

A tear rolled down her cheek, and I brushed it away with my thumb.

"I want to say yes. I want to throw myself in your arms and never let go," she admitted. "But I have this tug of war inside of me. One part says yes. The other says remember he hung you out to dry. Then I see how you are now. How you look at me. How I feel when you look at me. I'm terrified you'll hurt me again. Because this time, Ax... This time I won't be able to pick up the pieces. And that's what keeps me pulling away. If I'm broken, I'll be nothing."

"Baby. Fuck, I hate you feel that way, and I understand it. Just know I won't give up. I know my future, and it's with you by my side with my babies in your stomach."

She gasped and put her hand on her stomach. "And get stretchmarks? Have you lost your mind!" And just like that, the tension lifted.

She told me flat out how she stood.

Me, I was going to keep doing what I had been and make sure she never had to pick up any pieces again.

CHAPTER THIRTY
Indie

"DON'T BE NERVOUS. YOU KNOW THEM, AND THEY BOTH love you." Ax tried to reassure me, but I couldn't shake the nerves. I wasn't sure if it was one hundred percent because we were having a family dinner with Buzz and Bella. Oh, and Raid too. I hadn't had a chance to talk to Raid yet, and I knew it had to be done at some point.

"I know." The tray of sweets I put together was in my hands, threatening to fall to the ground if I didn't stop shaking. What the hell was wrong with me?

He was right when it came to his family.

But it wasn't just that. It was last night before Ax got there. I hated the feelings I was having. My gut told me I needed to tell Ax. After dinner. I'd tell him. It was eating me alive holding it in.

"Give me that." Ax took the platter in one hand

and my hand in the other. He squeezed tight, and I let out a huge breath.

Ax and I were still deciding what we were. Or, at least, *I* was still deciding. He proclaimed to already know what he wanted, and I was still terrified about putting my trust in him. He hadn't shown me a reason not to have faith, but I was still very leery.

Having a family dinner wasn't on top of my list of figuring us out. If nothing else it put another layer of confusion on top of all the other shit we had between us because I loved his mom.

Always had. Always would.

Bella had always treated me with respect, never harshly. When I was young, I didn't know how biker chicks were. While I knew my family would do anything for me, women like Bella were more take charge and fix the problem. She'd mentioned 'ride or die' several times to me.

When I asked her what it meant, she told me it was a symbol of family in the Ravage MC. No matter what happened, every single person in the club had each other's back. If one went down for something, they'd all go down and not think twice about it.

It was how I felt about Ax at one point.

Bella was a cut above the rest.

I didn't want to let her down if this didn't work. Hell, I didn't want to let myself down either. If I could scream, I would. Life was so tangled and twisted. I really didn't need any more kinks.

He stopped us by tugging my hand and pulling me to him. His lips met mine and everything around us washed away. It was just him and me on an island far away with no notes freaking me out. No creepy feelings of someone around me. All of it was gone. I absolutely loved kissing this man.

Ax pulled away and looked into my eyes. "Relax and have fun. Who knows what crazy shit Mom is gonna wanna do. She always comes up with somethin' that irritates my old man. Which is half the fun."

A smile graced my lips. "Okay. I'm good."

"If not, I can kiss you again. It would be a hell of a sacrifice, but for you—anything," he teased on a grin.

I shoved him playfully. "Smartass," I said just as the door opened, and Bella stood there.

"Smartass. It depends on the day. There's also dumbass, hardass, jackass, lazyass..." Bella started, making me burst out laughing.

"Ma, come on. She gets it. I'm an ass. Everyone knows it. Can we come in?" Ax asked his mom who opened the door and ushered us in.

"I know she does. I was just helping to move your conversation along. I'm that helpful, ya know." Bella made me laugh hard, and I felt it down in my gut.

"Truly, if you'd like to continue, I'm more than happy to listen," I replied, watching Bella smile wide.

"Oh, honey. The list is so long we'd be here for a year."

"Ma, seriously?" He leaned down and kissed his mom on the cheek. "She really doesn't need help figuring that shit out. She already knows, but thanks."

"What did you say to your mother?" Buzz came into the room, and I sucked in a breath at the look glittering his face. Holy shit. Was he going to deck his son?

"Hey, old man. Mom's givin' Indie a lesson in how I'm an ass. Told her she didn't need help in that area."

A slow smile crept on Buzz's lips as he wrapped his arm around Bella. "You wanna tell him. You go for it."

"Geeze," Ax responded.

A warm feeling came over me and filled me with something I didn't know I'd been missing. These people. This man.

"Well, come in and have a seat." Bella told us. "I'll go get some drinks."

"Oh, Mrs. Monroe. I'll help." I knew my mistake as soon as it left my lips. My hand went to my mouth, trying to take the words back, but they were out there swinging in the wind.

Her eyes narrowed. "What did I say about Mrs. Monroe?"

"Ma, you're welcome to lock us in a room, but when you hear moaning, you better not open the door."

Bella's gaze went from her son to me then back again. "Glad to hear that has worked itself out."

"Oh. We're still trying to figure that out."

Ax glared at me. "Figuring what out?"

"Us ... or..."

His finger came to my lips, halting my words. "Don't, because I'll take you in the back room and show you exactly how there's nothing to figure out."

My core quivered, and wetness pooled between

my thighs. How he did that with words I'd never know.

"Stop it," I said low.

"Then cut that shit out. If I need to remind you at any time, I have no problem doin' it."

"What the fuck is goin' on here?" Raid came in the door and stared all four of us down with question in his gaze.

"Indie."

I turned to Ax. "Indie? Are you kidding me right now? How about Ax?"

"Would you two just give in to each other and be done with this back and forth already? The sooner you do it, the sooner you'll be happy. This bickering is fun and all, but seriously you two are made for each other. You can do the back and forth about other shit. But you two are somethin' a lot of us only hope for." Raid burrowed past us, leaned down, and kissed his mother then moved into the house.

Me? My mouth was hanging open as my gaze followed the man.

Did he really just say that? Did he really feel that way?

A strong arm wrapped around my waist, and Ax pulled me into him. His lips were so close and he whispered, "See, even Raid sees it. Ma sees it. Dad sees it. GramO sees it. You need to see it."

He brushed his lips across mine, and I could barely breathe.

A small hand grabbed mine. "Come on, Indie.

Help me," Bella said, pulling me away from her son and leading me into the kitchen. Ax followed.

"Sit that down and go," Bella ordered Ax.

"Fine." Ax set the platter of sweets on the island, kissed my cheek, and moved out of the room. Bella who came to me and wrapped me tight in her arms.

I followed suit, just needing that comfort for a moment as my head spun. Bella pulled away and said, "Enough of that. You'll come to know what you want in your own time. Don't let my boys pressure you into anything."

I licked my lips. "That's the thing. I don't feel like Ax is pressuring me. He honestly believes we are supposed to be together, and he shows me. Helping my GramO, making me dinner, playing with Gizmo —all of it."

Bella squeezed my arms and then let go. "You're scared. Totally get it. Love my boys to the end of the earth. But..." This caught my attention. "Remember... He's a biker. Grown up in a biker family with a lot of men who knew who their women were immediately. When Ax is absolute about something, he doesn't waver. Won't waver. He tells you that you're it for him, then you're it for him. Buzz came at me like a raging bull, but I knew I loved him. Made him work for it, but I knew. When you know, you'll know."

Bella stepped away and moved to the other side of the counter. I rested my palms on it and hoped it would help me from falling to my knees.

"I do know. Doesn't mean he doesn't scare the hell out of me." I'd never admitted that out loud. That I knew he was it for me, and here I was telling his mother.

Bella smiled warmly. "Then you tell him. But that doesn't mean you don't keep him on his toes." She winked at me.

For the first time in a while, the binds that held me back from Ax began to fall away.

"Come on. Let's get the food to the table."

We began to do just that but were halted with the first dish as three hulking men came into our path. Ax held out his hand, and I put the dishes in it. "You go sit. I'll bring it."

I blinked rapidly and looked over to Bella who had Buzz doing the same thing. Holy shit. Even Raid went to the counter and picked up bowls, bringing them to the table as both Bella and I sat down.

"Are they like this all the time?" I whispered to Bella. "I mean, Ax cooks and cleans up, but I thought he was just trying to impress me."

"Nope. I'm already impressive," Ax said, setting down a bowl of salad then leaning close to my ear. "Told you—you're my queen. Anything and everything you need, I'm right there."

My eyes closed.

His lips brushed my ear and then he went back into the kitchen.

"Yes. My boys know how to treat their women. They can do all that badass stuff everywhere else, but not with their women."

"You did really good, Bella."

Her smile widened. "You called me by name. I love that."

"Yeah."

Dinner was actually fun. After all the heart to hearts and my laughter, I felt the tension drain from my body. When Ax draped his arm on the back of my chair and pulled me close to him after we finished eating, I leaned into him, feeling his heat.

When it was time to clean up we all pitched in, making the job fun and fast. I loved how Ax was with his family. Loved how he was with Raid and that bond no one could deny because it was so bold.

"Alright, Indie. It's your pick. We have Pictionary." Bella held up the board box. "Or Skip-bo. What's your poison?"

"Ma, do we really need to play a game?" Raid groaned, putting his head back on the couch. "Your food was so good it needs time to digest."

I leaned into Bella, whispering, "He's good."

She nodded. "Don't let them get away with it."

A laugh burst from my lips.

"Which one?" Bella dangled the two boxes like candy for me to pick from. My family was very close, but we'd never had a game night before. Truth be told, I'd never played either of them.

"I've never played either of them." I told her, and it was Bella's turn her mouth agape.

"What? You've never played board games?"

I shook my head. "It wasn't something big in my family. More free love and special weed."

Bella burst out laughing. "Gotta say that sounds

pretty good to me. Let's play Skip-bo. Boys!" she called, and all three of the men came back to the cleared off table.

Had to admit, I loved how they did exactly as they were told by Bella. But on the flip side, I knew bikers weren't always so accommodating.

By the third round, I knew this game and was good at it.

"Whoohoo!" Bella yelled, banging on the table as I dropped my last card and won the game. Lifting my arms, I danced in my seat and let the happiness and excitement fill me, feeling so comfortable with these people.

"What? No invitation for me?" A voice came from the front door, snapping everyone to attention. The man had blond hair that was greasy and looked like it needed a wash. His clothes were a bit dirty and eyes were wild.

Suddenly three guns were out and pointed at the man standing in the doorway. I didn't even know Ax had one on him. He took a step back, grabbed my arm, and pulled me behind him; once again shielding me.

What was going on? "Ax?" I whispered, grabbing onto his shirt as I tried to place this man.

"You're fine, baby. Just breathe." Hopefully he felt my nod because words escaped me.

Who on earth would just walk into someone's house without knocking? I mean, a house with men with guns. Did he have a death wish?

The tension in the house went from having fun at

zero to skyrocketing past ten to hostile and tense.

"What the fuck are you doing in my house?" Buzz clipped, moving to stand in front of all of us. Neither Raid nor Ax flinched. I tried to do what Ax said and breathe.

"Told ya. I need to talk to the club." His voice sounded jittery but not in a mellow high way, but a stimulant way. Made me wonder what he had taken and why he would come here in that state.

These men could break him when he was in top shape. Coming intoxicated was a death wish.

The man must've moved because Buzz said, "Stop."

"Hey, brother. Everything's cool," the man said, and it registered to me. He didn't mean brother as in the MC club, but brother as in blood. This had to be Ax's Uncle Nick who he didn't care for much.

Ax had only spoke about him once, maybe twice, but I did remember this man.

"Everything is not fuckin' cool. Do you have any idea what you've fuckin' done?" Buzz growled low.

"Haven't done shit," Nick said, and I felt Buzz take a few steps forward as the air began to pulse. Something really bad was going to happen here.

"You fucked the club. You fucked our family. You fucked the Monroe name," Buzz said.

"You sure as fuck did," Ax said low as I gripped him tighter. "You want to talk to the club. Sure. Let's fuckin' talk to the club."

Raid chuckled. Actually chuckled. I didn't see anything funny about this entire situation and felt very out of the loop. What did Nick do? And what did it have to do with the club?

"Really?" Nick asked with hope in his tone. How out of it was this guy? Even I could tell going to the club to talk wasn't something he wanted to do. Yet, here he was, excited.

"Yeah, really," Raid said, shaking his head.

"I really need the money. Now. Old Red he's comin' for me."

Who the hell was Old Red? And how much did Nick owe him?

"Oh, we know Old Red's comin'." Ax started. He made a move to step forward, but I clutched his leather so hard it made him stop. "He wants his money. Thought the club was gonna pay it. Imagine his surprise when we told him that wasn't fuckin' happenin'."

"What do ya mean?" Nick asked.

"Enough talkin'," Buzz said, and a shot went off, making me jump and scream as I muffled it in Ax's back.

"Fuck!" Nick yelled out loudly as a thud sounded in front of us. "You shot me in the foot! What the fuck?!"

"You're lucky it's not in your brain," Buzz said. "Raid..."

Raid moved forward from my right after a few moments, and Ax turned to block my view from the man at the door.

"Need you to go with Mom for a few. You can

either stay here or go home, but I've gotta handle this."

My head shook. "What's goin' on, Ax?"

He brushed his lips over mine. "That's my uncle. He fucked over the club, and we gotta deal with it."

My heart thumped hard in my chest. "What are you gonna do? I don't want you to get in trouble."

He smiled, the one I loved so damn much. "We won't get in trouble. Fuckin' swear it. This is club shit. Know this is my life. Two sides of a coin."

I remembered how he dealt with things at school. It was why no one came at him. He actually backed up his threats, so this was no surprise. I guessed it was a shock being thrown into the deep end like this.

"Know I'm yours, and trust me," Ax said, and damn I did.

I nodded instantly, and I didn't know what to make of that. "I'll stay here for a bit and then ask Bella to take me home."

"Not even a quiver in your voice. Fuckin' strong. Love you." He kissed me hard, and I sucked in the gasp of the words he just said to me.

Love me. He loved me. Sure, he said I was his and he was mine, but love? Oh my God.

He pulled away, and I couldn't get my mouth to move.

"Ma. Take care of her."

Bella wrapped her arms around me and lead me away from the room.

Holy shit. He said he loved me.

And he was going to do something to his uncle.

What in the hell was my life turning into?

"Come on," Bella said, pulling me through the house and down the stairs. I followed without a word, too stunned at what had just happened. Between the gunshot and what Ax said, I felt as if I was in an alternate universe.

Not paying attention, Bella put her hand on my shoulder, and I sat on a very comfortable couch and she sat next to me.

"Indie," she said, her face coming a few inches from mine, getting my attention.

"Yeah." The breath that left me felt foreign, not realizing I hadn't breathed for a while.

"It's okay, Indie. This is the part of life where you let the men do what they need to do, always knowing they will do anything and everything to protect you. Gunshots aren't a norm in most people's lives, and I get it if you're freaked by that."

But that wasn't it. Sure, my family was all about free love and happiness. Guns weren't a norm, but it was what he said to me.

"He said he loves me," I told her, and she smiled wide.

"Of course he did. He's loved you since he met you. He may have gone down the wrong path, but now he's on the right track. He's ready. Ready for you."

"He's gonna hurt me," I whispered low.

"It's always a possibility, Indie. Men are men. There's always a time when they'll hurt us in some way. But hurt you like he did... Really think about that. Talk to him. And I'll kill him if he does."

A smirk came to my lips. "I'll kill him with you."

"Loving someone means putting yourself out there. Putting your heart on the line. And with yours and Ax's past, there will be more bumps than not. But I promise. You stick with it, and it will be the love you've always deserved."

A tear rolled down my cheeks as the emotion took me over. The fear I had of being hurt was so heavy, but I understood her. I even knew it in my heart as well.

I loved him. Even though he was somewhere probably beating his uncle up, it didn't matter. Only he did.

Bella wiped my tears. "Yes. I know you love him too. It's okay. Take time together. Talk. You're not getting married tomorrow."

"What about the other stuff?" I asked her, looking at the ceiling and back to her. "Do you just act like it doesn't happen?"

She shook her head. "The more you connect with Ax, the more you'll understand."

"Right."

CHAPTER THIRTY-ONE

Ax

"GARAGE." MY FATHER ORDERED GUN STILL ON NICK, but other hand going to his cell.

"Nick's here." He said into it then turned it off.

"Why the fuck did you shoot me!" Nick yelled and spilled blood all over my mother's floor which pissed me off. Sure as hell pissed my father off too.

"Breaker's on his way you piece of shit." My father put his gun in the back of his jeans and picked Nick up by the shirt. "You're gonna hurt. Then hurt more. Then more. Then I'll give you to Old Red."

"Wait. What? What's goin' on?" Nick asked as Raid and I put our arms around Nick, took him outside and into the garage after my father opened it.

We tossed him to the floor missing the bikes. Raid and I moved everything out of the way leaving an opened space in the center.

Raid moved over to the workbench and tossed me

a rope then grabbed the ladder and I climbed up and attached to the winch in the middle of the room.

"Buzz. What's goin' on? You've already shot me. Let me go." Nick whined and my father landed a savage kick to Nick's stomach. He cried out and moaned.

"You fuckin' piece of shit." My father growled and spit down at his brother. "You'd be best to keep your fuckin' mouth shut!"

Raid went to Nick and wrapped his hands in rope. We both lifted him and attached him to the hook now hanging from the wench. We hadn't had to do this in our home before, but we still had what we needed.

We took turns with our fists and feet making him feel every single punch thrown. He cried out.

"As much as we want to finish you off, that would be too nice for what we have planned for you at the clubhouse." I growled in his ear reached in my pocket and pulled out my pocket knife.

"Can't stab him where he'll die." Raid reminded me and I looked to him rolling my eyes.

"Seriously? Do I look that stupid?"

Raid grinned. "Took you long enough to get with Indie. So stupid is debatable with you."

"Fucker." I growled and my dad touched my arm. "Yeah?"

"Want to wait until we get to the clubhouse?" He asked.

My head shook. "No. This is Monroe business." I pointed to the tattoo that Nick had across his abs.

"That needs to come off before we take him. He is not a Monroe. Never will be." The roar of the bike told me Uncle Breaker was here and it was time to do what we needed to do.

My father nodded as I stepped closer with the knife, Nick's eyes wild with fear. I soaked it in. Loved it. He needed to fear all of us.

Carving into his skin I removed each letter cutting a circle around each. Blood oozed from him as he screamed and cried. At some point he passed out, which made the last few letters not as much fun to carve out.

"Load him up. They're waiting for us. I'm riding behind." My father ordered and Raid and I did just that. Even put some old towels on the wounds to make sure he lived at least for a while longer.

"Get the plastic down first." It was Raid's turn to order.

"What the fuck is up with all the orders?"

Raid looked at me rolling his eyes. "Oh dear biker sir. May you please put the plastic down so the SUV isn't covered in blood?"

My hand shot out and I punched him in the arm. "Stop bein' a shit."

A chuckle escaped me. "Let's get this shit done."

It took a bit to load him, but once we had him ziptied and rolled up we took off towards the clubhouse.

"You care to tell me what the fuck you were talkin' about with Indie at the clubhouse? What's the shit you found out about her?"

Raid who was driving looked over to me and raised his brow. "You don't know?"

"Yeah. I know. I'm just wantin' you to repeat everything for the fun of it." I paused. "Fucker."

"Figured you'd talked." He said looking back to the road. "You know she went to college up in Seattle, right?"

"Yeah. Know that."

"Brother, she had a serious stalker there."

I turned hard to my brother. "What the fuck?"

"Calm."

"Fuck calm. Tell me what's goin' on or you'll be droppin' me off at Indie's and dealing with Nick's bullshit yourself."

I felt my heart pick up speed and the knot in my gut tightened.

"He's dead. She fuckin' killed him Ax."

This caught me off guard. My little Indie killed someone? Holy shit. How the fuck did I not know this. "Keep goin'."

"Older man she met in college and dated for a while." This made me growl low, but Raid said nothing and kept on going. "She dumped him, he didn't like it. So much so the cops intervened several times and she had a protection order against him. He didn't follow it. Sent her these fucked up rhyming letters and gifts daily. It came to a head in her apartment right after she graduated college. He hadn't been around for weeks and she must've thought she was safe. He showed up, beat the shit out of her, but she somehow managed to knife him in the side until the fucker bled out on top of her. Ruled self defense and she came home soon after that."

The entire time my brother spoke my heart was splintering and crushing. My girl went through all this shit and every day I saw her smiling at every customer that came in through her door. Watched her pour coffee and create cakes with not a care in the world.

Yet through all of that, she had to save herself by killing someone. It wasn't something I ever wanted her to have to do. Killing wasn't a thing anyone took easily. My beautiful happy Indie had to do it and no one would ever know the pain she had to go through.

Including me. I had no fucking clue. If I had, I honestly didn't know what I would do. Right now I wanted to murder the man again. Knowing it then, I wouldn't have waited for Indie to give me that sliver of an opening.

"He's dead?"

"Yep. Saw the certificate, autopsy, and pictures. She fought hard while he died laying on top of her. But yeah. The fucker is dead."

"Anything else happen to her?"

His head shook. "Self-defense. No question about it. How she got through it? I have no clue. But she did."

"And she did this shit by herself?"

"Her family was there for her. If I'd of known you really wanted to be with her, I would've told ya, but she'd been back for a while and you didn't have any balls to go to her. Thought it was for sure over."

"Fuck you." I barked back. "I don't need your shit."

I pulled out my phone and dialed Indie's number just wanting to hear her voice. I wouldn't tell her I knew, but just wanted to make sure she was safe.

The phone rang and voicemail picked up. I tried again, this time leaving a voicemail.

I switched to my mother who answered on the second ring. "How's it goin'?" She asked immediately.

"We're good mom. Is Indie with you?"

"No. She wanted to go home. She needed some time to wrap her head around what happened tonight."

"She's not answering her phone." I told her.

"She's probably asleep Ax. She was wiped. What's goin' on?"

My mother knew me well and I couldn't hide the feelings inside of me. Fucker dead or not, I wanted eyes on her.

"Can you run by her house and make sure she's good?"

"Why wouldn't she be?" She asked.

"Raid just told me some shit from her past. It's over with but raw for me. So I just want to make sure she's good."

"I'll go back and make sure. But you will tell me what the hell is goin' on later." She hung up the phone and I felt myself breathing heavy.

"Brother I'm sure she's fine. That shit was a long time ago. He's dead. Can't come back from dead."

My hand wiped my mouth and felt clammy. She

was so much stronger than I ever imagined and just made me have so much more respect for her. And I'd thought I couldn't have any more but this, just ratchet it up tenfold.

Fuck I loved her. Loved her more than my next breath.

We pulled into the club. "Let's get this shit done." Raid said pulling into the parking lot and moving through to the hole. It was where we 'assisted' people in telling us what we needed to know.

I tried calling Indie again and she answered on the second ring very sleepy. "Low…"

"You alright baby?" I asked her hearing Gizmo bark, but it wasn't loud more like she was annoyed to be woken up.

"Yeah. Just sleepin'. You okay?"

"Yeah. I'll be there in a couple hours."

She yawned. "Okay."

I heard Raid on the phone talking to our mother telling her she could stand down.

My heart still pumped hard. "Love you Indie."

"Love you…" She said so quietly I barely got it before the phone when dead.

"She's good. Let's handle Nick."

Sooner we dealt with him, sooner I'd be in bed with Indie holding her tightly and so fucking happy she was mine.

CHAPTER THIRTY-TWO
Indie

AN HOUR EARLIER...

"I'D LIKE TO GO HOME NOW." BELLA'S KIND EYES pierced me, and warmth filled my chest.

"I'll take you." She did just that, and my stomach was in knots.

I loved him. Even with a gun in his hand earlier and menace in his eyes, I realized I loved him.

"Are you alright?" Bella asked, pulling into my driveway.

I turned to her, smiling. "Yeah. I'm good. Just really want to see Gizmo and go to bed. It was a great night... Well ... anyway, thank you for bringing me home."

She reached out and grabbed my hand, giving it a squeeze. "You ever need to talk, you call me, Indie. I'm here always."

Leaning over, I wrapped my arms around her and hugged her tight. "Thank you."

She squeezed me back. "Anytime."

Getting out of the car, I made my way to the garage door and punched in the code, waiting for it to roll up. Bella didn't leave the driveway until the door had closed.

Resting my head on the door, I took in a deep breath. "Oh, Indie. What are you doing?"

Barking came from the other side, and I went in to hug my pup.

Curling up with Gizmo on the couch, I played Divergent and somehow fell asleep.

Dead asleep the phone ringing woke me. "Low…"

"You alright, baby?" Ax asked as Gizmo barked. She was a princess who did not like being woken up.

"Yeah. Just sleepin'. You okay?"

"Yeah. I'll be there in a couple hours."

I yawned loudly. "Okay."

"Love you, Indie." My heart filled so much.

"Love you…" I said, and I must've fallen back to sleep.

GIZMO'S constant barking woke me. She was worse than a damn alarm. Then I heard the knock. The movie was over, and just the black screen was staring back at me.

I must've been sleeping hard because I knew I'd

talked to Ax, and with the phone laying next to me I didn't remember telling him bye.

But I did remember the love you part. I think. Was it a dream? Shit, was everything a dream? It felt so real.

The doorbell rang. *Ugh*. Thought Ax could get into the house. He'd done it every other night. Why the hell did he have to wake me up tonight.? Too much had happened, and I really needed sleep.

Rolling out of bed, I walked through the house. Considering the lights were on, it was weird Ax was ringing the damn bell.

Looking through the peephole, because I wasn't a stupid woman, my breath stopped and I looked back at the clock. It was eleven forty-three. Why was he here at this time of night?

First, I picked up Gizmo and put her in the bedroom, then closed the door. Her running out the door would not be a good thing at this point, and she would. That I was sure of.

I left the chain on, unlocked the door, and opened it as far as the chain would go. "Blaine. What are you doin' here?"

He looked the same as he always did. Well put together in khaki pants and a polo shirt, hair styled like it wasn't the middle of the night and he hadn't made a surprise appearance. Especially after how we'd left things with him calling me a 'biker whore' and getting frog marched out of the bakery.

"Was thinking about you and wanted to see you."

Um ... what?

"That's nice and all, but I was sleeping. Is there something you wanted to see me about?"

"Will you let me in?" he asked, ignoring me.

"No. I'm goin' to bed, Blaine."

"I know he's not here," he said low, making my spine snap straight. Something was wrong here.

"Good night, Blaine." I started to shut the door and his foot came between the open space, causing the door to stop. My pulse ran faster, and panic hit me.

"I want to talk to you, Indie."

I tried taking in a deep breath, but it got lodged in my throat. "Then talk, Blaine."

"Not through the door," he charged back, and something started swirling in his eyes. Something wrong, and I'd never seen it before.

"Why don't you come to the bakery in the morning? We'll have coffee together and talk."

His smile wasn't the cute one I liked before. This time it was sinister. "Sure, we can do that. But your gonna let me in right now."

"I'm not doing that." Gizmo was going crazy in the bedroom, and I used it. "Gizmo's really upset. I need to go to her."

"Sure. You go ahead."

Relief flooded me. Thank you God.

"Okay. Take your foot out and we'll meet tomorrow."

"You got it," Blaine said, taking a step back. My hand shook as I pushed the door closed and went to the lock.

He lied. Of course, he lied.

I should've known it. I was that stupid girl from the slasher flicks.

My hope was so high he'd leave, but it was false.

Before I locked the deadbolt, the door was kicked from the outside, splintering down the middle, and the damn chain lock just hung there with the door dangling. Great use of something that was supposed to "protect" me.

"Blaine!" I screamed as he dove for me, and I took off running. My bedroom had a lock. A flimsy one, but a lock nonetheless. I needed to get to it. Or the bathroom. It had one too.

But my phone was in the bedroom. I needed my phone because the alarm panel which I didn't set was on the opposite side of the room, and there was no way I'd be able to hit the panic button.

He grabbed the back of the flimsy tank I wore to bed and wrapped his arms around me tight.

Rage filled me.

This could not be happening again. This just wasn't. No one should go through this shit once, let alone twice. And here it was. Staring me in the face.

I fought. Lord, did I fight. Kicking. Punching. Scratching. Elbowing. Biting. Any part of his body I could get to, I fought.

"Fucking bitch," he growled and touched something to me, and everything went black.

I woke in a black space that was clearly moving. When I bumped up and down, I knew I was in a vehicle. A trunk. I was in a damn trunk.

Blaine.

Shit. Blaine had me.

He said he wanted to talk, but this wasn't talking. This was kidnapping.

No. I wasn't going to allow this.

Reaching around the space, I could feel the hood of the trunk. Searching I noted the damn thing was very clean. Why couldn't it be like my trunk with everything and anything in it. I needed something hard.

Clean carpet. Not even a damn tissue.

Knocking on the floor it sounded hallow, which meant it was where the spare tire was. Maybe, just maybe, there was a jack or tire iron. Something.

No one would ever tell you when you're in a trunk it was next to impossible to lift up the plastic let alone reach inside of it.

I could feel my fingertips being sliced on something but continued to bend the corner of the plastic. Light would be great about now, but it wasn't an option.

Strength training. When I got out of this damn trunk, I was going to the gym to lift weights or whatever so this would be easier.

The car bumped and stopped and started several times knocking me around the space.

What were those people called that could move their bodies in weird ways? A contortionist. Yes. That was what I needed to be.

Getting the corner up, I reached around and felt the tire, but nothing else.

Where would the tire iron be? For the love of everything holy, please tell me it wasn't underneath the tire. I wasn't sure that would be an option. The space was so small, and the opening I made to the hidden compartment wasn't huge, but that plastic was so hard.

I flew to the side and tumbled when the car made a sharp turn, hitting every part of my body. It hurt. My side got the brunt of it. How I had no clue.

Feeling around, I went back to the plastic and began working again.

Light from the lip of the trunk came in, telling me someone was behind us. Not that I could open the trunk and get help.

Shit, this was not good.

CHAPTER THIRTY-THREE
Indie

EIGHT YEARS PRIOR...

LOVE? WHAT WAS IT? AFTER HAVING AX MONROE IN MY life, I didn't know what it consisted of.

But this... I knew it didn't consist of freaky rhyming letters.

Dating an older man, I'd thought it would cut through all the male bullshit, but I was very wrong.

Jacob said he loved me. Said we were meant for each other. Even asked me to marry him, which was strange considering we'd only been dating a year.

I'd been brushing off the letters. He hadn't approached me, and I could deal with a few notes.

Except, this one was a bit more possessive. Quite frankly, it scared me. I didn't want to be scared in my own apartment.

The police. I needed to take all the letters and show

them. Maybe get a restraining order, or they would go and tell him to leave me alone.

My cell rang, and Meadow's name popped up. I answered it. "Hey."

"What's wrong?" she asked, instantly hearing something in my voice that alarmed her.

"Another note. But this one is ... its just off. I don't feel right about it."

"I want you to call the police. Right now. Do you hear me?" she ordered.

"I am. Love you. Let me call the police, and I'll call you back." I'd hung up the phone and went to dial 9-1-1 when the door opened as if the person on the other side had a key. No one had my key but me and my landlord.

Jacob stood on the other side, and I rushed to the door and tried to shut it, but didn't make it. He'd already gotten in and closed the door.

He punched me in the face, and the force of the blow knocked me to the ground. Pain radiated in my face, my hand going to it.

"You stupid bitch. Seriously. You think you can just dump me and go on with your life? Fuck that." Jacob spit at me as his foot came into contact with my ribs several times.

I cried out in pain. "Please, Jacob. I'm sorry. Really sorry." Tears fell freely.

"Oh, you'll fucking be sorry," he growled. He gripped the back of my hair hard and yanked me to my feet. Sounds tore out of my throat that I'd never heard before.

My leg hit something hard, and I lost my balance, his

hand holding my hair the only thing keeping me from falling to the ground.

"You cunt," Jacob sneered and tossed me to the couch. He jumped on top of me and beat the hell out of me. Each punch and kick were intended to break my bones. I knew it.

Knew this man was going to kill me.

Everything inside of me hurt. Everything. There wasn't an inch of flesh that didn't ache excruciatingly. There had to be ribs broken my sides hurt so bad. At least he achieved what he wanted.

My heart hurt, and I called out for Ax. Why in that moment, I didn't know, but I wanted him ... here with me. To get this man off of me.

He wasn't going to come in on some white horse. If I wanted to live, I'd need to protect my damn self.

Jacob pulled out a pocketknife and opened it. "Now let's carve up your face so no one will ever want your whore ass."

If I'd thought it was bad before, this was going to be worse. A damn papercut hurt me. A knife?

It would just mingle in with all the other pain.

No.

No.

I kept chanting in my head as tears fell, and fear crushed me. He wouldn't stop until I was dead.

I wasn't ready to die.

Jacob knelt by me on the floor and pushed me over to my back. My body was so limp. So used and abused.

But as the knife got closer a burst of adrenaline hit me. Jacob didn't see the change. He thought he'd already *won. That he'd broken me and was now going to destroy me.*

It was the only reason he didn't see me coming. With every bit of strength, which let's be honest wasn't a lot, I was going to use it.

His hand held the knife loosely, telling me he really thought I'd given up.

Never.

I'd never give up.

As he came toward me, I lifted both my arms and my hands went to the knife. Turning the weapon, I pierced it through his right eye. I yanked the knife out with force, and blood coated me.

Adrenaline pumped through my veins, and I kept stabbing, aiming for his neck. There was a vein there, and if I hit it he'd bleed out.

Jacob screamed and fell back.

My body was spent. I was done. Completely done.

With a few gurgles, Jacob died right on top of me.

I was officially a murderer.

CHAPTER THIRTY-FOUR
Bella

"I can't get ahold of my boys or Buzz," I told Princess into the phone as my eyes watched the scene before me. A man had just put Indie in the trunk of a car and took off. I was right behind it.

Personally, I wanted to ram into the car to stop it, but knew if I did that, I'd hurt Indie. She was safe in the trunk. Or as safe as she could've been in this situation. With whoever behind the wheel, he was occupied.

Calling Ax, Raid, and Buzz didn't go through. They must have been in the hole with Nick still, and that place didn't have any reception. Going to the clubhouse to get them wasn't an option.

The next was the ol' ladies.

"What's wrong?" Princess said, and I heard rustling on the other end. She was on the move.

"A man has Indie. Need you and whoever you can

get to come to my GPS." It was one of the things that Buzz and I had an argument about. Him putting GPS shit in my car. Now. I was so happy it was there. It was in all the ol' ladies vehicles now, and we lived with it. Overprotective men and all. But we always seemed to find ourselves in trouble unfortunately.

"What do you mean *has her*?"

"Who, not fuckin' sure. Just know she's in the trunk of this car, and I'm followin' behind. Get the girls. Bring weapons. I only have my 9mill."

"On it. Don't go in without us."

She didn't wait for an answer as she clicked off.

Hands clutching the wheel, I followed. Fucking hell, what was going on here?

CHAPTER THIRTY-FIVE

Ax

NICK WAS ON THE GROUND IN THE DIRT, BLOOD COMING out of holes in his body everywhere. We'd all taken our turns getting our pound of flesh.

Not until the man couldn't move and was barely breathing did Cruz call us off.

"Patch him up and take him to Old Red," he ordered, leaving the hole, and many of the Ravage men followed, including my father and Uncle Breaker. They were officially done with their brother. He would be their brother no more.

Deke went over and grabbed the alcohol. He knelt next to Nick and pouring it into the thousands of cuts. Nick screamed in agony.

Deke stood up with a smile on his face. "He said patch him up. Gotta clean the wounds first. Wouldn't want him to get an infection." His sarcastic tone had us grinning.

Micah handed Dryerson a wad of oil-soaked rags. "Use these and the duct tape. Sooner we do this shit, the sooner this fucker is away from Ravage."

"Oil rags. Yeah, great idea to now have infections," I said on a chuckle.

Nick looked horrible. Blood everywhere and wounds open so deep I could see bone. At this rate Old Red was going to need to let him really heal before getting his retribution.

We got to work with the oil rags. The man was covered with duct tape, and it'd be a bitch when it came off. It was like a present Old Red would need to unwrap.

"Ax! Raid!" My father's voice came urgently from the stairway that led out of the hole. We moved fast.

As soon as he saw us he said the words I never wanted to hear. "Some fucker has Indie in his trunk. Your mother is in the car behind it. We need to go. Now. Tried calling your mom, and she's not answering."

As soon as we raced out of the hole our phones started going crazy with notifications. No doubt all from my mother trying to get to me. I opened the GPS app from my phone, found my mother, and took off like a bat out of hell on my bike. Several others followed behind me.

I'm fucking coming, Indie.

CHAPTER THIRTY-SIX
Bella

Several cars were pinging on my GPS. Princess, Tanner, Austyn and Ensley all came up. No doubt they had others in the car with them.

I called them all and put it on speakerphone.

"The blue car right in front of me is where Indie is. We need to stop the fuckin' car without hurting Indie," I told them.

"Let's box him in with the cars. Try to get him to pull over," Austyn suggested. She was so much like her mother. "Bella, you stay where you are. Tanner to the right. Ensley to the left and, Mom, you in front. Get him to slow."

"Of course. I'm in the front," Princess said with a smile in her tone. "Have me wreck my SUV..."

"Focus!" I yelled out. Loved their banter, but I needed to make sure Indie wasn't going to get hurt. "Let's do this before he gets out on the main road."

"I'll be in front with Mom," Austyn said.

"Stay on the line," Princess ordered, and we got into position.

The side cars came from the side streets and got in their places.

Princess' SUV came out of a parking lot, her tail-lights now all I could see as she began to brake. Austyn's truck came from the other side, and they created a wall in front of the car.

This was going to end up badly if he didn't stop. I needed him to stop.

Except, he didn't. Whoever this mystery man was sped up and hit the back of Princess and Austyn's vehicles, causing the car to swerve, but both Tanner and Ensley crushed the car between them.

Sparks flew as metal touched metal.

I was close, but far enough away that I could brake and not ram into the trunk.

"Motherfucker!" Princess yelled.

"Ryker is gonna be pissed as shit when he sees the back of his truck," Austyn said.

"Austyn," Princess said sharply. "We're slowing down. Get prepared. Sides sandwich him in."

Please, Lord, make this work.

CHAPTER THIRTY-SEVEN
Indie

WHAT IN THE HELL WAS HAPPENING OUT THERE? THE car was being jostled around and pushed from side to side, the sound of metal hurting my ears.

Each movement made me lose my balance and tumble from here to there in the confined space.

The car stopped suddenly, and I crashed hard in the trunk. A groan left me.

We didn't stop, though. Instead, there were ear-splitting sounds that had my hands going to my ears. Which was stupid considering my hands were all I had to balance with.

This caused me to tumble to the other end of the trunk where it would open in normal circumstances.

I felt like I was clothes in a dryer, and my head started to feel dizzy. I blinked it back. My hand reached out finding something hard, and I clutched it like my life depended on it, because it did. A tire iron.

Thank God. I had no fucking clue what was going on out there, but I had to fight.

Metal crunching and tires squealing, if felt like the car was getting some resistance from the front because we were starting to slow down.

What was going on!?

I clenched the tire iron as we slowed. The tires burned rubber as Blaine tried to move but was unable to do so. The smell grew and grew.

The car slowed to a crawl, and when it stopped, I held my tire iron, laid on my back, and kicked the lid of the trunk with all of my might.

When it popped open, I sat up and swung the tire iron.

"Indie!" Bella cried out, stepping back, but the iron clipped her face.

"Oh my God!" I cried, dropping the iron and climbing out quickly to rush to Bella. "I'm so sorry. Did I break something? Are you okay? What can I do?"

Guilt filled me, and the situation I was in didn't register.

Bella wrapped her arms around me tight. "I'm perfectly fine. You've got a good swing, though."

I pulled back to see blood spilling from her face. "I'm so sorry, Bella."

She smiled wide which I thought was unusual, but with her next words I knew why. "Took a tire iron to the face to get you to call me Bella again."

"You stupid piece of shit." I heard Princess' voice

and whipped around as I saw her punching Blaine in the face.

"Can we get him out of the car?" Austyn asked, and Princess punched him again.

"Now you can," she responded, smiling.

Twisted, but I got it. I felt it. The bond with these women. The "ride or die" coming out tenfold. And it was for me.

My heart warmed. Was that strange in this situation? Whatever. My life had turned into strange.

Tanner and Ensley came to Blaine's side as Austyn held him with his arm behind his back.

Not thinking or caring, I marched to them and hit Blaine in the dick so hard he fell to the ground in a moaning heap and everyone released him.

He cried out in pain, and I didn't care for one second.

"You know this guy?" Princess asked.

"Blaine. Dated but not serious. Him and Ax got into it at the bakery, and he called me a biker whore."

Austyn took her boot and kicked him hard up the ass then spit at him. He cried out. "You'll pay for that one too."

"How did you find me?" I asked just as the sound of motorcycles came closer and closer. I looked at Bella.

"He's coming."

Those two words meant so much. True, I got out of the trunk, but him ... I wanted to be in his arms. Everyone turned to the bikes that skidded to halts.

Ax jumped off, and I ran to him. Full out girly in a

romance movie ran to Ax and wrapped him in my arms, sucking in deeply.

"Are you hurt?" he asked, clutching me tightly.

"Few bruises. But I'm okay."

"Blaine," Ax growled so low it vibrated through our connection.

"He broke into my house and took me. He didn't say why or where we were going."

"I'll get him to talk," Ax said darkly, and it didn't scare me one bit. He was doing this for me.

I pulled back on a rush. "Gizmo! She's locked in my bedroom at the house. There's no front door!"

"I've got ya," Tanner said, racing to her car and taking off.

"Let's get the fuck out of here and back to the clubhouse," Raid said, his hand coming to my shoulder and giving it a small squeeze that I tried not to flinch at. "Fuck. Sorry, Indie."

"I'm okay. Just took a tumble, but I'm good."

"Pack him up. Clubhouse." This time it was from Buzz who had Bella wrapped in his arms.

"Come on, Indie. Let's get you out of here."

Not saying a word, I reached for Ax's hand and followed him to his bike. Once on, we took off, but not to my house.

When the gate to the clubhouse closed behind us, a sense of calm fell over me.

I swung off the bike, and Ax followed. He wrapped me tightly in his arms. "You okay, Indie?"

"Told you…"

"Know about your time in college. How you had

to fight and you killed. Now this bullshit of being kidnapped. Now are you okay?"

My heart sunk. I kept that information close to the vest. My family of course knew, but when I moved back here, I tried to forget it ever happened.

Now... Ax knew. He knew I was a murderer.

"I will be, Ax. How did you find out?"

He kissed the top of my head. "Raid."

Before asking him to elaborate, the gate opened and Blaine's car, being driven by Austyn, came into the lot. She moved past us and Banner Automotive into the field.

"He's in the trunk, isn't he?" I asked Ax.

"Yeah and soon to be dead."

I pulled back from Ax and he studied me, looking for my reaction.

My lip tipped. "Can we find out why first?"

Ax wrapped me up tight. "Fuckin' love you, Indie."

"Love you too."

CHAPTER THIRTY-EIGHT

Ax

OH, HE WAS MORE THAN DEAD. WHAT WE DID TO NICK didn't compare to what I was planning for this motherfucker.

Kidnapped my woman and put her in a trunk? He'd pay.

Having Indie in my arms felt like home. She was safe. I felt her. She felt me.

"Sorry I wasn't there, Indie." My heart cracked. I'd told her that I'd protect her, and then this shit happened...

She pulled back and looked deep into my eyes. "This was not you. This was Blaine. I trust in you fully, and I know if you knew, you'd have been there in a heartbeat."

"Wasn't there, though. That's a hard pill to swallow."

Her hands came to the side of my face. "Stop that

right now. I'm here. You're here. We're together. That is the only pill you need to swallow."

"I could give you something to swallow," I said on a wink.

Indie rolled her eyes. "Seriously?"

"Well, yeah."

"Your timing is impeccable," I deadpanned.

"Let's go!" Raid called out. Taking Indie by the hand, she was going to learn what being Ravage meant.

"Come on. Let's get some answers."

She didn't resist, following with me.

My mom fell into step beside Indie who asked, "How's your face?"

This made me pause and look over to the women. My mother touched the side of her chin. "It'll bruise like hell, but I'll be fine."

"What happened?" I asked.

"Your woman hit me with a tire iron," my mother replied on a smile.

I squeezed Indie's hand. "What the fuck?"

"I didn't know it was her when the trunk popped open. I thought it was Blaine. If your mom hadn't stepped back, I would've hit her hard. I'm so sorry, Bella."

"No more apologizing. You did that. It's done. Now let's get this done so we can find some damn peace."

I wasn't sure how to feel in that moment, but I knew Indie never would have done it intentionally.

She loved Mom. What I was happy about was Indie not getting her full shot in.

No telling how Dad was going to handle it.

I'd be right in front of Indie. She was mine. I was hers. Loved my father, but no one touched Indie.

It didn't take us long to get to the hole, but Cruz was there and stopped us. "It's not big enough. We're moving to the side barn."

"What's not big enough?" Indie asked.

"The hole," I answered, lifted my chin.

I entered the side barn, Indie right behind me and Mom behind her.

"I want to know what that is later," she said and stopped so hard my mother ran into her.

"Sorry," she said. My mother reached out and squeezed Indie's hand, ushering her through.

Blaine was strapped to a large table where he lay flat. His arms and legs were wide and shackled.

No doubt this had to be a shock for my woman, but she needed to know this was part of the life. We all trusted each other, and we were officially bringing her into the fold.

I hoped like fuck that she saw this.

"You good?" I asked as we walked closer to Blaine.

"Actually, yeah. I am."

Putting my arm around her and pulling her tight, I kissed her temple.

Fuck yeah. She was ready for this life.

CHAPTER THIRTY-NINE
Indie

THE BARN WAS VERY LARGE AND FELT AS IF WE WERE walking into a stadium rather than a building on the Ravage MC Property. Wide doors aligned several places and appeared similar to ones you'd see for a garage. There were several doors as well which were painted red. The large structure was all concrete blocks.

I had no idea how in the world something this large could be built with concrete blocks, but there it was.

Ax held my hand as we moved to the door then through it as I took in the space which was a bit intimidating. There were sectioned walls with doors that were shut. Couldn't help but be curious what was behind them.

We moved to the open section and saw a lot of the Ravage MC family. Not just the men, but the women too. The ones who came for me. My heart tightened at the thought.

I didn't know the rules but knew they had them. I'd thought Ax told me a long time ago that the women weren't part of "club business." Then again, this was "me" business. But with all the men here, maybe it was club business as well? I wasn't sure. Hell, I wasn't sure of anything at this point. Just that I was sore from banging on that trunk and trying to get the plastic up for the tire iron.

I never wanted to see the inside of a car trunk again.

All eyes came toward Ax and me, and I felt actual feeling from them. Not contempt or anger. No, I felt as if I belonged with this group. Like I always intended on being here in this moment. It wasn't what was about to happen. It was about all of them coming to take me back. It was trust. One I didn't realize how desperately I craved until actually getting here.

It was Buzz who came up to us first, standing in front of us. "You wanna lead?"

Around him was a large brownish table, and Blaine was strapped to it by his arms, legs, and torso. His fists opened and closed as they turned a bit purple meaning those cuffs were pretty tight.

I looked up to Ax who was looking down at me, awaiting my answer. Leading? What did that mean? Especially with all these people around, including the President of the club. I looked at Buzz. "Me?" Shock filled me as Buzz smirked, probably reading my thoughts, and nodded. "I ... what do you mean lead?"

Buzz looked to his son, and Ax turned me to explain. "Do you want to find out why he kidnapped you? Or do you want to stand back and have me lead it for you?"

Without thinking on it, I answered, "Yes, I do."

Ax nodded in a way that showed pride. Yeah, I loved this man.

Shouldn't I be freaked out about this? Shouldn't I feel like this was wrong? But I didn't. I felt justified. I felt as though I wanted answers from this man, and I was going to get them.

Releasing Ax's hand, I walked to the table where Blaine was strapped down. He was seriously worse for wear with blood oozing down his face from a large cut on his eyebrow. His eyes were already starting to balloon up and had a deep red tint to them. His lip was cut in several places and had blood caked there as well. It also looked as if his nose had been broken as it again had blood and the bone appeared at a strange angle.

He wasn't looking at me, just staring up at the ceiling vacantly. This was nothing like the Blaine I knew from coming to the bakery and hanging out with me. This was a cold, detached stranger.

"Blaine?" I asked, and his head twisted very slowly to me, him wincing with the movement. The blank, cold detached stranger disappeared, and in its place was the man I thought I knew.

"Indie. What's going on? Where am I?" He

sounded confused and unsure as if he didn't remember the past few hours and what he had done. Maybe a few too many punches to the head? Or was he playing a game? My gut told me this was a game.

"Why did you break into my house?" I asked him, crossing my arms over my chest. Self-preservation? I didn't know.

He clenched his hands into fists then released. "I didn't break in, Indie."

His voice was so calm that it sent a shiver up my spine and my arms fell, but I didn't step back. He was playing a game.

Something old, cold, and dark filled me. A place I went to many years ago. A part I closed off because thinking about it made me relive it.

As this feeling flowed through me, my spine straightened and shoulders went back. I moved closer and rested my hip on the table, looking down at a man whom I thought actually liked me.

"Yes. You did. You also put me in the trunk of your car and kidnapped me. Why?" There was no inflection in my tone. It was harsh, demanding he answer.

Blaine shook his head as if I were the crazy one here. Sorry, buddy, but no. "No. I would never do anything like that."

"Bullshit," I spit. "Have you been sending me letters?"

"Letters?" Ax asked next to me. I'd never gotten a chance to tell Ax about them because of Nick showing up and the night going to hell.

Blaine heard it, though, because he smirked like

he was proud he knew something Ax didn't. Like he one upped him, and that pissed me off.

I balled my fist up and punched down hard into Blaine's gut. He tried to move but was strapped down tight, and there was nowhere to go.

Fire burned in my veins as the anger took over. Why was I being gentle with this man? He broke into my house, knocked me out, and put me in the trunk of his car. Not to mention, where the hell was he planning on taking me? He could've drove off, and I would've never been seen again.

I'd have fought, of course, but one never knew the minds of sick people.

"Stop that right now. You either answer me, or I'll let Ax get the answers from you," I growled at him.

Blaine chuckled, which I did not like. "Awe, you didn't tell your biker bastard about my notes."

That pissed me off again. I gripped Blaine's finger and bent it back as far as I could. Blaine cried out, the laughter now gone as it stretched in my tight grasp.

"Answer me!" I demanded. When he didn't, I bent the finger harder and heard him cry out.

"Why did you come into my home and take me?"

Blaine chuckled. "Wouldn't you like to know..."

Anger bubbled inside me, but bending the man's finger back and punching him wasn't getting me anywhere. What else could I do? Blaine was already beaten up, and that didn't make him want to talk. I wasn't sure what to do.

I looked at Ax in question. "What do I do if he doesn't talk?"

"You do whatever you want to do."

This didn't help. "That's what I'm asking you. What is the 'whatever'?"

The sound of metal scraping along the floor caught my attention as the tire iron hit my foot. Head swinging up, Bella's gaze met mine. "Only if you're comfortable. If not, you let Ax get your answers."

I bent down and picked up the iron, feeling its weight in my hand. It was the one I swung at Bella with, causing me to give her a cut on her face. I'd thought it would be Blaine. For that, I placed the iron over Blaine's crotch and put a bit of pressure on it. His eyes widened.

"You know I hurt Bella because of you? I like her, and I don't like you. What would happen if I pushed down harder on the iron? Think it would hurt?" I did what I warned.

"Don't!" Blaine ordered as if I were going to listen to him. All I could see was the cut across Bella's face and the pain I'd felt doing it.

"I will." He was sorely mistaken, and I pressed harder. He cried out, and I felt as though I was going to get somewhere. "Tell me why, Blaine."

Again when he didn't, my knuckles turned white as I pushed down and demanded answers from this man.

"Indie!" Blaine cried out. "Stop."

My head shook. "Not until you tell me."

He shook his head and tried again to move, unable to.

When he still didn't tell me, I gripped the iron

with both hands, went up on my tiptoes, and he cried out so staggeringly that I had to be completely crushing his balls.

"You murdered my father, you whore!" he screamed out. I instantly dropped the tire iron, stepped back, and my hands started trembling as inside I couldn't breathe.

"Jacob?" The name came out in a breath.

"Yeah, you fuckin' bitch. And I'll fuckin' beat ya and kill you too!" he screamed out.

Ax was right beside me, his arms going around my body, which I was thankful for because I felt as though my knees were going to give out.

"You're Jacob's son? He didn't tell me he had a son." Disbelief hit me. Jacob would've told me that. Right?

Blaine clipped, "He didn't know I existed, you fuckin' bitch, and now he never will."

Ax stepped in. "You mean to tell me Daddy didn't know you were born and all of this shit was payback?"

"Fuck you, asshole." Blaine spit up at Ax who moved out of the way, the spit just covering Blaine.

Ax didn't take kindly to it and balled up his fist and went down so hard on Blaine's leg that I could've swore I heard something crack.

Blaine screamed out in pain, so maybe Ax broke his leg with one punch?

I was shook from the revelation and needed to know. "Where were you going to take me?"

"Don't fuckin' know. Just away from all these fuckers!" he yelled loud, the pain taking over him.

"My turn now, Indie," Ax said, then looked behind me. "Take care of her."

Only then did strong arms pull me away from the table. Looking up, Raid was there. "This is nuts, Raid. Am I dreaming?"

He gave me a small smirk. "Unfortunately, no."

I could hear Blaine's cries of agony, and I didn't want to be here anymore. "Can I leave?" I asked him.

"Mom." Raid grabbed Bella's attention, and she came right away. "Can you take Indie to Ax's room here?"

"Of course."

She put her arm around me and guided me out of the barn, all along hearing the sounds of Ax beating the hell out Blaine.

And Blaine's screams.

CHAPTER FORTY

I watched as I washed the blood from my body, and it flowed down the drain in the hot shower. I wanted to go right to Indie, but I didn't want to contaminate my woman with that fucker's blood.

Blaine was gone. Never to be heard of or seen again. He would never hurt Indie or anyone else for that matter.

My rage had simmered after Blaine took his last breath, but it was still there, just under the surface.

That motherfucker was going to beat my woman and kill her.

That was the fact that ate me up inside.

She never told me about the notes she was receiving. Warning signs that I could've looked into. Fuck, Raid had waited to tell me about Indie killing Jacob. It could've been avoided. At least that was what I was telling myself.

Putting my head under the water, the warmth slicked my skin as the last remnants of Blaine washed away from me.

I couldn't blame Raid or Indie. I knew it.

I was just upset I wasn't there to protect her. She was supposed to be safe in her home.

Swinging my hair out of my eyes, I turned the water off, got out, and dried off.

Indie was laying on the bed, under the covers, and her gaze connected with mine. Keeping the towel around my waist, I got in beside her and pulled her into my arms. She rested her head on my chest.

"You okay, Indie."

"No," she said softly, and I squeezed her. "He was going to kill me, Ax. That scares the hell out of me."

I kissed the top of her head. "He's dead and gone. He'll never get his hands on you again."

"Doesn't make that fact go away," she said.

"True. But know that shit won't happen ever."

"He's really gone?" she asked.

"Fuckin' swear it."

"How do I know there's not another one of Jacob's spawn coming to find me?"

"Raid's on it, going through all the DNA databases and any records he can find."

Her body fully relaxed into mine. "I can't believe I crushed his balls with the tire iron."

"You had all the men in the room crossin' their legs."

Her hand clutched my chest. "I should feel bad

about it, Ax, but I don't. I'm happy he's gone. Does that make me a bad person?"

She was dealing with an inner turmoil, and I hated that for her.

The life I led, killing was a necessity. Extracting information was a necessity. Yes, Indie took a life, but that was in self-defense. She wasn't a fighter in the physical sense. Every other way she was hard as a rock. The woman had more inner strength than she was giving herself credit for.

"Fuck no, Indie." I pulled her up my body so our gazes met. "You're a beautiful person inside and out. He was going to kill you, but you fought." I pulled her hand up to mine and kissed each one of her scraped fingers. She'd done a number on them in the back of that car. "You are the best fuckin' person I know."

"It feels like a strike to my soul. Not only one man, but two."

I kissed her lips softly, then stared into her eyes. "Your soul has no strikes on it, Indie. None." She had no idea what a real strike on the soul was. I had a ton of them. "You're strong and did what you had to do. Never think all of this makes you a bad person. You are not. There are horrible people out there, Indie. Trust me. You are not one of them."

"I love you, Ax."

"Love you, Indie. So fuckin' much."

Our lips connected and I deepened the kiss.

When she pulled away, I didn't stop her. Before I knew it, she was sound asleep on my chest.

Indie was here.

She was safe.

She was mine.

CHAPTER FORTY-ONE
Indie

"I CAN'T FIND GIZMO WITH ALL THE BOXES." I searched through the field of stuff Ax had brought to my house. Gizmo barked, and I went toward the sound, searching.

Ax came from the kitchen holding Gizmo in his arms. "This furball?"

"I thought you lived at the strip club?"

He smirked. "Used to."

"So how do you have so much stuff?"

Boxes lined the living room, stacked here and there. I'd never lived with a man before, and it was a bit overwhelming.

The door opened and Bella walked in with Buzz on her heels, carrying another box.

"How many more are there?" I asked, and Bella smiled wide.

"Only a few. We'd been storing these at home until he found a place. Now he has a place, and I can get my basement cleaned out," she said as Buzz sat the box down. "Some of his toys are in there. High school yearbooks. Tons of albums that I made with pictures. Now they're all yours."

My head tipped up to the ceiling. "Lucky me," I grumbled.

Strong arms wrapped around me, and Gizmo licked under my neck. "I'll go through it and get rid of what needs to go. I'm gonna move it into the spare bedroom so you don't have to stare at it."

"You sure you wanna move in here?" I asked him. Loving that he didn't live in a strip club anymore, but also on edge as we'd never lived together. What if he threw all his dirty clothes around the room or that he didn't know how to do laundry? "Do you know how to do laundry?"

Buzz, Bella, and Ax burst out laughing. "No worries, Indie," Bella spoke. "Taught him to cook, clean, do laundry and everything else a man should do for his woman."

She was right. It was the nerves talking.

"You tryin' to kick me out already?" Ax asked me.

The door swung open again, and Raid came through. "Hell, I'd have already done it."

"Take that to the spare," Ax ordered, and Raid flipped him the bird. How he did it holding a box, I sure didn't know. He was one strong man.

"Everything will be fine, Indie. Do you love me?" he asked me, and my arms went around him tight.

"Yeah."

"Then all the other shit will fall into place."

He was right. Not that I'd tell him that. I didn't want him getting a big head and all. He was already too cocky for his own good.

"I'm gonna go order the pizzas so they can get delivered," I told Ax who reached around him and pulled out his wallet, handing it to me.

I closed my eyes, opened them, and took the wallet. He'd asked me to give him this, and I told him I would. It was unusual having a man at my side who wanted to make my life easier. But damn, I loved it.

Ax released me, and I moved into the kitchen, grabbed my cell off the counter, and ordered the pizza.

Looking up, Raid entered the room and sat at the island.

"Thank you," I said into the phone, moving to the opposite side of the island and tossing my phone down to it. "You okay, Raid?"

"Was gonna ask you that."

My brow quirked. "You worried about me, Raid?" I teased him.

The side of his lip tipped up. "Always, Indie. You're family. Family watches out for family. Remember that."

My head nodded as the warmth grew in my chest.

"Want ya to know. I searched everything I could. Then had Micah and Deke search. There is nothing left of Jacob. He has no other children. Went through all the women he'd ever been with that we could find, which fuck me was a lot, no children."

"What about Blaine's mother?"

"She passed on about a year ago. It was probably why he started looking for his bio dad."

"He's really gone then. Blaine, I mean." I asked, leaning my hip against the countertop.

"Yeah. He's gone."

"Thank you, Raid. Can you thank the boys for me too?"

He nodded but seemed to have more on his mind.

"What's up?" I asked him, curious.

"I'm so fuckin' sorry, Indie. That tape that went around school..."

I made to say something, but he shook his head.

"No. Please give me this?"

I nodded, staying quiet.

"When Baker blackmailed me, I was pissed and let that cloud my judgment. I'd thought if Ax and I knew what we were doing that Baker would never actually put that tape out there considering it would be his ass too. Alas, he did. I'd wanted to talk to you. Wanted to tell you it was a line of shit and that Ax wasn't in there and you had nothing to do with it. And I'm so fuckin' sorry you were pulled into that mess. Wish I could go back and change shit. Wish I would've gone to the club sooner. I'd tried livin' my life with no regrets, but leavin' you to hang in the wind was my biggest. I'm so fuckin' sorry, Indie."

I moved around the counter and wrapped Raid in

my arms, hugging him tight. "It hurt. Bad. Made my life hell for quite a while. It's also something I'll never forget. But I do forgive. It's in the past, and we need to leave it there."

"What the fuck?" Ax barked as I pulled away from Raid.

"You ruined a very good moment between me and your brother," I barked.

"What. The. Fuck?" Ax said again.

"Knock it off." I looked to Raid. "He's being an Axhole."

Raid burst out laughing, and a smile tipped my lips. "Axhole? I'm fuckin' usin' that one."

Ax came and stood in front of me, my eyes lifting up to his that were burning hot. "Seriously, Ax? He was apologizing for high school, and you came in being yourself."

Only then did he relax.

"You really think I'd hit on your brother?"

"No," Ax replied, wrapping me in his arms. "Just got you back. Hate seein' anyone holdin' you in their arms."

"And on that note, I'm out," Raid said, slapping Ax on the shoulder.

"That wasn't very nice. He's your brother."

"Love him to the end of the earth, Indie. But you're my other half. The half that has been dead until you came back in my life. Nothing will take that away from me again. Nothing."

"Love you too, Ax. Always."

. . .

PLEASE CONTINUE TO THE EPILOGUE
PREORDER BOUND BY PASSION TODAY!

EPILOGUE
Indie

THE CLUBHOUSE WAS ROCKING, AND THIS TIME IT FELT different to me. I knew it was because Ax had his arm around me, and I was officially his. We'd moved in together, and life was falling into place.

Every person in the Ravage MC had my back and I felt at ease.

It wasn't like before when I delivered the cake and was on pins and needles worried I'd see Ax. This time was the complete opposite, and I was happy to have Ax's arm around me.

We laughed, danced, and drank ... a lot.

When a whistle came out over the crowd, everyone stopped to look.

Ax stood in the middle of the clubhouse and crooked his finger to me. I rolled my eyes to Ensley. "Seriously?" I asked her, not waiting for an answer but hearing her laugh as I made my way to Ax.

The music was down and some of the lights were up.

"You beckoned?" I sassed as Ax fell down to one knee and pulled out a dark blue box, opening it wide. Inside was a beautiful emerald square cut with diamonds around it.

My hand flew up to my mouth.

"You're gonna marry me," he told me instead of asking.

I cocked my hip. "You're supposed to ask me. Not tell me."

Chuckles went up all around us as I noted all eyes were on us.

"Not this time, Indie." He reached for my hand, took the ring out, and slipped it on my hand. He then kissed it and stood up. "You're mine. I'm yours. We're makin' that official."

A cough came from the right, and Buzz handed Ax a leather cut. Ax turned it around, and it read *Property of Ax* on the back. All the other women had one just like it, only with their men's names on them.

Ax held it up, and I slipped my arms through it. He leaned down right to my lips. "Be mine forever, Indie. Will you marry me and be my ol' lady?"

Tears welled in my eyes. "Yes."

That was when he kissed me so hard my panties were on fire. "We need to go home," I told him, and he smiled wide.

"Fuck yeah we do. We're out." He raised his hand to the crowd and led me out of the clubhouse. Shit. I was getting married to Ax Monroe. Something I'd always wanted, but never thought I'd ever have. Now it was mine for the taking.

Hand in hand, Ax lead me out to his bike. The cool night air caressed my skin as the alcohol was burning in my system. Moving past the grassy area of the club, I stopped dead in my tracks.

"What the hell, Indie?" Ax asked as I tugged him to look at what I was seeing.

"Is that Liam from high school and your brother?"

Raid was down on his knees in front of Liam, head bobbing back and forth. Not going to lie, it sent a bolt of lust through me. It was hot. Sue me.

"Yeah, let's leave them alone."

Ax pulled me to his bike, and all I could wonder was *what was Raid's story, and how did I find it out?*

Please continue to the bonus

BONUS
Raid

Down on my knees, Liam's cock slid far down my throat as he groaned loud. Humming increased the sensation for him.

He loved it when I was down on my knees in front of him, which let's be honest wasn't often. Twice...maybe.

Loved me sucking his cock just like this. It made him feel as if he had the power. Even if only for a brief moment.

Liam was right there, his hand coming to my shoulder, and I pulled him out of my mouth and rose.

"What the fuck, man?" He said and I smiled.

"Remember me on my knees. Remember me suckin' your cock. Remember me takin' you to the edge. Also, remember me while you walk around with blue balls for tryin' to top me." I grabbed his shirt and pulled him close to me. "I'm always on top. Don't fuckin' forget it."

I kissed him hard, turned around, and walked away.

Yeah. This was fucking fun.

Bound by Passion (Ravage MC #20) (Bound #11)

Raid bled the blood of the club. Undeniably loyal.
Focused on family. Determined.
His thought processes would make any other man cringe. Calculating. Meticulous.
Always thinking.
Guilt to this day for ruining his brother's life due to his actions.

Liam grew up in Sumner, Georgia always on the outside looking in.
He didn't come from money or a good family.
The only happy times he could remember was in high school with Raid and Ax who were his best friends.
Until the day he took it too far with Raid.
Leaving Sumner in his rearview mirror, he never wanted to come back.
Unfortunately, life had other ideas, throwing him back into Sumner.
Back into the tornado of Raid's world.

Nyx wanted to blend into the background, work and live a life of peace.
Something she never had growing up in the system and desperately craved.
She'd never had a home, and in choosing Sumner, Georgia she'd hoped to find one.
Undetected and under the radar.
Always fighting for every scrap of happiness she was tired of fighting.

The three of them were lost in different ways.
Each soul desperately clinging to find ...

Pasts never in the past.

When Raid, Liam, and Nyx come together, sparks erupt, both figuratively and literally.
But these types of relationships never last.

Jealousy is an evil b*tch.

Was there a way for the three of them to find peace?
Or was it all going to blow up in their faces?

A NOTE FROM RYAN

Thank you so much for reading Bound by
Temptation.
I hope you enjoyed their story as much as I do.
If you could please leave a review I'd appreciate it!

ACKNOWLEDGEMENTS

Thank you to my entire team.
You're the best.

Chelsea Camaron—My sanity keeper, critique
partner and bestie.
Natalie—My right hand who keeps the ball rolling
when I'm down on the ground.
Beta Readers & Expert Team—Thank you for your
feedback and help during the writing process.
Silla—Best editor around. You're amazing. Thank
you for being part of my team.
Linda—Thank you for your keen eye!
Sinners—Always. Thank you for staying with me.
Blogger, Influencers, ARC readers—Thank you
from the bottom of my heart!

Love to all of you!

ABOUT RYAN

Ryan Michele is the *Wall Street Journal* and *USA Today* **Bestselling author** of over 40 romantic suspense novels. She found her passion bringing fictional characters to life, being in an imaginative world where anything is possible. Her knack for the **unexpected twists and turns** will have you on the edge of your seat with each page. She is best known for **her alpha, bad boy bikers and strong, independent heroines who refuse to back down.** When she's not writing, you can find her on her swing, watching the water ripple in the pond and daydreaming about her next book.

Join my Reader Group:
https://www.facebook.com/groups/RyansSultrySinners/

Sign Up for my Newsletter:
https://www.subscribepage.com/918Backmatter-SignUps

Come find me:
www.authorryanmichele.com
ryanmicheleauthor@gmail.com

facebook.com/authorryanmichele

twitter.com/Ryan_Michele

instagram.com/author_ryan_michele

bookbub.com/authors/ryan-michele

tiktok.com/@authorryanmichele

Thank you for reading!

Ryan
Michel